Pine Tree's War

Kicking out, David overturned the heavy table. The mayor shrieked, scrambled for cover with an agility that belied his ancient limbs. At the same time, shots rang out. Armed men dashed from the cover of the curtain, from the back room, the kitchen, where they had been hiding. An ambush! A hail of lead thudded into the heavy planks of the table, and David winced as splinters flew. The whitewashed silence suddenly shattered. Orange flame splashed the gloom, men cursed and yelled, the air thickened with the stench of burning powder.

As the brown-uniformed men poured over the table, trying to get at him, David heard someone yell, "Save him! Do not kill him! Save him for me, I tell you!" David caught a glimpse of Saenz through the clamor and smoke, waving a pistol and gesturing.

He emptied the magazine of his pistol, hurling the useless weapon in the face of a man with sergeant's stripes who clawed at him, trying to drag him from behind the table. The sergeant had probably been the first man to rush from the kitchen, for he wore ridiculously draped around him the remnants of the flowered gingham curtain, torn from its rod in his rush. But suddenly, as the man's big hand grabbed David's collar and hauled him triumphantly across the warped planks of the table, a fresh fusillade broke out. David Pine felt the grasp on his collar relax; the sergeant's look of triumph faded to a puzzled questioning look.

BORDER RIDERS

Robert Steelman

LEISURE BOOKS NEW YORK CITY

A LEISURE BOOK

Published by

Dorchester Publishing Co., Inc.
6 East 39th Street
New York City

Printed in the United States of America

Chapter One

He got off the Southern Pacific and stood on the platform, watching the rails shimmer westward in the heat of the afternoon. In the distance a few black clouds hovered on the horizon. But now, under the khaki shirt, rills of sweat stitched down his chest. No one was on the platform to meet him; he was not really expected. The SP agent, he noticed, was new. Six years before, when David Pine had left for the East and a career, old man Riggins was in the tiny office. Otherwise, Roosevelt, New Mexico, looked the same.

In late afternoon somnolence the town sprawled across the SP tracks. To the south, between the tracks and the new barbed-wire fence with its border gate, lay San Andreas, where he and Maruja and Paco had been friends. The Anglos called it "Chili Town." On the northern side of the tracks was the Anglo community—the "business district" of small groceries, a hardware store, the Plains Bank, Doc Menick's office, and a haphazard sprinkle of weatherbeaten frame houses. Now there was even a sales agency for Dodge trucks and a garage for the motor cars suddenly popular with miners and oil men. But Pop Cooper, Mom said in her letters, still drove old Atlas and the buggy.

Walking along the tracks, boots deep in dust, he saw

another sign of change. In 1911 the border crossing had been manned by a drowsy and indifferent customs clerk. Now there was a detail of soldiers, a Benet-Mercier machine-gun mounted on a new Locomobile truck, a latticed tower with a searchlight. A corporal saw David Pine's gold bars and snapped a brisk salute. But David pretended not to see. There was enough military courtesy—too much—around Fort Bliss. Anyway, he was only a Quartermaster Corps lieutenant.

Standing before his old house, porch sagging under the bougainvillaea vine, the entryway looking like a jungle with Mom's plants in tomato cans and old vases, he felt a chill as one of the vagrant clouds passed over the sun. Perhaps it was the excitement of seeing them again that made him tremble and feel cold. Perhaps it was only the approaching storm, one of the quick swirls of wind and dust and chill air that in summer rolled down out of the mountains, bringing little rain but often a cannonade of hail. Perhaps it was even the uncomfortable errand Colonel Hayden had fobbed off on him. Or perhaps—perhaps it was after all something new and strange about Roosevelt, New Mexico. There were few people in the streets. Even the dogs did not bark at him. No children played in the dust or called to each other, even in San Andreas. There was instead a feeling of tension, of waiting.

When he knocked at the peeling front door, no one answered. Uncertain, he walked to the back of the house. Everything seemed the same; Mom's washboiler on a pile of whitewashed rocks, clothesline swinging in the wind on wooden props, the sagging shed for the old horse, Pop's buggy. After the army life he had lately led, the homely clutter seemed odd and endearing. Below, in the shallow canyon, stood the chinaberry tree. The rope swing still hung from a limb, and there stood the remains of the fort he and Paco Mora had built from scrap lumber, rocks, and tarpaper.

Feeling the wind build, he shivered. When a grain of

hail bounced on the rim of his campaign hat, he hurried to the back door and pounded on it.

"Mom! Pop! Are you in there?"

They came suddenly, Mom wide-eyed in disbelief, Pop in his undershirt, gnarled hands holding a cup of coffee.

"David! Why, Coop, it's David!"

There was much hugging and tears, Pop's leathery handshake, a gruff pressing of his cheek against David Pine's.

"Jesus Christ, Davy, whyn't you let us know you was coming?"

Pop took his suitcase and they went into the parlor, Mom hanging tearfully to David's arm.

"I didn't know myself till this morning," he explained. "The colonel gave me a twenty-four-hour pass and I decided to ride the SP for a visit."

The parlor was the same as he remembered, seldom used except for company. Now he was company, and he felt vaguely uncomfortable. On pegs over the fireplace hung Pop's old Spencer carbine, unfired in anger since he was a corporal in the Eighth Cavalry during the Indians Wars. Lace doilies covered the backs and arms of the chairs. The room smelled of dust, cloth, furniture polish. On the round table with its pie-crust fluting stood the polished glass dome that fascinated him when he was a child, a shiny bell filled with dried flowers, colored pebbles, a stuffed woodpecker with only one staring glass eye. The other had long since fallen out and disappeared among the pebbles.

Hat balanced on his knee, he sat stiffly on the best brocade chair. "How have you all been?"

Mom bustled about, flicking with the hem of her apron at the powder veiling the furniture. In Roosevelt the wind blew most of the time—the air was always filled with talclike dust—but New Mexico was mining country, Pop's country.

"Fine and dandy, David! Oh, Coop's hip bothers him

a little, but—"

"Right now," Pop admitted, "it does twinge me a little, seeing it's drawing on to storm." As if in confirmation, a drumfire of hail rattled on the corrugated iron of the front porch roof.

Mom sat down and straightened her apron. "This place gets to be such a mess! Tell us, Davy, how do you like El Paso?"

He shrugged. "To tell the truth, I haven't seen much of it. They keep us pretty close to the post. But I should get an assignment soon."

Pop lit his pipe and said nothing. It had been Pop Cooper's fondest dream to see David Pine become a cavalry officer with Pop's old Eighth. Pop had never ceased trying to get David into West Point. But David had not been a soldier, nor much of a scholar either. In boyhood gangs it had been Paco Mora who was the fighter, the doer, the planner of raids against other juvenile bands. And in school it was always Maruja Cruz who was the scholar. David just got along. So after high school he had gone east with a hundred dollars and the Coopers' blessings to become a struggling accountant. It was only the budding Mexican War, the operations of General Black Jack Pershing against Pancho Villa, that made a bookkeeper valuable. Someone had to keep the troops fed, housed, paid every thirty days, warehouse cannon and shells and medical supplies for them.

"How's the mine?" David asked.

The Little Alice had never paid Pop Cooper much for his labors; the ore showed minimum silver, less lead and copper. But Pop was always sure he was approaching a rich lode.

"So-so," Pop said and did not carry the conversation further.

"Still work her?" David asked. Remembering, he rubbed a thumb against the palm of his hand. There had been callouses there, rough two-bit-sized callouses where he had gripped the handles of the rusty wheelbarrow. He could still smell in his memory the dry coolness of the Little Alice diggings and tunnels, the tingling odor of the air after a blast. The Little Alice was where Coop had taught the gangling boy about stopes and levels and cinnabar and dynamite.

"Not much anymore," Pop sighed. "It's my back. If 'twasn't for my tired old bones, I'd of broke through to a real Golconda by now."

David shifted uneasily on the brocade chair. "When I came in on the SP, the town seemed kind of—strange. Not many people in the streets, no dogs barking. Even San Andreas looked like a graveyard."

Pop chewed hard on his pipe, looking at the ancient Spencer on its pegs over the fireplace.

"Ever since the bandit Villa raided Columbus, down the line," he said, "everyone's been kinda jumpy. I tell you, Davy, no one knows where that rascal will strike next! All the troops the Army's got strung out along the border from Brownsville to Yuma don't seem able to catch him! Why, Black Jack hisself is roaming Chihuahua with five thousand men and can't lay a finger on him!"

"Well," David said, "I guess I've got General Villa to thank for my job. I was starving as an accountant, but now at least I've got a regular salary and a place to eat and sleep."

"What they need," Pop grumbled, "is the old-time Army, my old outfit." He shook his head. "This new Army . . ."

David grinned. Pop Cooper considered the old Eighth the finest fighting machine in the world, several cuts above the Roman legions.

"Well," he said, "times change, I guess. They say almost a hundred thousand green National Guard troops are coming to Fort Bliss soon. Maybe I'm not a cavalryman, Pop, the way you wanted me to be, but I'm still pretty important. Someone's got to feed and clothe all those recruits. Supply is first priority at the post now, furnishing the troops with ammunition and remounts and canned beef."

"My goodness!" Mom jumped up, smoothing her apron. "Speaking of beef made me think! Davy, you must be *starved*, and here I am just sitting and gabbing when I should be making supper!"

David protested, but she hurried to the kitchen. A few minutes later he smelled pork chops frying and coffee boiling.

"No, there ain't but one way to deal with Villa," Pop said. "That general of Carranza's has got the right idea. General Pineda rides into a village, and if anyone's been dealing with Pancho Villa—selling him corn or beef cattle or ammunition—old Pineda just strings 'em up to the nearest cottonwood!"

"That seems unjust," David protested.

"Only way to do it!" Pop banged the dottle hard from his pipe. "Pershing can sashay all over the state of Chihuahua, but as long as the damned greasers are hiding Villa and helping him, there ain't a Chinaman's chance of running him down!"

The hail on the porch roof slacked its drumming, and a mizzling rain began to fall. Mom called them and they went in to the kitchen to sit at the oilcloth-covered table. Pop scratched a match on the seat of his breeches and lit the coal-oil lamp. Electricity had come to Roosevelt, but only a few of the stores and some of the wealthier citizens had installed it.

"Any pretty girls in El Paso, Davy?" Mom asked, spooning pork gravy over the mound of fried potatoes on his plate.

He blushed. At least, he supposed he blushed. It was something never conquered, this sudden reddening, this awkwardness, when women were concerned.

"I guess so," he admitted.

In her letters Mom hinted rather heavily that it was getting time for him to think about marriage. After all, he was twenty-four years old. She and Pop Cooper had married when they were eighteen.

"There's that pretty Louise Trilling you went to the prom with," Mom reminded him. "The blonde girl—you remember, Coop—her father was head teller at the Plains Bank. I'll bet Louise would be glad to see you, Davy! Why don't you just—"

"Now, Mom!" Pop warned, and David was grateful.

"I thought after supper I'd just walk over and see Paco and Maruja," he offered. "We used to be such good friends, the three of us."

He sensed the sudden tightness, the restriction. Pop and Mom never cottoned to David's Mexican playmates. The chinaberry tree and the fort in the canyon were out of sight from the Cooper house, and that was where the three of them spent most of their time. Paco and his hot-tempered cousin Maruja were not invited in for milk and cookies the way the Anglo kids were.

"I'd be a mite careful," Pop said.

"Careful?"

Mom got up and went noisily to clearing and rinsing dishes in the tin sink.

"Careful," Pop repeated. "You been away a while, Davy. I guess maybe you don't understand how things has changed around here. After all, Villa shot up Columbus and killed a good many US citizens. Since that, there ain't much love for the Mexicans. Things are kinda strained. They even put up bob-wire around the Plains Bank. If I was you, I wouldn't go down to no Chili Town, especially in that uniform. It ain't safe no more."

David was incredulous. "But I know everyone down there! Paco and Maruja were always my best friends! And there was old Senora Jimenez and Ruiz the druggist that had all the seaweed and dried spiders and *brujo* stuff in his pharmacy, and—"

"I know," Pop said heavily, "that you and Paco was great friends onct, but a lot of water has run under the bridge since then. I mean it kindly, son, but a U.S. uniform in Chili Town might cause trouble, with everyone on edge so."

"To think of it!" Mom complained in a spatter of soapsuds. "Those Mexicans, after all we've done for them! Built a new school so as to educate their children, and the Baptist church sews for the poor ones every Thursday! But do they show gratitude? No!"

Pop poured coffee into his saucer while Mom wiped the oilcloth clean with a soapy rag.

"Used to be," Pop said, "the Anglos and the Mexicans got along fine. Everyone knew his place, and there wasn't no trouble. But lately there's a lot of hotheads been causing trouble in Chili Town."

"But Paco?" David shook his head. "We had some scrapes when we were kids, Pop. You remember the time old Fitz put us in jail for throwing firecrackers into the stove in Pettit's grocery. But Paco and I never did anything against the *law*."

"Nevertheless," Pop said. "Nevertheless." He sipped carefully at the saucer. "There's them that say that Paco Mora's been seen lately down around Lago Guzmán, in Chihuahua. The El Paso *Herald* told that's where Villa stopped to organize, just before he hit Columbus."

David laughed. "Lago Guzmán? That doesn't mean anything! Paco's uncle Jaime lived at Lago Guzmán!"

It was true. There was a time, long ago, when David Pine and Paco Mora ran away to Lago Guzmán and *Tio* Jaime, leaving Maruja Cruz behind to weep at being excluded from the company of gentleman adventurers. They hitched a ride south on a freight wagon, intending to find a gold mine in Chihuahua and make their fortunes. David remembered the courtly white-mustachioed Don Jaime and the good *queso fresco*, the fresh white cheese the old man made. Under a gnarled oak on the sunbaked little ranch was a press fashioned from a section of sewer pipe with an iron weight pressing on the cloth-wrapped cheese. Cats congregated under the press, opening pink mouths to receive the liquid that dripped from the cheese. When the *queso* was firm and white and creamy, Doña Ana gave the boys slices to wrap in fresh-cooked tortillas. Boylike, David Pine and Paco Mora had sworn a blood oath never to reveal where they had spent those three days. It was humiliation enough to be sent home by Don Jaime. They had not found the gold mine, either.

"Well," Pop shrugged, "maybe there ain't nothing to it. But I'd be careful, just the same."

Through the kitchen curtains shone a low orange sun in the west, a fiery orb half hidden in a leaden bank of clouds. Mom raised the window. It had stopped raining; to David Pine's nostrils came the fresh evocative scent of wet desert plants, the clean dampness of sand, a rain-washed desert dusk.

"Well," he said, "it still wouldn't be right to come back after almost six years and not see old friends, war or no war! Pancho Villa is a passing thing, Pop. But Paco and Maruja and I were friends long before Pancho, and we'll be friends long after."

Of course, that was true. But there was another reason for going to San Andreas, the reason that made him feel somehow guilty, ill at ease.

"All right," Pop shrugged. "You're the doctor, Davy."

"Be careful, David!" Mom begged.

They were uncomfortable, standing on the front porch to watch him go, half lost in the vines and greenery. A freight train rumbled into the setting sun, loaded with trucks and fieldpieces. David waited patiently at the grade crossing. When he looked back at the house after the train had passed, Pop and Mom Cooper were still standing in the twilight, watching, as if their surveillance could somehow protect him. He sighed and turned toward San Andreas. He did not like this business of being a spy.

In San Andreas lights glowed against the dusk. The air smelled of *chile colorado* and beans and woodsmoke Somewhere, expert fingers strummed a guitar against a rhythm of female hands slap-slapping tortillas. At this hour few people were in the grandiloquently-named Cinco de Mayo Street, and to David Pine it seemed they turned quickly away as he approached.

At the corner a lace curtain fluttered at an iron-barred window. He wondered if old Señora Jimenez recognized him in his uniform. The old lady never missed anything. Of course, she might be dead. It was almost six years since he had set foot in San Andreas.

At the drugstore, Señor Ruiz had just turned down the lamp and locked the door of his tiny shop.

"*Buenas tardes*," David said politely. "*Hace tiempo, señor, que no le veo.*"

He slipped easily into the forgotten Spanish, so gentle and courteous a language it recoiled from ever impinging a verb directly against the name of a person. You could never *see Juan* in Spanish, you had to *see at Juan*. What was called the "personal *a*" must always intervene. Paco Mora had despaired of him ever remembering.

"Who is it?" Señor Ruiz asked, fumbling with his thick spectacles. "*Conozco la voz*—I know the voice—but—"

Suddenly he recognized David Pine, saw the uniform. With a mutter that might have been recognition, or apology, or simply distress, the druggist turned quickly away and disappeared, account books under his arm, toward the adobe shack where he lived with his cats. Everyone in San Andreas, and many in Roosevelt, owed Ruiz the druggist for medicines and charms and potions.

"Señor!" David called. "Wait!" But there was only silence, the dusky street, the inquiring *miaow* of a kitten that came from the shadows to rub against his boots.

Things *had* changed. He felt a stranger—he, David

Pine, of whom Mom Cooper once predicted he would turn into a tamale himself if he didn't stay out of that heathenish place. The familiar sounds of San Andreas—the smells, the tumbled adobe and tin and lumber of the structures—all seemed suddenly foreign, threatening. Was there indeed some great conspiracy going on?

Paco Mora had lived with his father in a brush and wattle lean-to, pieced out with scrap boards, that leaned against a livery stable. Señor Mora was an expert mechanic for the Southern Pacific. After being crippled in an accident, the railroad let him go with a fifty-dollar settlement and their good wishes. Somehow, Felix Mora eked out a living doing odd jobs around Roosevelt.

The Mora place was a rabbit warren of adjoining rooms made from cardboard cartons, rusting sheets of corrugated iron, and whatever came to Felix Mora's skilled hands. David walked the familiar dark passage behind the livery stable, a passage smelling of ammonia from horse urine mingled with the perfumes of vines that hung over the Mora place, which softened the harsh outlines of salvaged lumber, scraps of cardboard and tin, the roofbeam of rusting iron pipe that stuck into the street like the keel of an overturned ship.

The shades were drawn, but a slit of light showed at the edge of the rough plank door. He knocked. No answer. He knocked again, seeming to hear a muted rush of activity and soft voices.

Puzzled, he called, "It's David, Davie Pine! Is anyone there?" Then he remembered, and said, "*Hola, amigos! Soy David El Pino! Esta Paquito?* Is Paco there?"

David El Pino was an old joke with old-man Mora—*David The Pine Tree*, because he was so tall and gangling.

This time he heard a sound as of a chair knocked over. There was a stirring of air, perhaps a hidden door was opened. Something rustled, seeming to brush him in the darkness. He whirled, but the man or whoever it was had disappeared. Or was it *men*? There had been more than one. Though he heard no footsteps, saw no sign, the back of his teeth recognized the gritty feel of dust raised by hurrying boots.

Short hairs raised on the back of his neck. He remembered what Pop Cooper said. "I wouldn't go down to no Chili Town especially in that uniform." An itch sprang into being between his shoulder blades. He wondered if it was some relict of an old instinct, a flinching before an expected impact of club, the lean gliding-in of a knife.

Suddenly the door swung open, bathing him in light. Maruja Cruz stood there, Maruja as always; hair shining in the lamplight, eyes dark pools in the shadows cast by the coal-oil flame.

"David?" Her voice was hesitant. One hand clutched at the starched snowy collar of her black dress.

"It's me," he said. "It's just me, Maruja. David."

Grateful for the sudden light and safety of the room, he stepped quickly in, closing the door. He wondered if he had caught a glimpse of old Señor Mora, a white face looking out from a curtained recess, only to quickly disappear.

"What are you doing here?" he asked. He had been sweating, standing outside in the dark, and ran a finger over his forehead. Then he remembered to take off the broad-brimmed campaign hat. "What are you doing here, in Paco's house?" he asked again, this time in English. Maruja had always been proud of her English, better than his, and corrected him when he split infinitives.

"David," she said, touching his cheek with her fingers. "You—you have come home."

Once it had been a kind of home, a haven where David Pine was always welcome, no matter what transgressions he had committed in his stepfather's house.

"What's going on here?" he insisted, puzzled.

"Where's Paco? And who were all those people I heard?"

The hand holding the lamp seemed to tremble. Shadows danced on the wall—on the Plains Bank calendar, on the picture of the Virgin of Guadalupe before which guttered a candle.

"Well?" he demanded.

When she did not speak, only continuing to stare at him with that bemused look, he took her hand. She put down the lamp and sat beside him on the sagging sofa Felix Mora had rescued from an Anglo junkpile.

"I—I shouldn't be here with you—a man—alone!" she murmured.

So many years away, it had not occurred to him that Maruja Cruz was now a young lady subject to the punctilious code that governed the behavior of unmarried Mexican females.

"Wasn't that Señor Mora I saw when I first came in?" He gestured toward the curtained recess. "We're chaperoned then, aren't we?"

"Papa Mora is not here," Maruja said.

"And Paco?"

"He is not here either. He has not been here." She seemed uneasy.

On the heavy arm of the sofa was a glass ashtray. Butts smoldered in other makeshift devices—salmon cans with soldered rests for the smokes—and empty bottles of Modelo beer stood about. The air smelled of coffee, along with an exotic musky smell that reminded David Pine of the Egyptian cigarettes Colonel Hayden smoked.

"Well," he said, "someone has certainly been here. What's this all about?"

She disregarded his question and playfully toyed with his fingers. "Are you a detective or something, David Pine?" But when she saw the shadow of concern in his face, she said, "My goodness, it was only a meeting of the Holy Name Society of the Church, with Father Herrera. They are—well, they are making plans for a big fiesta in September. That is all."

"But why did the meeting break up so fast when I knocked?"

She shrugged. "These are uneasy times, David. And you surprised me so! That is why I acted so funny, I guess. Who would expect to see you, David Pine, after all these years!" She drew back to look at him. "Ah, you look so fine and handsome! Tell me, how do you come to be here?"

Still unsatisfied, he said, "I'm stationed at Fort Bliss. After the two years in college, I went to work for a firm of accountants in Camden. That's in New Jersey. Then I tried to start my own little company. I worked night and day, but I was going broke, until I heard the Army was looking for bookkeepers like me to keep the supplies in order. So they gave me a commission in the Quartermaster Corps, and here I am."

"Did you—did you see Mr. and Mrs. Cooper?" She did not say Pop or Mom, and he knew a little wrench for that.

"I had dinner with them. But I couldn't wait to come down here and see you and Paco and Papa Felix and all the rest of the people I liked so well when I was a kid."

With a sudden gesture he drew her to him, pressing his cheek against hers. The gesture had nothing of passion in it; at least he did not intend passion, only love and affection. It was a gesture common in San Andreas households. But he was unnerved by her closeness, her softness, the unexpected rich scent of hair and skin and body. Awkwardly he drew back, managing in his discomfiture to knock the ashtray from the arm of the sofa.

"David!" Maruja giggled and knelt to pick up the scattered debris. "Ah, David!"

Red-faced, he knelt beside her to help. She sat for a moment on her legs, smiling. "You have not changed! You are still the same awkward, big, blushing-faced nice boy!" She brushed her cheek against his shoulder. "The uniform has not changed you. Nothing will ever change you, I guess—and I hope."

Face flaming, he sat beside her again, gruffly asking, "Where is Paco then? That's who I came to see."

The new Maruja drew from her bosom a packet of the *El Tigre* cigarettes he and Paco used to smoke in hiding. Never before had he seen Maruja smoke, and he was not sure he liked it. Tipping the smoky chimney of the lamp, she held the tip of the cigarette over it and drew hard till the cigarette broke into a glow.

"Ah, Paco," she murmured, blowing smoke through the delicately chiseled nose. "Well, Paco is very busy. He has things to do, you see?"

"What sort of things?"

Fleeting emotion, it seemed to him, passed over her brow. But he was not expert enough with women—had never been, would never be—to understand.

"I can not tell you, David," she said. "I will not lie to you. We are too old friends for that. But you know that Paco is adventurous. He always liked new things, new places, new ideas. So he is—busy." She looked thoughtfully down at the smoldering *El Tigre* in its smoldering paper. "Knowing you, David Pine, I know also that some day you will be proud of Paco when you understand."

Still he was not satisfied.

"We never kept secrets from each other before, did we?" He gestured toward the door. "A lot of people attending a Holy Name Society meeting don't break and run when someone knocks at the door! And why is Señor Mora hiding back there?" He saw the curtain move a little, tremble. "Why can't he come out of there and say hello to me?"

"I have told you all I am going to tell you!" In the old way he well remembered, she flared up. "I do not have to tell you any more, David Pine! I cannot tell you any more!" In her anger and frustration she broke into the mother tongue. "*Por favor, te ruego, no me molesta*!

Do not press me!"

He picked up his hat. "All right, then. Anyway, no matter what's going on, I'm glad I came. And if you see Paco—"

Contrite, she followed him to the door.

"I'm sorry" she whispered. "Ah, David, things are not the same anymore. It is not your fault. It is not my fault. It is not Paco Mora's fault. We should still be friends as always, the three of us."

"I—I guess so," he faltered. "Sure. Well—"

She held the door open, and he went out onto the sagging porch. Reaching out her hand, she touched him, a small uncertain brush of fingers. Then she closed the door and was gone.

Feeling a sad and bittersweet emotion, perhaps the death of childhood, he walked down Cinco de Mayo Street. The Mexicans had given that grand name to the dusty lane. The Anglos never referred to it at all; for them it hardly existed.

All was quiet. Houses shuttered, shops closed. The kitten emerged again, mewing in inquiry. There was faint starshine and a distant light in the SP station down the tracks.

He was walking toward the comforting beacon of the SP light, puzzled and bewildered, when he heard a rush of feet, saw dark shadows move, smelled the rusty scent of danger. He started to run, but shadows came from other recesses, blocking him. Someone called out softly and mockingly. "*Eh, gringo*! *Que haces aqui en nuestra calle*? What are you doing here in our street?"

Someone snatched off his hat, someone else grabbed his wrist, twisting it in a bone-cracking hammerlock. He was forced suddenly to his knees. A boot thudded into his ribs.

"*Gusano*!" a voice jeered. "Worm! Play soldier!"

Slumped on his knees, he tottered and would have fallen, but a hand grasped his collar to haul him erect. In the starshine he could see the twinkling blade of a knife. Was he going to die—here, now, in the dust of Cinco de Mayo Street?

Time stopped. Frozen into immobility, he stared at the wink of steel, saw it approach, ever closer, to his strangling throat.

"Let him alone, you fools!"

It was a new voice, a crisp commanding voice, that called from the shadows before Señor Ruiz's pharmacy. The raised knife trembled, hesitated.

"Let him alone, I tell you!"

The shadows mingled, flowed together, dissolved into the night. David Pine stood alone in the dust, stomach churning, ribs numb and aching from the kicks. Slowly his pounding heart began to return to its natural rhythm.

"Who's—who's there?" he called.

No one answered. There was only the night and his terror. The kitten came to him and meowed, frightened too by the sudden violence, the fleeing attackers.

"Who's there?" he called again, his voice shaky.

No one answered. After a while he knelt to retrieve his hat. It was gone; the ruffians had stolen his hat. He was out of uniform. The lamp still burned steadily in the SP depot, having taken no notice of his danger and deliverance.

Shaken, still trembling, he walked toward the reassuring depot light. The angry voice that had spoken from the shadows sounded very much like Paco Mora. It had been six years, and Maruja Cruz had said she did not know were Paco was, but the voice from the shadows was very like that of Francisco Mora—Paco Mora—David Pine's friend, Paquito.

Chapter Two

From his office at Fort Bliss, David Pine watched the dusty confusion. A hundred thousand National Guardsmen were pouring into the post from Illinois, from Kentucky, from Montana and California and the Dakotas. Fresh-faced young men came from unlikely-sounding places like Rabbit Forks and Dismal Swamp, Gumtree, Blue Springs and Pisgah and Sutton's Corners. President Wilson had spoken. Unless Mexico could bring the lawless Pancho Villa under control, war was imminent.

The post was bursting to the seams with soldiery, the Quartermaster Corps headquarters a madhouse. At the motor pool under his window Lieutenant Pine watched mechanics noisily breaking in new Jeffery Quad trucks. Motors raced, sergeants bawled commands, everyone sweated in the June sun.

"Sir?" Sergeant Acton inquired.

David closed the window against the oily roar of a lumbering Curtiss R-2 airplane going over. The First Aero Squadron was now at Fort Bliss.

"Yes, Sergeant?"

"Colonel Hayden would like to see you in his office."

The corps commander was a lean whip of a man, trig in blouse and Sam Browne. Sitting beside Hayden was a bright-looking captain with staff officer insignia on his collar and a row of colorful ribbons.

"Ah, Lieutenant Pine!" The colonel indicated the staff officer. "This is Captain Mason, from General Funston's G-2. Mason, David Pine."

David took the indicated chair while the colonel briskly cleared papers from his desk.

"Mason here is interested in what you found out at Roosevelt, David. You've already told me your story, but G-2 thinks there may be more to it than reported."

"No criticism, of course," Captain Mason said reassuringly. "But sometimes a chap has to have the proper training to understand what he sees and hears."

David decided he didn't like Captain Mason very much. The intelligence officer affected a British accent and wore with some ostentation a massive silver watch on his wrist in the style of those same Britishers.

"I've already told the colonel everything I knew," David protested.

Colonel Hayden lit one of his Murad cigarettes. "Now, David," he said. "Mason does have a point. And he's trained in intelligence techniques."

"That's right," Mason said. "Let's not quibble, shall we, old man? The situation along the border is too pressing to waste time. With General Pershing deep in Chihuahua, we don't want any monkey business to cut off his supplies."

Colonel Hayden was a good CO, and David wanted to please.

"All right," he said. "First, I talked to my stepfather and stepmother. They spoke of some kind of trouble they weren't too specific about." He could not bring himself to mention Paco Mora to Captain Mason. After all, there was no real evidence that Paco was involved in anything.

"Then what happened?" Mason was making entries in a small notebook with a silver pencil. "Didn't you go down to Chili Town? I mean, San what was it? San

Andreas?"

"San Andreas," David said, rolling the *r* to let Captain Mason know where he, David Pine, stood. "That evening I walked down there—it's only a half-mile from my folks' home—to see an old friend."

Mason's pencil poised expectantly. "Name?"

"Mora. Francisco Mora. We used to call him Paco."

Mason looked puzzled.

"That's the nickname for Francisco," David explained. "Like Frank."

"Oh."

"Paco wasn't there. A girl I used to know named Maruja—that's the same as Maria—was there. Maruja Cruz." He paused. Obviously, there *had* been something strange about that covert meeting in Felix Mora's house. On the other hand, with the situation tense between Anglos and Mexicans, perhaps even the Holy Name Society was being careful. "Maruja Cruz," he repeated. "She was cleaning up after a meeting of the Holy Name Society at Felix Mora's. She said Paco was—"

"A meeting? Of what?"

"A Catholic society. Father Herrera is the head. Does good work in San Andreas."

Captain Mason riffled quickly through his notebook. "Ah, let me see. Yes! Doesn't Miss Cruz work at the Plaines Bank?"

"I don't know," David shrugged. "I've been away a long time. Anyway, she said Paco was gone someplace. Then I left."

Colonel Hayden cleared his throat. "David, you mentioned some unpleasantness later. A street fight or something?"

He nodded. "A gang of kids—young toughs, I guess—roughed me up on the street afterward. They kicked me, threatened me with a knife, stole my hat." He paused, wondering whether to say anything about the voice that had come out of the darkness to rescue him. Finally he decided. This cloak-and-dagger stuff was silly. "They ran away, finally," he concluded, "and let me alone. I went back to Pop Cooper's, and the next morning took the train back to El Paso."

Mason looked sharply at him.

"Did you see any of their faces, recognize any of them? The ones that assaulted you, I mean."

David shook his head. "It was too dark."

The intelligence officer was not satisfied. Time after time he led David Pine over the details of the experience. Finally the colonel, an expert at handling difficult personnel situations, took over.

"Guess we've run that rabbit far enough," he said. "Mason, I'll have Lieutenant Pine dictate a complete statement for your files and send it over with suitable copies to G-2 this afternoon. Fair enough?" Without giving the staff captain a chance to object the colonel picked up a pointer and went to a map hanging on the wall, eyes squinting against the smoke from his cigarette.

"David, I'm going to let you in on something. Corps says they need an additional depot at Agua Fria to handle the increased load when the National Guardsmen all arrive. A depot commander usually rates a major, at least, according to the TO, but at the moment you're all I can spare."

David Pine was astonished. "Me? A depot at Agua Fria, sir?"

Colonel Hayden looked pleased at his enthusiasm.

"That's right. You know the lay of the land, the people, the railroad men and all. As you probably know, the citizens of New Mexico are critical of the Army. It will help our case if knowledgeable people like you can somehow put in a good word for the Army, explain the Army way."

David was eager, ebullient. He almost forgot his annoyance at the persistent Captain Mason. His own depot at Agua Fria, not three miles from Roosevelt!

"Yes, sir!" he said. "There's a local businessmen's association at Roosevelt, and another over in Minas Grandes! I could speak at one of their meetings!"

"There's another thing, too, Lieutenant." Mason's voice was G-2 again, smooth and contained. "There's something rotten in Roosevelt, perhaps a cell of Villista sympathizers intending to make mischief. The new Agua Fria depot will be an ideal cover for a small group of G-2 people, enlisted specialists and a capable officer or two, to keep an eye out." Mason smiled companionably; his decorations glowed in the dusty office.

David hesitated. "Are you—" He broke off, uncertain, then turned to Colonel Hayden. "Is he—"

Captain Mason didn't wait for the colonel. "I'll be in charge of the Intelligence activities, Lieutenant," he said. "Glad to have the chance to leave the desk, get out in the field again! Oh, not as Captain Gerald Mason, U.S.A.! Perhaps—well, I'll pick a good name. Maybe Corporal Jerry Mason, QMC. My men will be truck drivers, warehousemen, clerks—whatever. All with assumed identities, of course. That way they can mingle with the locals and not be noticed."

"Sir," David said to Colonel Hayden, "I'm very pleased to be chosen as CO of a depot. I'm young and very junior, and I must admit I never saw myself as a great military brain. I'll do the best I can, and hope to be a credit to you and the corps. But I don't like this business of spying! I know the people along the border. They get riled, understandably, when they think the Army isn't protecting them properly. But they're still honest and loyal citizens! I can't imagine treachery on their part!"

Captain Mason smiled. "Even the greasers?"

"The Mexicans I know," David snapped, "are fine people! They're generally oppressed by somebody, but they still manage to bear up and lead peaceful, law-abiding lives, which is more than I can say for some of the Anglos along the border!"

Colonel Hayden was anxious to pour oil on the waters David Pine and Captain Mason were troubling. "Most of them are, I'm sure. But they attacked a U.S. Army officer in uniform. That's serious!"

"A gang of young toughs!" David protested. "Why, it happens right here in El Paso! Every night they roll enlisted men on Cathouse Row!"

Colonel Hayden shrugged, pinched at his mustache. "Well, these are difficult times for everybody, I guess." Searching in a bulky file, he came out with a memorandum in a paper folder. He handed it to David Pine. "Here's Plan FA20, David! Everything written down. Complete instructions for establishing the depot. Basic authorizing letter from Corps, detailed schedules and deadlines—everything. SOP."

Colonel Hayden was well organized. Some day, David knew, he would get a silver star to replace the eagle on his collar.

"What *isn't* spelled out there, you understand," Hayden added, "is the fact that you're to work closely with Captain Mason on the intelligence side of the operation, render him every assistance you can. Do you understand?"

"Yes, sir," David said unwillingly. "I understand."

At Fort Bliss, amid the confusion of a peacetime Army plunged into a Mexican campaign, David Pine had been little more so far than an interested observer. But the lumbering Army system had finally caught up with him; he was needed, he had a job, he had a *command*!

Pleasurably he threw himself into the thousand and one details of FA20. It was the colonel's own brainchild, and David had been assured everything was SOP—Standard Operating Procedure. But as he and Sergeant Acton toiled in warehouses, typed out manifests, rummaged through file cabinets, requisitioned trucks, haggled with overburdened SP officials, it became apparent there were a lot of things that put him strictly on his own.

There were few precedents. He remembered a weary instructor at the QMC school saying, "Book learning, rules, regulations—they're all good. But in the last analysis a supply officer is a bandit!"

He became a bandit, and a good one. "Moonlight requisitioning," it was called. They needed an extra truck; Sergeant Acton appeared the next morning with a brand new Locomobile, and no questions asked. The SP claimed they did not have enough flatcars for his loads, so ten dollars from unappropriated funds bribed a yard clerk. They were short eighteen reels of field wire; David himself wheeled them from a warehouse while Acton shared a bottle of bourbon with the armed guard.

He and Sergeant Acton and thirty enlisted men were one day dumped by the SP into the mesquite-studded desert at Agua Fria, three miles east of Roosevelt. Flatcar after flatcar was off-loaded until the sandy waste was littered with boxes, cartons, barrels, canvas-shrouded fieldpieces, crates of rifles smeared with cosmolene, drums of gasoline and oil, chests of spare parts. David hired local carpenters from Roosevelt and Minas Grandes and Sage and Buena Vista to throw up warehouses of two-by-fours and tarpaper. He put advertisements in the Roosevelt *Patriot* and the Minas Grandes *Citizen* and the Sage *Weekly Rancher and Miner* offering five dollars a day for clerks, warehousemen, truck mechanics, draymen. He sweated and cursed and cajoled, signed legally-questionable documents, became even thinner and certainly tougher, grew brown-faced and long of hair. There was little time for the Mexican barber who set up shop just outside the gate in the new wire fence surrounding the Agua Fria Quartermaster Depot.

But one day in September it happened. The Depot was complete and functioning. He sat back at his desk, hands clasped behind his head, looking with pride at the string of dusty trucks loading supplies. Someplace, down in Chihuahua, a weary cavalryman would open a can of beef from the Agua Fria Depot—David Pine's Depot—and stay his hunger. Somewhere, at a place called Pueblo Morales or Candelaria, an infantryman would break open a packing case and take out a Springfield greasy with preservative but deadly and efficient once cleaned with kerosene from a metal drum supplied also by the Agua Fria Depot. It was all very satisfying.

He did not suspect what an important man he had become along the border. The Depot gave employment to dozens of citizens, the Depot bought many of its supplies from local merchants, the station's complement of enlisted men grew to sixty-five who spent most of their fifteen dollars a month in Roosevelt and Tres Minas and Sage. The Plains Bank bulged with new money; everyone had dollars to spend. And David Pine—"you remember Davy Pine, Coop and his wife brought him up after his folks died"—David Pine began to rank in importance with the editor of the *Patriot*, the president of the Plains Bank, the head of the Border Cattlemen's Association.

Fortunately, Captain Mason from G-2 gave him little trouble. He knew Mason had moved in once he saw the staff officer captain in dirty overalls and an old baseball cap checking off Peerless trucks from a manifest as they rolled down a ramp to the New Mexico sand. Mason had some enlisted men, too. David Pine did not know who they were; he suspected everyone but Sergeant Acton. Each time Mason saw David he gave a conspiratorial little wink, but it amused David Pine that the captain still wore his massive silver wristwatch. It did not fit the dirty coveralls and the corporal's stripes.

So busy, he had not been able to visit Pop and Mom Cooper, he accepted an invitation to address the Roosevelt Boosters Club at Druid's Hall. Sergeant Acton grinned. There was a free-and-easy association between them, one not to be countenanced in the real fighting Army at Fort Bliss.

"Sure, I'll go along with you,' the leathery sergeant chuckled. "I ain't tied me one on for a long time, Lieutenant." He rolled his eyes in mock salaciousness. "I can't wait to see the bright lights of Roosevelt! Is it true it's such a wicked town?"

David laughed. It was legend that Roosevelt rolled up the sidewalks at nine o'clock each night.

"I'd like you to meet my folks, too, Henry. And maybe you could draw a few charts to show the organization of the QMC how many dollars we've put into Roosevelt pockets since we've been here."

Acton polished up the station's shabby Studebaker touring car while David Pine spent fifty cents at Mando's *Peluqueria* for a haircut, a shave, and a liberal dose of pomade to plaster down the sunbleached hair. At seven of a blistering September evening they stopped at Pop Cooper's.

"Whyn't you come for supper?" Pop complained. "Mom baked a ham and made biscuits!" He shook hands with Acton, eyeing askance the sergeant's collar insignia with the sword and key crossed on a wheel, surmounted by a flying eagle. But when he learned Acton had started out in the cavalry, Pop was mollified.

David wanted them to ride into town in the Studebaker, but Mom shook her head.

"Coop's hip is still troubling him, Davy. He can't sit still too long on those hard chairs. Besides, there'll be a lot of your old friends there, people anxious to shake your hand afterward. Coop and me likes to get to bed early. You and Mr. Acton just clank along in that smelly thing, and we'll follow."

David smiled, looking at the old Spencer carbine stuck crosswise behind the buggy seat, the bandolier of cartridges. "Whatever are you taking that blunderbuss along for, Pop? Indians around?"

Pop Cooper was nettled. "Mexican Indians!" he snorted. "Pancho Villa Indians! Just you take a look at some of the ranchers and miners that's goin' to be at Druid's Hall tonight. Them fellers know the situation; they don't go nowheres without they pack a pistol."

Druid's Hall was packed. Everyone in town came; the streets were deserted. Uneasy, David peeked through a hole in the curtain. There must be a hundred people in the audience. He saw Mr. Mills, president of the bank, Sam Haywood from the Cattleman's Association, Miss Houghton, the high-school teacher who had taught Paco and Maria and him all they knew about Shakespeare. There were many others, including a blonde girl with an aquiline nose and marcelled hair to make sure the cowlick stayed in place.

"Shall I take this chalkboard out front now?" Sergeant Acton asked. "It's almost time."

David jumped. "Oh! All right."

Actually, it came off very well. After the first few minutes when he turned brick-red and forgot his carefully planned recognition of the mayor and other dignitaries, he got into the swing of it. He did know a lot about supply, about business and payrolls and inventories, and the citizens were warm and encouraging. He even managed to crack a few jokes. When it was over he felt relieved and a little proud.

Mom was helping Miss Houghton at the punch tables, and the blonde girl was passing cookies.

"David," Mom said, "you remember Louise Trilling." Handing him a cup of punch, Mom giggled. "You and Louise used to be pretty sweet on each other!"

Uncomfortably he shook hands with Louise Trilling. Her hand was small and well manicured inside his brown paw. "Sure," he said. "Sure, I remember. How are you, Louise?"

"Coop and I are leaving," Mom announced, tying a shawl over her gray hair. "Davy, we were real proud of you tonight! Now you young folks just get together and talk—enjoy yourselves."

Pop winked at David and peeled the wrapper from a stogie. Sergeant Acton lit it for him, which pleased him greatly. Then he and Mom waved goodbye and went outside.

David and Louise Trilling were standing in a corner next to a potted palm, sipping the purplish punch, when she jumped a little, spilling some of the drink, and said, "Heavens, what was that? That yelling outside?"

"I didn't hear anything," David said. He got a napkin and sopped up the spill on the worn boards of the floor.

"My goodness!" Louise said. "I'm glad I didn't get any on this dress. It stains horribly." She went on talking. "It's so good to see you again, David. I'm sorry we didn't really know more of each other in school."

"Yes," he agreed. "Me too."

"After school," she smiled, "you never seemed to be around much. You were always down in Chili Town with those kids." She wrinkled her brow. "What were their names? Paco and—"

"Maruja," he said. "Paco and Maruja."

There seemed to be a commotion at the stairway leading down to the street. Someone leaned out the window and called below. A few of the ranchers and business men ran down the stairs.

"I thought I heard a noise," Louise said. "What's happening, do you suppose?"

Sergeant Acton came over to them, holding the campaign hat politely over his broad chest. "Lieutenant Pine, sir, there's some kind of a fracas going on below. Hadn't we better—"

"Louise," David said, "this is Sergeant Acton, from the Depot. What kind of fracas, Sergeant?"

A horse neighed shrilly from the street. A faint rumbling sounded, one they seemed to feel on their faces, in their bodies, rather than hear. The old hall swayed gently, heaved under their feet. There was a tinkle of broken glass.

Louise Trilling dropped the punch cup and clung to him. "David, what's happening?"

He pushed her away and went to the window. Below, in the light shed by the electric bulbs in Druid's Hall, a pall of smoke lay in Main Street. Broken glass was everywhere, shining in the moonlight. There were riders in the street, men on plunging horses, men in broad-brimmed sombreros with cartridge belts crisscrossing their chests. One had a fat canvas sack slung over his shoulder. The door to the Plains Bank hung askew on its hinges; inside, something burned with a hot glow.

"*Vamonos*!" a rider shouted. "*Ya lo tenemos!*"

A scattering of gunfire broke out. One of the riders fired and there was a ragged volley in return. Some of the ranchers and oil men were behind wagons, behind motor cars, behind horses, wherever they could find cover, firing back at the *bandidos*.

"Come on!" David cried.

Neither was armed, but he and Acton clattered down the stairs. The clock in Goodwin's Grocery said exactly ten thirty when a wild shot splintered the glass.

"It's Villa," Acton muttered, "or some of his *dorados*!"

"They've robbed the Plains Bank!" a woman's voice screamed.

Almost under David's feet, a crouching rancher held a heavy Colt in both hands, squinting, finger tight. But as he squeezed off the shot his chest suddenly caved in, as if hit by a heavy timber. He toppled slowly into the dust, hunched in that strange position. David snatched up the Colt and fired at a bearded man on a bay horse with the red saddle blanket of the Villistas. He saw the man drop his rifle and clap a hand on his thigh.

"Pop!" David called. "Get the hell out of here!"

The Coopers had not yet left; they were caught up in the robbery. Pop had the old Spencer carbine propped on the dashboard of the buggy. Mom, white-faced, cowered behind old Atlas.

"Pop!" David shouted. "Get down! Get down!"

Pop squeezed the trigger. The big man on the capering bay fell off and lay flat. Main Street was filled with dust, blood, rearing horses, the sound of gunfire, orange stabs of flame. Acton picked up a dropped rifle and swore at a breechblock he could not close.

There was a pounding of hoofs, a cloud of dust, a fusillade that bit splinters from a hitching post beside David Pine's face. It riddled the Studebaker, whined down the moiling street and smacked into board fronts. David ran into the street, firing until the cylinder spun, then threw the gun at the nearest rider. Beside him Acton swung the useless rifle, butt first, and disappeared under a rearing horse.

Suddenly David remembered Pop Cooper. As he swung to look, a careering dark horse hit him in the shoulder and spun him around. He fell as the bandits ran over the dogged defenders, rode them down, disappeared toward the border fence with a pounding of hoofs and a cry of, "*Arriba Villa*!"

He ran to the buggy. Pop Cooper sprawled over the dashboard; the reins hung loose. Old Atlas, inured to everything, looked at David and made a snuffling noise.

Sergeant Acton, a smear of blood across his face and his hat gone, helped David lay Pop gently in the street. Mom Cooper stood near, face white, lace handkerchief to her lips.

"Is it—David, is he—hurt?"

He got up from his knees. His eyes burned, and he realized he was crying. It had been a long time since he cried.

"He's hurt," he said. "Mom, it's bad. He's—he's dead."

In the dust the body of the bearded man on the bay horse lay flat and still, too. A wounded horse neighed. One of the ranchers, cursing in a steady monotone, walked over and put a gun to its ear. A knot gathered around a wounded SP clerk named Leighton, who insisted he was all right but died as they carried him into Doc Menick's office.

"They got away with all the cash!" someone said. "Blew the bank vault! Dunno how much. Mr. Mills says it might go as high as ten thousand!"

David snatched up the old Spencer carbine. There was blood on the stock, and he wiped it clean with his palm. It loaded through a hole in the buttplate; he examined it carefully, deciding there were still cartridges in the magazine. From the buggy he snatched up the bandolier of ammunition.

"Acton?" he called.

"Yes, sir."

"Will the Studebaker run?"

The sergeant turned on the ignition and spun the crank. One of the Studebaker's headlights had been shot out, but the engine coughed, coughed again, and finally broke into a galloping stutter.

"Cylinders ain't all firing," Acton reported, "but I guess she'll go."

Mom Cooper pulled at David's sleeve. Pressing the handkerchief over her mouth in disbelief, she asked, "You're not—you're not thinking of—"

"Don't worry," David said. "Take care of Pop." Not bothering to open the door, he threw a booted leg over the seat and climbed in beside Acton. "The border gate," he said. "Fast!"

At the border the hashmarked corporal was trying to instill courage into two frightened recruits. Acton jumped on the brakes. The Studebaker slid to a stop in the glare of an electric searchlight mounted on a latticed wooden tower.

"Where the hell were *you* bastards?" Acton shouted. He pointed back toward Druid's Hall. "There was a battle up there! Villistas robbed the Plains Bank!"

The corporal saluted David Pine and said, "I got my orders! We ain't to leave the gate unguarded!"

David looked at the gate, a hastily carpentered affair

of new yellow wood and barbed wire. It was closed and locked.

"Didn't they come this way?" he demanded.

"Hell, no—excuse me, sir," the corporal said. "I mean no, they didn't come this way." He went to the latticed tower and pulled an arrangement of ropes and pulleys so the light swiveled to search along the barbed wire fence. "Must have cut a hole down below someplace. Private Burke thought he heard something about a half-hour ago."

Lago Guzmán, David thought. Lago Guzmán, where Paco Mora's uncle lived, Don Jaime. Was it possible that was where the bandits were heading? There had been no more than a few of the Villistas, and at least one lay dead in Main Street before the bank. The bandits were on horses, but he and Acton had the Studebaker and Pop's carbine with plenty of ammunition.

"Open up!" he commanded.

"Can't," the corporal said. "Orders, sir. No uniformed personnel to cross the border without a pass from Corps!"

"Goddamn it!" David cried. "Open that gate! We haven't got time to argue!"

The corporal's face hardened. While the soldiers looked on with wide eyes, he took a step back, raising his Springfield. "I don't open no gate!" he said in a voice half defiant, half pleading.

Sergeant Acton put the car in gear, intending to turn the car in a half-circle and return to town in the face of this impasse. But David Pine was angry in a way he had never before been angry. Given time to think, to cool off, he would have agreed with Sergeant Acton's decision. But there was no time. In sudden fury he jammed his left foot down hard on Sergeant Acton's, which was resting on the accelerator, at the same time jerking at the wheel.

The Studebaker gears screamed. The car slewed in a cloud of alkali dust and rammed the gate. The corporal pulled the trigger; there was a roar and a blast of flame. But they careened across the washboarded crossing and jounced crazily down the rutted road toward Lago Guzmán. Behind them other shots were fired. The long finger of the searchlight swiveled, caught them for a moment, then faded as they dipped into a shallow wash.

"Keep going!" David said between gritted teeth. Holding the Spencer carbine across his lap, he tried to keep from being jolted from the car. Part of the border gate hung over the bonnet of the Studebaker, the rest dragging alongside, banging and clattering.

"Yes, sir!" Acton muttered. He looked almost fearfully at David Pine. "Whatever you say, sir!"

Chapter Three

The moon was bright, giving some illumination of the road in addition to that cast by the single functioning headlamp. Acton, muttering under his breath, drove hard, slewing the car to avoid rocks and chuckholes. At times the car flew into the air, coming down to bottom the springs. Again, careening madly around a boulder, the Studebaker swayed so that the metal rims of the wheels bit into rocky ledges with a shower of sparks like a grinding wheel with a metallic scream.

Far into Chihuahua, the border miles behind, the engine coughed, spat, and quit. They rolled to a stop. Acton said, "Out of gas."

David climbed out and stood in the pockmarked road that meandered through tall *cardon* and *pitahaya*, ghostly monuments in the moonlight. "Isn't there a five-gallon can in back?"

Acton poured gas into the tank. Then he dragged the wreckage of the border gate from the bonnet of the Studebaker, found a bulb from a spare-parts kit, and got the damaged headlight to operate. From his silence, he disapproved of the whole crazy undertaking.

"We should have come up with them by now," David said.

Acton only shrugged. David squatted in the road,

picked up a dusty horseapple, looked at it, then tossed it aside.

"Well," he altered, "I—I guess we better . . ."

He did not know quite what to say. The fever had cooled; he began to think more rationally. They could both be killed by the bandits, if indeed they ever caught up with them. Sergeant Acton was also unarmed. The Studebaker—how much longer would it take punishment of the rutted road? A good and hitherto reliable QMC officer, David realized with a sinking feeling that the car was charged to him, to Lieutenant David Pine. He was accountable. Still . . .

"I'm no Yaqui," he said, "but I'll bet those bastards are still on this road. They haven't taken to the hills yet, the way I'd expect."

Acton only leaned against the fender, arms folded, and said nothing. David took a deep breath, trying to make a decision. Into his mind came the vision of Pop Cooper lying like a rag doll over the dashboard of the old buggy, riddled by bandit fire. He remembered Mom's pale worried face, and heard her ask, "Is it bad, David? Is it bad?"

"Well," he said finally, "I'd like to keep on for a little while at least."

Sergeant Acton spoke. "Wish I had at least my sidearm." He dusted his hands, washing them free of any responsibility. David saw, and understood.

"It's my doings, Henry," he said. "I'm responsible, whatever that's good for. I ordered you to cross the border with me."

Acton's lips twisted in the semblance of a grin.

"Yes, sir. I guess you could say you ordered me across the border." He limped back to the car. "Jesus, my goddamned foot is about broke where you stomped on it back there!"

Wary of the worsening road, they now drove more slowly. It was rougher, more rocky, than David remembered, winding down shallow washes studded with ledges of rock and clumps of cactus. At times they could go no faster than a man could walk. Once they had to stop and pour water from a can into the laboring engine. Finally, somewhere, in the middle of the night, they blew a tire.

Acton jacked up the wheel and took off the flat. In the light of the headlamps he pulled out the tube, found the hole, patched it, and replaced the tube. The operation took over an hour, including the time to pump up the tire with the ridiculously inadequate hand pump.

"I'll write a letter to someone about that pump," David said. He squatted in the road again, looking at the stew of hoofprints and fresh droppings.

"I'd guess," he said, "these aren't very old. Look how sharp and clear the prints are, even though the sand is dry. And the droppings are warm."

Acton came unwillingly to look. Finally he said, "Sir, begging your pardon, this is one hell of a crazy thing we're doing. You're a QMC officer, without no combat experience, and I'm an old Army relic with a Pistol Expert Medal." He flipped the decoration with his thumb and added, "But without no pistol. It looks to me like we're fixing to get killed."

"Just a few miles more, Henry!" David pleaded. "Just a few! If we don't spot something in, say, half an hour, I'll be willing to give it up as a wild-goose chase!"

Acton spat into the dust. It was obvious these antics were beginning to annoy him. He had soldiered in the Indian Wars, Cuba, and the Philippines. David Pine's authority in a QMC depot was one thing, pursuit of armed Villistas another.

"All right," he finally sighed. He took an Ingersoll from his pocket. "It's now three o'clock in the morning. At three thirty, come what may, we turn back. Right?"

"Right," David said.

Resuming their journey, they were increasingly aware

of perilous noises from the car. From the way it pulled to the right, it was obvious also that another tire was low. Sometimes the engine pulled smoothly, at other times it fired on only three cylinders, staggering and bucking like a rodeo horse. But after a while they came to a fairly smooth and level area, apparently the dry bed of an ancient lake, where they could make fifteen miles an hour.

"This is more like it," David said, encouraged.

The smooth lake bed was their undoing. Bouncing over an unseen ledge of rocks, the undergear of the abused staff car dragged the ledge with an appalling screech. The Studebaker stopped in midflight, hung up on the ledge so that the wheels spun uselessly.

"Christ!" Acton swore. "Now I've gone and done it!"

The Studebaker made a desolate wheezing sound as water left in the radiator flashed into steam. Acton, on hands and knees, reported the pan torn completely away. David knelt beside him, saw the spreading black stain under the car.

"I guess this is it," Acton said.

"I guess so." David squatted again and in discouragement scanned the faint trace of road. "We lost their tracks, too," he said. "Somewhere near here—we probably passed the place—they turned up one of those washes and headed for the hills."

The barrel of the old Spencer carbine was cold and lifeless in his fingers, cold with the dawn wind. He looked down at the gun and ran a remembering thumb over the worn stock. Pop Cooper had taught him how to shoot with that old relic.

"I guess I lost my head," he admitted. "You were right, Henry. And I certainly had no right to take someone else into Chihuahua on my own personal war."

Acton wrapped his arms about him against the cold. "So what do we do now?"

David shook his head. "I don't know."

"We must be twenty-five, thirty miles from the border. That's a long walk for an old man like me."

"Well," David said, "I expect when we're missed, they'll send a patrol to find us."

They climbed into the wrecked car and sat. David wondered how long it would take for a lieutenant's pay to buy a Studebaker staff car. The engine still made querulous complaining noises, the steam in its bowels bubbling and hissing. Finally even that sound ceased.

"Must be another hour or so till morning," Acton muttered. He glanced at the sky. "Maybe they'll send out one of those newfangled airyplanes to look for us."

The desert air grew sharper and colder. In the east there was a gradual fading of the blackness. The stars paled. Miserable with the cold, David climbed out of the car and slung the Spencer over his shoulder.

"You stay with the car," he ordered. "I'm going up on that ridge and take a look. Maybe I can see something, now that it's growing lighter."

Henry Acton rummaged in the tool kit, coming out with a heavy tire iron. "You better not go up there without me, Lieutenant. Suppose you did stumble on them, and—"

"I won't stumble on anybody," David said wearily. "But stay with the car anyway." Not unkindly, he added, "That's an order!"

Acton tossed the tire iron back in the box.

"All right," he said. "But be careful. Just be careful." Glumly he climbed out of the car and stood with legs propped wide apart before a fat barrel cactus, trying to pass water. "Guess I had it all scared out of me," he muttered.

In the growing dawn David scrambled up the wash toward the distant ridge, the bandolier of cartridges bouncing against his chest. He had a strange salty taste in his mouth. When he touched it with inquiring fingers, they came away speckled with blood. Only then did he realize he had a jagged gash on his cheek. The barbed wire of the border gate had probably done that.

He still did not understand why they had not long ago caught up with the fleeing bandits. Had they too paused someplace, perhaps to rest, or to meet other confederates? He and Acton had come so fast in the Studebaker; the Villistas could certainly not have galloped their mounts all that distance. Where were the bandits? Ahead or behind?

Nearing the top of the ridge, his boots lost their purchase in the wind-scoured sand. He lost his balance and fell, scratching his hands on a spiny *cholla*. A pinkish coil lay under a nearby bush, and he scrambled quickly away to avoid the snake.

The first slanting rays of the rising sun were beginning to touch the mountains to the west, the *sierra*. Far ahead wound the road to Lago Guzmán. He squinted tired eyes and gripped the Spencer tight. He was bone tired, exhausted. He was staring hopefully at a patch of cottonwoods in the distance, wishing to see movement of some kind, when he felt something cold and hard against his neck.

"You fool!" a voice said in Spanish. "Oh, you great fool!"

Carefully, David dropped the carbine. The foppish Captain Mason at Fort Bliss had been right. There *had* been something suspicious going on in Roosevelt.

He turned, very slowly, and Paco Mora was smiling at him.

"*Buenos dias*, David," he said. He gestured. "Push the gun over here, very carefully, with your foot, eh?" He spoke very softly, in Spanish, and scooped up the bandolier of cartridges.

"Where the hell did you come from?" David blurted.

"*Habla espanol, hombre*?" Paco said. "Speak Spanish, eh? We are not in Yankeeland now."

"But—"

"You know well where we came from," Paco said.

"You have been following us half the night. We came from Roosevelt, where we took a lot of money from the Plains Bank. We would by now have been farther into Chihuahua except we had to stop to let a man die. A boy, really, Manolo Garces, only sixteen. Someone shot him in the streets before the bank." He prodded David with the barrel of the Spencer and draped the cartridge belt over his shoulder. "*Vamos*! Let's go! The rest of my *tropa* are up there."

Stumbling before him, David spoke bitterly.

"Someone shot Pop Cooper, too! He's dead. Did you know that? They shot him dead, an old man like that!" He cursed, a thing he did not remember doing for a long time.

Paco stopped, holding the carbine at the trail. He took a deep breath, blowing it out so that the long tips of his mustachios wavered in the air.

"Truly, *hermano*? *Ay*, I did not know!"

"Don't call me brother any more!" David cried. "Not any more, you aren't my brother!"

Paco took off his steeple-crowned sombrero, finely worked with gold braid and colored threads, and wiped his forehead with his sleeve. "*Ay, que lastima*!" he said. "What a pity! When you and I were boys, David, Pop was not very kind to me and Maruja, you will remember that. But I did not bear him any ill will. He was only another Anglo."

"Yet you killed him!"

Angrily, Paco flung out his hand.

"Then he should have stayed out of the fighting!"

"But you were bandits, robbing the Plains Bank!"

"We are not bandits!" Paco shouted. "We are revolutionaries! And a revolution can not be made without bloodshed! They were all shooting at us, those people. You saw that! We did not want a battle ourselves; all we wanted was money for General Villa, our Invincible General! We planned for a long time how to carry out the raid without spilling blood. But we did not know all those people were going to be in Roosevelt that night. When we last heard from Maruja, she said—"

"Maruja? Was she in on this too?"

Paco shook his head and motioned to David Pine to walk forward again. "I do not want to talk about Maruja now."

A little knot of men, swarthy men, well armed, waited for them in the bushes atop the ridge.

"My *tropa*," Paco explained. "My company of irregulars."

They captured Sergeant Acton with no trouble; he was unarmed. One of the *tropa*, a sullen, gray-faced man they called Dr. Saenz, wanted to shoot David and Sergeant Acton at once, but Paco overruled him.

"David Pine," he explained, "is an old friend of mine. I do not shoot a friend, even if he is so misguided as to wear a U.S. Army uniform. Besides," Paco hefted the canvas bag which David supposed contained the loot from the Plains Bank, "in Chihuahua, things other than gold can be valuable. Maybe a U.S. lieutenant and a U.S. sergeant can be exchanged for some of our Villista brothers now held in jail by General Pineda and his *colorados*."

Still Dr. Saenz persisted. "But we can not take them with us! It is too much for the animals! They will have to carry double, and they are already tired!"

Paco and Dr. Saenz were still quarreling when they heard the noise. It was a faint buzz, like a faraway bee foraging flowers for nectar.

"An airplane!" Dr. Saenz muttered. He had a gray desiccated look to him, a dry juiceless look, and he wiped quickly at a corner of his lips with a handkerchief. "They have got an airplane after us already! Paco, we should have left Manolo to die and gotten out of here quickly as I advised!"

They had all heard of airplanes but never seen one. The Yaqui called Nacho made ritual signs for protection and scanned the dull sky with frightened eyes, gripping his rifle tightly.

"So it is an airplane," Paco shrugged. "What harm can an airplane do us? We will be at Lago Guzmán soon. Anyway, the U.S. airplanes are not any good. Maruja talked to a soldier at Fort Bliss, and he said there is a lot of trouble with them. They can hardly go fast enough to rise off the ground, then they crash back again."

Suddenly they saw the airplane, a golden speck on the horizon. Paco ordered everyone to take cover in the chaparral. Nacho, the Yaqui, pinched his mount's nostrils shut in the old Indian way, to keep the animal from nickering and thus betraying them. Paco grinned. "No need to do that," he said. "The airplane can not hear us. It makes too much noise by itself."

The craft flew a zigzag course, casting back and forth like a hound on the scent. The *tropa* shrank farther into the head-high brush, watching the propeller of the craft make a silver disk in the rising sun, hearing the needle-like droning of the engine.

"So their airplanes are no good!" Dr. Saenz jeered. "So they fall back right away to the ground, eh? What is this then, Paco Mora? A big bug of some kind?"

The boy called Luisito and the grizzled, barrel-chested man known as Café both crossed themselves and looked fearful. While they watched, tense and nervous in the dawn chill, the airplane soared nearer in its methodical stitching of the countryside. It seemed to be flying a prescribed search pattern.

"I told you we should have hurried!" Dr. Saenz muttered. With shaking fingers he lit a cigarette. "We should have been safe at Lago Guzmán by now!"

Nacho was trying to wrap a marihuana cigarette in brown paper. In his fright he spilled the grasslike stuff. "Ah, see it come!" he muttered, eyes fixed on the advancing airplane. "*Que caray!*"

It lumbered toward them like a great ungainly bird, spitting and roaring and trailing a wisp of oily blue smoke. Suddenly it seemed to find the wrecked staff car in the dry lake below. While the craft circled the spot, the observer peered over the side. They could see him plainly.

"That's the First Aero Squadron, I'll bet!" Acton muttered.

David knew one of the officers of the squadron. It was common knowledge at Fort Bliss that the Curtiss R-2 had only a bare minimum of horsepower. An engineer was rumored to have calculated the Curtiss had only four horsepower more than necessary to sustain it in level flight, with no margin for maneuvers. Still, turning to make a long level approach, the pilot felt for the ground, finally setting the airplane down in a cloud of dust.

"I do not like this!" Paco muttered. "The word is out for us! They have probably telegraphed from Roosevelt to Fort Bliss to send out this damned airplane! Soon we will have some of Pershing's men on our trail, as well as David Pine and his old Spencer gun!"

The observer, in helmet and flying suit, white scarf wrapped around his neck, climbed from the cockpit. The propeller was still turning, though the engine now only ticked slowly over. The man circled the wrecked staff car, a pistol in one hand. As they watched he bent over and stared into the tonneau.

"Listen!" Paco said. "Listen, Nacho! I do not want that airplane to get away with any information about David Pine, about us, about anybody! I do not want it to get away at all! You are always bragging, *hombre*, about what a good shot you are." He pointed to the airplane. "Do you see that silver round thing spinning there? That is called the propeller. That is what makes the bird fly. If it is damaged, the bird can not rise off the ground and fly back to Fort Bliss to inform on us. So, *hombre*, shoot the bird in the propeller, eh? Right in the middle of that spinning silver thing!"

There was not much they could do, but David Pine,

hands bound behind his back, decided to save the airplane, somehow. It was their only chance of rescue from this bandit band. "Listen!" he muttered to Acton. "When I—"

Paco looked at him, frowned. "*Callete*, David!" he ordered. "Be quiet! We want absolute quiet here while Nacho performs his miraculous marksmanship."

It was indeed a difficult shot, several hundred yards. Nacho lovingly patted his rifle, propped it across a large boulder. Squinting through the sights, he muttered to himself. "Three hundred meters. Or four hundred? But this is an easy shot for a Yaqui. And I have never shot at so big a bird before. I can hardly miss!" He pressed his cheek against the stock, squinted again. "I squeeze the trigger, just so—"

At the top of his lungs, David screamed. It was a long way to the airplane, and against the noise of the idling R-2 engine, but there was just a chance the pilot might hear him. Acton, startled, stared at him for a moment. Then he too opened his mouth and bayed like a coonhound. Nacho looked up in surprise; the aim of the rifle wavered.

"Fire, you idiot!" Dr. Saenz shouted. "Nacho, you fool. Shoot! Quickly!"

Nacho squeezed off a shot. Alerted by the caterwauling, however, the aviator was already running toward the airplane. The shot kicked up a puff of dust at his heels.

"Fire!" Paco shouted. "Everybody shoot!"

The *tropa* loosed a hail of lead at the fleeing man, at the spinning silvery disk, at the airplane itself. Spouts of dust sprinkled the desert, and some bullets undoubtedly ripped the fabric of the airplane. But the observer vaulted into the cockpit and the engine roared. The propeller spun rapidly; the big bird staggered forward. A wing caught on a bush so that the R-2 spun sideways. Still it lumbered on, gaining speed. Now it seemed to be coming toward the ridge, directly toward them. They redoubled their fire.

"Kill it!" Nacho screamed. "Kill it before it hurts us!"

The airplane hit a rock and a tire blew. At the same time something—perhaps it was the shock of the blowout or a lurching upward over a rock—threw it heavily into the air. Engine roaring, the R-2 caught the air. Propeller blades bit deep; the airplane soared over their heads. Undaunted, the goggled flyer leaned over the side and fired a pistol at them.

Paco was furious. Though both David and Sergeant Acton's hands were tied, he hit them hard, shouting curses. Nacho, too, his chance for a spectacular kill gone, struck them, driving them to their knees as they endeavored vainly to keep their faces protected against the blows and kicks. The others—Luisito, Enrique, and the rest—joined in too. Dr. Saenz only watched from afar, moodily sucking on his cigarette.

"I told you, Paco," he called. "We should have gotten rid of those two immediately."

Anger finally exhausted, the *tropa* relented. Some still wanted to kick and beat and pummel, but Paco drove them away.

"I am sorry," he said to David Pine. "It is not right to hit a man when his hands are tied. But David, you caused me trouble, much trouble. Perhaps Saenz was right. I have no case anymore. Perhaps you should be killed."

Now the airplane was only a golden speck in the distance, dwindling straight as the crow flies toward Fort Bliss and safety. It would there deliver a report on the whereabouts of the *guerrilleros* who robbed the Plains Bank in Roosevelt, New Mexico, the night of September 18th, 1916. Fort Bliss officials would also know where Lieutenant David Pine and Sergeant Acton had disappeared.

During the heat of the afternoon the *tropa* holed up in a pile of sunbaked rocks that held greenish water in shallow pools called *tinajas*. Sore and angry from the beating, David Pine sat beside Henry Acton and stared northward, where a smudge on the horizon indicated a distant Roosevelt. Paco came over with a canteen of water and offered them a drink.

"I was very angry, David," he said in an attempt to make amends.

David said nothing.

"Come, *hombre*!" Paco urged. "We can be friends! After all, you are not dead. You have me to thank for your life. Dr. Saenz would have killed you long ago. He is a very powerful man, our liaison officer with General Villa's *Division del Norte*. I can not afford to antagonize him, you know. And he was right about our poor horses carrying double. Look at the weary beasts, blowing and wheezing at the water there!"

David turned cold eyes on him.

"You killed Pop. You and your damned gang came into Roosevelt—your own town—and killed people you'd known all your life!"

Paco made an angry gesture. "Roosevelt is not my town! It never was! They have signs there, remember, saying: DOGS AND MEXICANS KEEP OUT. Now it is our turn. The revolution has come."

"Don't talk to me about revolution!" David shouted. "Pop Cooper didn't have anything to do with your revolution!"

"But I am only fighting for my people, for *la raza*!" Paco protested. "Do you understand that?"

"I understand you and your bully boys rode shooting into Roosevelt!" David said bitterly. "I understand you robbed the bank, killed people! I understand that, all right!"

Paco's smile was hard as he held up the sack of

money never far from his side.

"Don't you understand, *hombre*? This is blood money! Money taken from every overworked, underpaid *peon* who ever worked on your oil rigs, chopped cotton, washed dishes and cleaned house for fat *gringo* women! This money really belongs to us, to *la raza*!" Lowering his voice, he leaned forward. "David Pine, do not be stubborn! I am sorry, very sorry, about your Pop Cooper! But the struggle has to be, you see. It is the only way." In a sudden change of subject he put a hand on David's knee. "Do you remember how it used to be with us, *amigo*? How we used to be together all the time? You, me, Maruja?" He laughed. "Ah, the fun we had! The oaths, the great oaths sealed in blood, we swore!"

David said nothing.

"Let us be together again!" Paco urged. "David, our General Villa needs Yankee experts. Already some are with our artillery, our infantry, our mounted troops. The general, I hear, pays well—in gold. David, come with us! Fight with us, help us in our struggle for freedom! Really, you are a part of us, I know. Your heart was always with the poor people!"

David shook his head. "You're a fool to put such a proposition to me! I'm a commissioned officer in the Army!"

Paco got up, slinging the canvas bag over his shoulder.

"I do not know," he said, "which of us is the fool, David Pine. After all, the situation you have gotten yourself and the sergeant into does not exactly recommend you as a sage!" He patted the bag. "But when I deliver this money to our Invincible General, I become an important man. I may become an officer myself. The general may possibly make me a captain or a major in the *Division del Norte* for my services. and it is my intention to make good. I do not intend to let anything interfere with my success, not even my friendship with you, *hombre*."

Dr. Saenz stubbed out a cigarette. He seemed to David Pine to be always smoking a cigarette. His face was angry.

"It is time to go, Paco!" he growled. "What this *tropa* needs is action, movement, not so much talk! I will speak of this in my report!"

Late the next morning they came out on a ridge above a sprawling *rancho*. David recognized it; it was Don Jaime's home at Lago Guzmán. Beyond the whitewashed buildings sparkled the waters of the lake. Wild geese punctuated its surface. Even farther beyond was the spidery trace of the Mexican Northwestern Railroad, running from El Paso and Ciudad Juarez all the way to Colonia Dublan and Madera and Guerrero. No trains were on the track, and the little *rancho* appeared calm and peaceful.

"Home!" Paco Mora said. "This is my home, David!"

Cautious, the *tropa* set their horses atop the ridge, watching. Finally Paco said, "Everything looks all right. Let's go down."

The keen-eyed Nacho shook his head. "I don't see Don Jaime's cows!" he protested. "They are always grazing on that green stuff around the lake. Where are they?"

Paco took out field glasses and studied the land. "I don't know, *hombre*. Maybe they are in the shed, and Don Jaime is milking them." He turned to David. "It takes a lot of milk to make the good *queso fresco*, eh, David?"

The sun rose higher. Still they watched the buildings of the *rancho*, wary. "Where is everyone?" Luisito demanded. "Don Jaime and the señora? The boys, too?"

"And Pablo Corral and Pedro Mirón and the rest we left to guard the place?" Dr. Saenz asked. "Paco, this does not look good to me!"

Fearing an ambush, Paco sent Café and Nacho to circle the outbuildings and approach from the lake side. It took a long time to ride through the brush and scattered rocks. Finally the scouts signaled with waving arms, followed by three shots in the air.

"*Vamonos*!" Paco cried. "Let's go!"

He dug his spurs into his mount's flanks and they all clattered noisily down the hill. In a moment they knew why Don Jaime's *rancho* was so still and quiet.

Nacho met them. He was weeping, an unusual thing for a Yaqui. "Pineda and his *colorados* have been here!" he cried. He swept out his arm. "Look!"

From a gnarled juniper in the yard—a tree David Pine remembered himself and Paco Mora climbing on that time so long ago—hung the bodies of Don Jaime and two stripling boys. They had been hanged then shot. Slowly their bodies twisted in the sunlight. At Don Jaime's feet lay a small black and white terrier. When Paco approached, the dog looked up, as if beseeching him to do something about this terrible thing that had happened to his master.

"*Ay, Cristo*!" Paco moaned.

In the bare-swept yard lay the body of Doña Ana, skirts about her head, fat bare legs showing immodestly. She had been bayoneted to death. More bodies were scattered about, those that had been left behind to guard the *rancho* while the *tropa* robbed the Plains Bank.

Still others seemed to be missing. Café called off the names in a kind of dirge. Rodrigo, the Aguirre brothers—twins, Pedro Mirón, Eufemio Bolanos. The whitewashed buildings of the *rancho* were splayed with bullet holes.

"They died bravely!" Luisito muttered. "*Por Dioś*, there was a fight! But too many *colorados*, I think! *Caray*, the dead shrink so!"

There was no sign of federal troops in the vicinity; they had apparently carried away their own dead and wounded.

"They went away on that damned MNR train!" Dr. Saenz said. He turned toward David Pine. "See, *gringo*, what butchers your government supports—Pineda, Carranza, Obregon!"

Now everything was peaceful, the peace of death. There was only the incense of dead fires, the smell of a pan of dough for tortillas, an overlooked hen scratching busily in the gravel. Those things—and the three bodies twisting in the cheerful sunlight.

"Good God!" David murmured, the words sticking in his throat.

He stared at Don Jaime, swinging a little like some horrible pendulum. He did not want to, but he looked at Doña Ana's plump body sleeping in the sunlit yard. First Pop Cooper, now the courtly old man and his wife. They had all been good to him. Suddenly his thoughts were confused. He did not know what to think.

Chapter Four

They buried the bodies beneath rude crosses; now it was time to return to the business of the living. The men watered and fed the exhausted horses. Nacho found Dona Aña's little stone trough and resignedly began to grind corn for tortillas. It was woman's work, but there were no women. Café boiled water for coffee, while Paco emptied a painted rawhide trunk belonging to Don Jaime and stuffed the loot from the Plains Bank into it. Dr. Saenz watched, smoking a cigarette. David remembered the scent of Egyptian tobacco in Felix Mora's house in San Andreas. Dr. Saenz must have been there, one of the plotters, that night, the musky smell was the same. Saenz, like Colonel Hayden, fancied Egyptian cigarettes.

Seeing David Pine's eyes on him, Dr. Saenz took a Mauser cartridge from his crossed bandoliers and tossed it in his hand. The metal winked dully as it spun toward the ceiling. David and Sergeant Acton sat side by side on a rude wooden bench before the smoke-blackened fireplace. A crucifix with a carved Jesus hung over the hearth. David fixed his eyes on the crucifix.

"We have got to move quick from this place," Dr. Saenz said, playing with the cartridge. "Here, on this level plain of the lake, we are unprotected." He gestured toward a window, to the flat southern land bathed in sunlight, to the distant bulk of the *sierra*. "The *colorados* will come back, and then where will we be?"

In a corner of the room Nacho squatted impassively, precious rifle across his knees. Luisito went on carving a piece of bamboo into a rude flute. Dona Aña's old Singer sewing machine stood silent and motionless in the sunlight that moved across the floor of pounded earth. It seemed strange to be looking at so homely, so familiar a thing, when death might be near. David took a deep breath, wondering if it were one of a numbered sequence remaining.

"Well," Paco finally said, "I have a plan, Saenz." He gave the strap of the painted trunk a last hard pull and sat down on it. Paco, even now, looked very young. Almost innocent, David thought, with the innocence of childhood. The curl of black hair dangled over his eyes, and his chin was cleft. Gracefuly he lounged on the painted trunk, one booted leg crossed over the other. "You say General Villa is with Colonia Dublán now. Right now?"

The gray-faced Dr. Saenz tossed the cartridge high, catching it with an expert twist of his wrist. "That was my most recent information."

"Then," Paco said, "we go to Colonia Dublán."

Dr. Saenz's eyes narrowed. He looked at David and Sergeant Acton. "But about these two *gringos*?"

Paco grinned. "We take them with us!"

Saenz snorted. "What foolishness! It is a journey of two hundred and fifty kilometers, and the land swarms with *colorados*! Anyway, we do not have enough horses!" He turned to Nacho, to Luisito, to Café. "Listen to how foolish Paco talks! It is our lives he is trifling with—and our money, too! Just because this *gringo* officer was once his friend! No, I say kill them both now and get out of here quickly, with no more talk! Luisito, Nacho—you, Café! What do you say?"

They only stared at Saenz, then back at Paco.

"You see!" Paco grinned. "They are my men, sworn to me, Saenz! Do not try to start any trouble. I command this *tropa*, even what is left of it, and I make the decisions. Anyway, all you ever want to do is kill people!"

Café scratched his stubbled chin. "But Paco, our horses are few, and they are tired. How—"

"Do you trust me?" Paco demanded. He strode about the room, spurs clinking, heavy cartridge belts rustling. "I have a plan."

Dr. Saenz continued to look at the painted trunk.

"All right," he grumbled. "A plan."

"We do not use horses. We go by the Mexican Northwestern Railroad." Paco clapped Luisito on the back. "This boy used to be a *telegrafista*, no? What could be easier? We do not even have to buy tickets! We slip into the MNR station at Guzmán tonight, shoot the guards, put Luisito here at the telegraph key. We tell the dispatcher to stop the next train for cattle to go to Colonia Dublán, to feed the *colorados* there. When the train stops, we cut the telegraph wires and get on board. That way, you see, we ride in style all the way to Colonia Dublán! Just before we arrive, we wreck the train and mount our horses. Before the *colorados* know what has happened, we deliver the money to General Villa! In addition, we have all had a nice train ride and wrecked a lot of MNR rolling stock too!"

They were taken by the boldness of the plan. Use the *colorados'* own railroad to ride to Colonia Dublán and deliver the money to Villa, then twist the bull's tail by wrecking the train! Café whooped with delight, Luisito tootled a martial air on his bamboo flute, even the impassive Nacho grinned. Dr. Saenz only shrugged, saying, "Maybe it will work. But General Villa himself would have shot these two, I know that, and not traveled with extra baggage!"

Excited, the bandits squatted together and made plans over a map spread on the floor. David was thirsty. Morning cool was gone from the adobe dwelling; now the whitewashed walls simmered with heat. Behind him he twisted his wrists, but the rope had been expertly knotted. He looked helplessly at Acton. Acton stared grimly back.

During the day a lookout called a warning. The *tropa* were instantly alert, poking guns through the wooden lattices of the windows.

"*Por Diós*!" a voice shouted. "Put away your guns, *compadres*! It is only Pedro Mirón! *Por Diós, dejenlo!*"

It was the rest of the *tropa*, the ones driven away from the rancho by the federal troops. Delighted, Paco and the rest crowded around the new arrivals, calling out greetings. "Pedro! Eufemio! Enrique! *Que tal*?"

"They came on us at dawn," the new arrival named Pedro said. He was a tall man, burned almost black with the sun, carrying an ancient fowling piece that might have been left from the French. All bore the stains of battle. Some had bloody bandages, one man hobbled on an improvised crutch. Few had modern weapons, most carried machetes and brush hooks. "We fought them hard," Pedro explained. "We gave them as good as we got. But after a while we ran out of bullets." He pulled at his cartridge belt, letting it flop emptily against his chest. "They drove us back and back." Looking around the bullet-pocked room his eyes filled with tears. "Don Jaime," he wept. "And Doña Ana! Paco, we wanted them to flee with us! But they said this was their home. They said they had done nothing wrong! So they stayed."

"I know." Paco nodded toward the rude crosses in the dooryard. "Now they stay here forever, *hombre*. But that was the way they would have wanted it."

The men took off their sombreros. For a while no one spoke. Finally Paco broke the silence.

"Well," he said, "we are going for a little ride on the

railroad!" Quickly he explained the plan to Pedro Mirón, the Aguirre brothers, and the rest of the scattered *tropa*.

Now that they were together again, the *tropa* was exultant. They would extract a sweet revenge for the loss of countrymen, of friends, of relatives. Perhaps they had lost the battle of the *rancho*, but they could strike back against Pineda and his federal forces, the hated *colorados*.

"*Vamonos*!" Pedro Mirón shouted, brandishing the old shotgun. "Let's go, eh? Paco, what are we waiting for?"

Only Dr. Saenz seemed unmoved. He took out a fresh cigarette and lit it, staring moodily at the painted trunk.

In the glow of a waning September moon they sat their horses atop a hill overlooking the Guzmán telegraph station of the Mexican Northwestern Railroad. They were almost thirty now, a sizable band. The moon sprinkled them with silver dust, a motley collection of ragged farmers, lame horses, and ancient weapons. The only signs of uniformity were the red saddle-blankets of the Villistas. Some had dyed old blankets red, and the dye ran on the sweating horses. Others had pieced together remnants of bright clothing. But all proudly carried the scarlet sign of the Villista army, the Division of the North.

Below, the tracks of the MNR railroad traced southward in the moonlight. It was a warm evening, desert plants scented the air. Beside the tracks was the telegraph station, a wink of lamplight in the darkness, surrounded by outbuildings. There were soldiers at the station. By squinting his eyes David Pine could see a glimmer of the white hand-woven cotton shirts and pants they wore, hear an occasional laugh, see the sputter of a match as a guard lit a cigarette.

Hands bound, he urged the old mare with the

pressure of his knees to come close to Paco Mora. In a few minutes they might all be dead, but first David had something on his mind.

"Paco," he said, "no matter what has happened, I'm grateful to you for saving my life that night in Roosevelt, when I came to your father's house."

Paco was puzzled. "Saving your life, *amigo*? What do you mean?"

David was annoyed. "That night! When I left Maruja, a gang jumped me in Cinco de Mayo Street. You were there! You know!"

Paco grinned. "Oh, that, *hombre*! But I did not save your life. The boys were just having a little fun with a *gringo* soldier, innocent fun!" He pushed the big sombrero far back on his curls. "Bah! They would not have killed you, David! You were my friend, no matter the uniform you wore! I gave orders you were not to be harmed, really harmed. But I heard you did lose that fancy hat with the gold and black cord!"

He rode away, shouting orders. David Pine and Acton were left under guard by an old man armed with a musket. Pedro Mirón and Café led a small group down a canyon to the west, where they were to create a diversion to draw away the guards while the bulk of Paco Mora's men captured the station.

"I done me a heap of soldiering," Henry Acton muttered, "but I never figured to be mixed up in anything like this!" With his bound hands he tried unsuccessfully to blow his nose, but the old man became alarmed and prodded him with the musket. "All right, all right!" Acton grumbled. "Keep your pants on!"

The night became more still. A bat fluttered by. David's mare shied, tossing her ancient head. Away in the distance the *sierra* shone luminous in the moonlight.

"Some day," Acton murmured. He hesitated, staring at the *sierra*. "Some day I'll forget all this crazy business! I've got in my thirty years, and won't I shake the dust of New Mexico off my heels in a hurry! I'll find me a little shack where I can fish and hunt and—" At the sound of distant shots he broke off. Silently they sat the horses, watching, listening. Long minutes later the lamp in the station went out, then reappeared—twice, three times, in the agreed-on signal.

The old man chuckled. "We have them!" He clapped his heels into the ribs of his spavined paint horse, drawing them after him with the long *maguey* rope he had tied to his prisoners' bridles.

At the station the telegraph operator sat frightened in his chair. Nacho held a gun to his head. Pedro Mirón and his companions soon swept into the station with a thundering of hoofs. Pedro flung himself off the horse with a rumbling chuckle.

"Paco! Ah, Paco! Those guards are running yet, I tell you!"

Paco Mora looked up from a sheaf of papers taken from an iron spike on the telegrapher's desk. "What happened, then?"

Pedro's eyes crinkled in amusement. "When we shot at them—just once, mind you, just once—they dropped their guns and ran away in the night! I think they are running yet!"

Café found the station coffeepot and was pouring himself a cup. "They were probably *pelados*," he explained. The word meant "the peeled ones," the people of *La raza*, deprived of land, liberty, and money by the grasping landlords and an oppressive government. "They did not want to fight anybody. But Pineda pressed them into his army and gave them guns. It is all right that they got away!"

In a yellow circle of lamplight they crowded around Paco Mora. "What do we do now, *jefe?*" someone asked.

Paco folded the documents carefully and stuck them in his pocket.

"According to these papers there is a train coming at six in the morning. But it will not stop. We have to talk on the wire to the operator at Ciudad Juarez and tell him to stop the train here." He turned to the frightened operator. "Senor, what is the call sign for the station at Ciudad Juarez?"

The operator was a sallow man with a green eyeshade and sateen sleeveguards over an expensive silk shirt. His sweaty face shone in the lamplight. Frightened, he only stared at them.

"*Cabron*!" Dr. Saenz nudged the operator with the muzzle of his rifle, catching the man under the chin with the front sight and forcing his head up. "Did you hear, *cabron*? We do not have time to play games! What is the sign?"

The man only stared glassily.

"I think he has wet his pants," Pedro muttered.

"No matter!" Dr. Saenz said. "I know how to make him talk, wet pants or no." He grabbed the terrified operator by the collar of the fancy shirt and dragged him out onto the platform.

Paco shrugged and turned to Luisito. "*Hombre*, do you know what to do with these instruments?" He pointed to the rough wooden table before the window. There were shiny brass sounders in wooden cases, clacking relays, a large lead-lined box full of electrical cells.

Luisito slipped into the operator's chair and fingered the knob of the telegraph key. "Does a fox know what to do with a rabbit? Ah, Senor Paco, my father was the agent at Parral! I was weaned on battery acid!"

They jumped when a gun went off, outside on the platform. Dr. Saenz sauntered in, slinging the Mauser rifle over his shoulder.

"Cuidad Juarez is CJ now," he reported. "That is logical. Guzmán—the station here—used to be GZ, but is now LG. If we want to talk further down the line, then Colonia Dublán is DD and Parral is PR."

For a moment they were silent, staring at him. Finally Luisito said, "Well, that is very good! That is all right!

But if the agent told you the signs—"

"Yes, that's right!" Pedro Mirón protested. "There was no need to kill him!"

Dr. Saenz smiled a gray smile. "A man who wears a silk shirt like that is a pimp, I think. Anyway, he said some very bad things about General Villa."

Paco shrugged, looking tired and drawn. David Pine, standing in the shadows with Sergeant Henry Acton, realized they all had been long hours without sleep. The world seemed suddenly unreal. He thought of his familiar office in the QMC compound at Agua Fria—the row of pens and pencils, his adding machine, homely sheaves of manifests and bills of lading, the dusty electrical bulbs hanging overhead, warehouse smells of grease and wood and metal. What was David Pine, an inoffensive supply officer, doing here, bound and weary in a Mexican railroad station while outside a man in a pink silk shirt bled out his life in the gravel of the MNR roadbed?

Henry Acton, too, looked near exhaustion, much different from the capable non-com of Agua Fria Depot. The sergeant swayed on his feet, unavailingly twisting his bound hands behind him. "Can't even feel my fingers no more," he complained. "Wish they'd loosen these ropes!"

David called to Paco, asking him to loosen the bonds for a moment, but no one paid attention. They were all drawn into the game of waylaying the train from Ciudad Juarez. In a pool of smoky light they crowded around the wooden table, jostling each other for position, watching Luisito with respect and admiration as he worked the shiny brass key.

"Any answer yet?" Paco asked.

Luisito started to speak, then held up a finger for silence. The sounder in its wooden box clattered. Luisito listened, then giggled.

"What is it?" Dr. Saenz demanded.

Luisito scribbled on a scrap of paper, holding it out

for them to see. "The operator at Ciudad Juarez says he does not recognize my fist. He wants to know where Jorge is!" Happily Luisito tapped the key, sending a message in return. "I tell him Jorge is drunk, and I am taking his place until he sobers up!"

There was a howl of laughter, but Paco was still concerned. When the clacking of the sounder ceased, he asked, "Did he believe you?"

Luisito nodded. "I think so." Tapping the key, he requested the Ciudad Juarez operator to stop No. 124 at the Guzmán station for cattle ordered by General Pineda to feed the *colorados* at Colonia Dublán.

Afterwards, there was long and anxious silence.

"Do you think he suspected anything?" Paco asked.

Luisito shook his head. "*Jefe*, I know how to make train orders! I learned to read from my papa's train orders at Parral." Suddenly he held up his hand again. "Listen!"

The sounder tapped out a message. Luisito jumped to his feet, doing a little dance in triumph. "*Compañeros*, it is all arranged! The train will stop here at six in the morning!"

After a hot day, the night turned cold and crisp. David remembered this was, after all, late September; autumn was at hand. The *tropa* lit fires along the railway to warm themselves. Though Paco was too busy organizing the attack to talk to him, David finally persuaded Pedro Mirón to loosen their bonds. Pedro, who seemed to bear them no ill will, found a burr-studded blanket for them, even bringing coffee and a few cold, tough tortillas.

"For," he explained, "our chief enemy is Pineda and his *colorados*, along with his master Carranza. You *gringos* are not bad people! You mean well, but sometimes good intentions give bad results. *Mira*—I knew a *gringo* lady once at Carrizal! She gave us food and money and took care of my children when my wife, my Concepción, was in her last illness."

At dawn, the two prisoners were thrust on a pair of mules and taken up a draw to a mesa well above the railroad. The old man, who was called Don Antonio, was angry at not being allowed to participate in the matter of the train. He took out his resentment on them, jabbing them with the muzzle of his musket.

"Goddamn it!" Acton exploded. "Stop poking me with that blunderbuss, you old fool!"

Half hidden in a screen of chaparral, they watched the sky brighten, glow gray and misty. It became faintly luminous, finally streaking into pink and green and yellow and mauve. Below, Paco and Dr. Saenz were directing the tactics of the operation. Horses were concealed in the outbuildings. Half the *tropa* remained hidden in the station, ready to pour out on command. The rest took cover in culverts and piles of brush along the tracks, each small group with specific orders: capture the brakeman, board the engine and hold the engineer and fireman at gunpoint, seize the conductor, shoot the handful of armed guards that normally accompanied No. 124. The flat land around Lago Guzmán was not a terrain of concern for the railroad officials; it was usually in the *sierra*, the mountainous stretch from Colonia Dublán through Cumbre Pass to Madera and Guerrero, where raids might be expected.

The dawn grew, strengthened. Birds woke in the cactus, flitted from *cardon* to scraggly mesquite to *pitahaya*. David shivered in his thin khaki shirt. The garment had been torn and soiled since his capture; one sleeve hung only by threads. His boot had lost a heel, and there was an annoying itchy stubble on his chin and cheeks. Sergeant Acton divined his thoughts, saying, "Me, too, Lieutenant! I look like a scarecrow! I'm beginning to smell gamy, and my britches could stand without me in 'em."

Utterly miserable, David tried to think of something pleasant. Maruja Cruz came to mind. Perhaps it was only in contrast to his own dirt and rags he thought of her, of that night in the *casa* Mora, sitting on her legs on the floor to pick up the remnants of the broken ashtray. Maruja, he thought. Ay, Marujua! So dainty and soft, so gentle with her humor at his awkardness, so womanly. Lost in thought he stared across his mule's neck, across the *maguey* rope binding him to the old man and his bony mare, across the valley, far toward the peaks of the *sierra* to the south, only now tipped with the first splash of gold from the rising sun. Fresh, clean, soft, he sighed to himself.

"There!" Don Antonio pointed with his musket. "Senores, look!"

To the north was a sooty plume of smoke that rose up and then mushroomed flat as it struck a layer of stagnant air. David could see a puff of steam. Seconds later he heard the toot of a whistle. No. 124 was on schedule.

Below them, the station appeared deserted. The lamp still burned in the window, but its brightness was lost in the growing day. A small figure paced the platform, and David thought he saw a pink shirt. They had taken the dead agent's shirt and someone was wearing it to make things appear normal. Jorge was sober again. Jorge, the agent, was on the platform with his papers and manifests and bills of lading.

Swiftly the train approached. Now they could hear the steady beat of the drivers, the rumbling of the flatcars and gondolas and box cars, smell coal smoke as the wind shifted in their direction. Don Antonio licked his lips in anticipation, jerking the *maguey* rope hard to pull David and Sergeant Acton farther into the brush. "No one must see us!" he hissed. "Ah, to take a train! All my life I wanted to ride on a train!"

Below them No. 124 ground to a halt. Paco's men suddenly burst from the station, swarmed aboard. From culverts and canyons and clumps of brush others of the *tropa* rose, firing, yelling. The guns seemed to pop harmlessly, and cottonlike wisps of smoke arose;

even the shouts and cries seemed staged and unreal.

But men were shot and killed. They dropped weapons, staggered, and fell. From a box car poured a stream of red-badged guards. They fell on Paco's men with a volley of precise fire, signaled by a man with a sword and a red sash who must have been an officer.

Beside him, Henry Acton sucked in his breath.

"Guess your friend bit off more than he bargained for!" he muttered. "Cuidad Juarez got suspicious and beefed up the guard on the train!"

For Paco Mora and his *tropa* the fight was not going well. Outnumbered and outgunned by the disciplined *colorados*, they were forced steadily back to the shelter of the station building. The platform was littered with bodies, some trying to crawl, others limp and still.

"*Por Diós*!" Don Antonio cried in his shrill voice. "They are defeating us!"

The old man watched the struggle, chewing at the fingers of his wispy mustache. Then, in sudden resolve, he banged the mare in the ribs with his musket and let out a battle cry. Neighing in alarm, the mare gathered her stringy haunches and galloped down the slope toward the battle, Don Antonio shouting and brandishing his musket.

Jerked by the *maguey* rope, the mules clattered after, slipping and sliding on loose rocks. David Pine, no horseman, was almost thrown in the wild rush. He gripped hard with his knees, hands still pinioned behind him, bending over the arched black neck of the mule in a desperate effort to hang on. Before him, Don Antonio, riding like a youthful cowhand, lifted the musket and fired. "Hoo!" he yammered, like a man calling pigs. "Hoo! Hoo!"

David clamped his legs hard on the mule's ribs, but solid ground dropped from under them. The bank down which they slid had been cut away at the bottom to form a cattle-loading chute along the tracks. All of them—mare, mules, riders—dropped into the corral in a maelstrom of thrashing hoofs and clouds of bitter dust. Whinnies split the air. The mare and the mules rolled and kicked, teeth bared and eyes white with fear. David Pine found himself still astride of the mule, which was down and trying to stand. As the dusty black body heaved under him, he jumped aside and sprawled on all fours in a stew of cattle droopings.

Somehow in the fall his bonds loosened. The twisted rope hung free from one wrist. Near him a red flash lit the boiling dust; a shot boomed. He staggered to his feet, pawing at blinded eyes.

"Acton!" he cried. "Henry, where are you?"

As the morning wind blew aside the dust, he saw the iron bulk of the engine. Nearby, in a shallow gully, two men in brownish-green uniforms crouched over a Browning machine gun on a tripod. A fourth was lifting a belt of cartridges preparatory to feeding it into the gun.

Giddy, disoriented from the fall, he started to run. He didn't know where. Near his ear a bullet whistled, and he threw himself down, finding himself lying across Don Antonio's frail body. The old man's head was twisted askew; David realized the skinny neck must have broken in the fall.

In an action more instinctive than reasoned he snatched up Don Antonio's musket. For a moment the *colorados* at the machine gun stared at him. The man holding the snakelike belt half rose from his crouch.

"Henry!" David yelled. "Where are you?"

The gunner made up his mind. The snout of the tripodded gun swung around, traversed past David Pine, then swung back. The man with the belt crouched again. They were going to shoot him!

There was no time to think. In three long-legged strides David Pine hurdled the tracks, scrabbled for a moment in the ballast to regain his footing, then jumped into the gully, swinging the musket like a club. A startled coffee-brown face below a red-badged cap loomed in his vision. He slammed the iron buttplate hard against the mouth and teeth; the long cartridge belt dropped in a tangle. Tugging at a sidearm, the non-commissioned officer yelled a command to his startled detachment. Then the wide-swinging musket caught him between chin and shoulder. He went down like a steer in an abattoir, the pistol going off in the air.

David snatched up the pistol, but by that time the remaining *colorados* had fled the gully and were running away, climbing into a box car. He emptied the clip after them, suddenly aware the tide of battle had turned. As he watched, standing alone above the silenced gun, the defenders of the station burst out in a wild charge. Firing pointblank, swinging machetes and brush hooks, they drove a fierce wedge through the encircling foe. David watched the wedge split into two wings, the wings instantly spreading wide to flank the besiegers. In moments it was all over. The swirling counterattack dissolved the federal discipline; earth-colored uniforms fled this way and that, pursued by cheering farmers who might have been hunting *javelina*, the wild pigs of Chihuahua. In a few minutes there were only two kinds of *colorado* at the Guzmán station: dead ones or distant fleeing specks, running terrified into the sparse vegetation along the rails of the MNR.

Trembling, David stepped out of the gully and onto the tracks. Where had time gone? The sun was impossibly high; the battle had lasted longer than it seemed. Captured pistol hanging from nerveless fingers, he stumbled along the tracks. He was very hungry, very thirsty. Yet he was sick, too, and could not stomach food; his throat was constricted and he could not swallow. So this was battle!

"Henry!" he muttered, and dropped the pistol.

Henry Acton, late sergeant of the QMC, lay across the tracks, face staring into the blue sky, hands still bound behind him. Dr. Rafael Saenz was near the body, knotting a soiled handkerchief around his own bleeding hand.

"Your sergeant," Saenz grimaced. "He tried to escape to the damned *colorados*! He kept running toward them and yelling, 'Friend! Friend! U.S. soldier!' "

David knelt over the shattered form. "Henry," he murmured, "I'm sorry! I'm damned sorry."

The rest of the *tropa* drew near. They ringed David and the dead sergeant, respectful and reverent. Already someone was stoking the locomotive for the run to Colonia Dublán. A shovel rang against a firebox door. A shower of soot fell on them. They heard the hissing of released steam.

"Perhaps," Dr. Saenz went on, pulling the soiled handkerchief taut with his teeth, "you have something else to be sorry about, too, Lieutenant Pine." David followed Saenz's pointing finger. Down the track, in a litter of crumpled green-brown uniforms, was a patch of what looked like khaki, U.S. Army khaki.

"No. 124," Dr. Saenz grinned, "had on board, it appears, soldiers of Pershing's cavalry! A liaison group, perhaps, going to Parral. Anyway, they are dead now—and you helped kill them!"

Chapter Five

Café and Luisito squatted beside the open hole watching David Pine dig a grave, a large grave, for the dead U.S. cavalrymen and the late Sergeant Henry Acton. They said nothing, only smoked their homemade cigarettes, watching David Pine, stripped to the waist, dig deeper and deeper. Luisito took out his little bamboo flute and blew a note or two. Café frowned at him.

"Now is a very serious time," Café reproved. "This is not a time for flute music, *hombre*!"

The sun was hot. After a while Café laid down his rifle and took the shovel from the sweating David Pine. David protested, but Café kept a firm hold on the shovel.

"I know how it is with you, señor," he said politely. "These are your people. One of them was your friend, and a good man. It is an honor for me to help you. *Verdad*, these dead men were on the wrong side. But then no two people see a cat of the same color."

David knelt beside the blanket-wrapped bodies, searching pockets for indentification. The bodies were still warm, limp, like tattered rag dolls. His hands trembled as he touched them, but he found wallets, notebooks, a sheaf of faded photographs. He forgot the names almost as soon as he had tied the effects in a rag.

They were anonymous names, names like Jenks, Roberts, Smith, names that had no more meaning. Unremarkable enough at first, death had wiped away any shred of meaning.

Luisito helped him carry the bodies, already stiffening, to the grave and lay them beside each other. Afterwards, David tamped the dry dusty earth with the flat of the shovel. Luisito brought a handful of white pebbles and outlined the grave. Café broke off a dead agave stalk and fashioned a rude stalk which he stuck at the head.

"Señor," Café asked, "are there not some holy words you should say? A small prayer, perhaps?"

It would take a very great prayer to absolve David Pine from his sins, but perhaps a small one would do for these newly dead. "Henry," David said, "I'm sorry. Where you went—" He swallowed. "Where you went I hope there's hunting and fishing, like you wanted. You other fellows—" Tears stung his eyes, and he shook his head to clear the vision. "God help us all," he murmured. "And amen."

The captured MNR train had been a rich haul. Breaking open the cars the *tropa* found new Mauser rifles, sidearms, cases of dynamite, tools, canned milk and canned beef, cigarettes. There was plenty of bottled beer and whole cases of Monopole champagne. But they had taken heavy losses in the battle of Guzmán station. Ten had been killed—both the Aguirre boys, Pablo, Enrique, Victor, several others—and some wounded. If it had not been for David Pine capturing the deadly Lewis gun, there would have been more casualties.

"Did you see him?" Pedro Mirón demanded, champagne dripping from his huge mustachios. "He stood like a tall pine tree, high over those miserable *cabrones*, and smashed them flat!"

"*Que caray*!" Eufemio said admiringly. "He crushed their skulls like eggshells! It was like being struck by lightning!"

Luisito sounded a few notes on his bamboo flute. "I am going to compose a song," he decided. "A song about *El Pino*—our great pine tree—how *El Pino* killed the *colorados* and took their machine gun, all to the greater glory of *la raza*—the people!"

Someone found a rocking chair in the station. They roped it in place atop the coal car and gently placed the body of Don Antonio in it. "For," a man explained, "the old one always wanted to ride on a train. Is it not the will of God that he finally do so, even dead?"

From nowhere the *soldaderas*—the *tropa*'s women—appeared to climb on the train, accompanied by small children and even some old people, perhaps grandfathers and grandmothers. On piles of sand in the box cars the women built fires and cooked food. They began to wash clothing and do all the homely things as if they were on their own hearth. The men buried their dead, pulled horses aboard the train, cut telegraph wires. By backing the engine onto a siding they managed, with a huge chain someone found, to uproot several hundred meters of MNR track between Guzmán station and Ciudad Juarez.

Paco Mora, standing atop a box car, waved a captured *colorado* flag to signal Café, who held his pistol on the terrified engineer and his fireman.

"Let's go!" he shouted.

Steam hissed, drivers gound on sanded rails, smoke belched from the stack. They were off to Colonia Dublán to join General Villa, the Centaur of the North, the Invincible General.

The first car was taken over by Paco for a command post. The leader sat in one end, the rawhide chest his throne, loading clips for his rifle. Dr. Saenz looked at a map and explained something to Pedro Mirón, who had an unlettered man's reverence for anything printed, and especially in several colors. An old woman named Elena cooked on an earthenware *comal*. Grinning, she offered David Pine a spoonful of beans wrapped in a hot tortilla. It was good. He had not eaten anything for a long time.

Watching from the open door, he saw black smoke streak overhead as the train gathered speed. The turquoise sky, the blue sky of Chihuahua, held only a few lamblike clouds. Women stood on the flat cars, their draperies windfolded, excited by the unfamiliar sensation of speed. Men squatting in sarapes looked like colored toadstools. Someone started to sing the revolutionary song "*La Adelita.*" All the way to the end of the train voices joined in, heard still above the rumbling of iron wheels, the hiss of steam:

> *"Si Adelita se fuera con otro*
> *La sequiríria por tierra y mar.*
> *Si por mar en un buque de guerra,*
> *Si por tierra en un tren militar.*
>
> "If Adelita went away with another,
> I would follow her through earth and sea.
> If by sea, in a warship;
> If by land, in a military train."

This was a *tren militar*, indeed. And they were all going to seek Adelita, the sweetheart of the revolution.

Nacho, the Yaqui, had been told to guard David Pine. Now he squatted at David's feet, beloved rifle cradled across his knees, looking like an Aztec idol. The only sign of life was the quick darting of his eyes this way and that.

Paco put the last clip in the belt slung across his chest and swaggered forward. "David! Ah, David—*Señor El Pino,* that is!" He pinched his lip, looking thoughtful. "But it is a waste of our good Nacho to guard prisoners!"

"Let me go, then!" David urged. "Let me get across the border. Let me go back to Agua Fria!"

Paco shook his head. "No, *hombre*. First," he ticked

points off on his fingers, "first, you know too much; who we are, where we are going, what we will do with the money."

Dr. Saenz must have overheard the last word.

"I want to count that money soon, count it myself, Paco," he called. "I want to make an accounting of the amount of bills, coins, other items." He laughed, but it did not sound genuine. "Sitting on that money like an egg, you will not hatch it!"

No one laughed. Paco seemed not to have heard.

"Second, you might be valuable in an exchange of prisoners. And third—well, you would not last one day, *hombre*, in Chihuahua without my protection. This place is crawling with *colorados*, bandits, with frightened villagers who shoot anyone, friend or foe, who comes near."

"Let me go to Parral," David suggested. "Pershing is at Parral, I hear."

"Even if you got that far, the U.S. soldiers would probably shoot you when you tried to cross their lines! *Hombre*, you do not look like an officer. You look like a ragpicker!"

That much was certainly true. But Paco went quickly on to establish the case even more convincingly.

"Who knows how the U.S. command at Parral would receive you anyway? In this country, news travels fast by the brush telegraph. Already there is talk about *El Pino*, the hero of the battle of Guzmán station. And is it not a fact, David Pine, that you fought with Paco Mora's gallant *tropa* against the *colorados* of General Pineda, who are allied with your Pershing? Fought even against your own khaki-clad soldiers, who died back there at the Guzmán station?"

Till now David had not felt the full impact of those still khaki figures.

"That couldn't be helped!" he protested, his voice hoarse with the remembrance. "Anyone in my position would have had to do the same thing! Those *colorados* were going to kill me with their machine gun!'' It sounded lame, very lame. Desperately he plunged on. ''No one could call me a traitor for that! That was just something that happened, that's all! Fate, or whatever you want to call it! But whatever happens, I'm still an officer in the Quartermaster Corps!''

Paco shrugged. ''In any event, old friend David, you have put me in a very difficult position by sticking your nose into our business, the rightful business of the *tropa*. You are in effect an embarrassment. We are few now—we lost many at the battle back there—and every man in the *tropa* must do double duty. Yet here is the good Nacho, our best marksman, wasted on simple guard duty over a prisoner.'' He sighed. ''Believe me, *hombre*, it is difficult for me when there is such a simple solution!''

David frowned. ''What simple solution?''

As soon as he asked, he knew. Paco looked toward the gray-faced Dr. Saenz, who was probing a wounded man's bullet hole with a penknife. The man sitting on the floor cried out in pain as Saenz gutted the wound with the knife. Yellow fluid poured out. The man fainted.

Saenz grunted in satisfaction. ''Good!'' he said. ''Very good! The putrefaction has been drained. Everything will be all right now!'' He cast a brief glance at Paco and David Pine and said, ''Putrefaction *must* be cast out! Only in that way can the body be made healthy and whole again!''

''You see?'' Paco murmured. He took off his big sombrero to wipe an arm across his forehead. Morning cool was still in the racing car, but Paco was sweating. ''This business of being a leader of patriots is very difficult, David Pine. Robbing banks, that part of it is easy, and exciting. But commanding a *tropa* and keeping everyone happy is a hard task, I tell you!'' He shook his head gloomily, then took David by the arm. ''Do you remember when we were children? The oaths you and Maruja and I used to swear? Blood oaths? We cut our wrists and let the blood mingle. Only Maruja wouldn't go that far."

David nodded. That was a long time ago, when life was simple, when choices were simple.

"And when we ran away," Paco continued, "to Don Jaime's *rancho* and would not tell our parents where we had been?"

David remembered a body back there, hanged to a tree, twisting slowly in the sun. "Yes. I remember."

Paco put the sombrero back on his glistening curls. "We never broke that oath. I did not. Did you?"

"No."

"Well, then, I propose to you a new oath."

David was puzzled. "Swear to something, you mean?"

Paco spoke slowly and quietly. "Here and now, David Pine, give me your word not to try to escape. It is the only way out for you—and for me. Swear here and now, on our old friendship, on the body of poor Don Jaime, killed by the *colorados*, that you will not try to escape, will not attempt to do me or my *tropa* or our cause any harm."

David frowned. A thought stirred in his mind, something concerning a convention. The Hague Convention, the one about the rules of warfare? Henry Acton would have known. The sergeant knew all the regulations, the laws, the rules under which military men lived and died. Vainly David tried to recall some military law. Name and rank—that was all he was required to furnish a captor. But what about parole? What did the Convention say about parole?

"Well?" Paco prodded.

Acton would tell Paco Mora to go to hell, but David Pine's position was very different. The sergeant had found a solution for all his problems at the Guzmán station.

David temporized. "Why?" he asked. "Why should I

accept parole?"

Paco shrugged. "Anyone can see that. It is the only path remaining. You are an old friend; perhaps—even now—my best friend. I do not want to see you harmed."

"But—"

"If you do this for me," Paco said, "I swear to release you unharmed once I have gotten the Plains Bank money to General Villa. I will give you an escort and see you safe to Parral or El Paso or wherever you choose. But now I am too busy with other things, and you are a problem. Old friend, what do you say? I must have your answer and quickly."

David glanced around, almost as if in hope of finding an answer within the swaying box car. Luisito was tootling on his bamboo flute, Café drinking coffee, the old woman tending a pot of beans. The car smelled of smoke, unwashed bodies, corn-husk cigarettes, festering wounds.

"All right." His voice was husky. "But on one condition."

"Eh?" Paco frowned. "Do not push me too hard, David Pine! Really, you are in no position to make conditions."

"Nevertheless," David said doggedly.

"Well, then?"

"In the future, if anything happens to change my mind, if I decide to try to escape, for instance, I will first tell you so. Then the parole is off. Agreed?"

Paco stared, fingering his lip. "It is a strange arrangement."

David wondered if the Hague Convention spoke of revocable parole. It was indeed an odd arrangement. Still, the circumstances were strange, too. Circumstance had tricked him, mocked him, piled blow after blow on him. Too, the *colorados* were brutes. His heart, as Paco insisted, was indeed with *la raza*, the little people of Mexico, endlessly ground between the millstones of one oppression after another.

"Well," Paco said, "I guess it is all right." He held out his hand. "We do not have to draw blood on this, David. There was enough blood—too much blood—back there at the station." He spoke quickly to Nacho. "*Dejelo, hombre*! The *gringo* does not require a guard any longer."

Dr. Saenz looked up from his patient, eyes half closed against the smoke curling from his scented cigarette. "*Que pasa, Paco*? What is going on?"

They all turned to look—the old woman Elena and her beans, Café watching over the rim of his tin cup, even the wounded man staring dull and uncomprehending.

"David, here," Paco announced, "has given me his parole. I know and trust him, and so have accepted it. From now on he agrees he will not attempt to harm us, not betray us, not try to escape. From now on he travels with the *tropa* as one of us."

Dr. Saenz scowled.

"He is to be treated with all respect and consideration as a paroled prisoner," Paco said, "and that is all there is to it."

"I have never heard of such a thing!" Dr. Saenz complained. "Not in this kind of a war anyway, Paco! What kind of a foolish business is that?"

Paco sat down again on the rawhide chest.

"There is no further discussion," he said. "This is Paco Mora's *tropa*, and Paco Mora commands. Does anyone want to make something of it?"

Dr. Saenz shrugged and turned away. Over his shoulder he said, "I tell you now, Paco Mora, you have done a thing that can ruin us all, perhaps endanger even the revolution itself."

But the rest seemed to welcome David Pine in his new status. Café clapped him on the back, Nacho twisted his thin-lipped mouth in an unaccustomed grin, Luisito tugged at David Pine's sleeve.

"Listen," he said. "Listen, *hombre*. I have composed a new *corrido*—a ballad—a song about the great *El Pino*."

After her mother died in January, Maruja Cruz lived in the Mora place, cooking and keeping house for old Felix. Though Paco's father was crotchety and difficult, it was a good arrangement. Maruja had no family ties, and with Paco gone the old man would have neglected himself without someone to see that he ate properly and wore clean clothes.

From eight in the morning till six each night, Maruja cleaned and dusted at the Plains Bank, and at night saw to Felix. The old man's mind was clear and sharp, though he was failing physically. Maruja appreciated his help in compiling her weekly intelligence report to General Villa's *Division del Norte*.

She did not know how the intelligence gathering system had been set up, but apparently Paco Mora had had a great deal to do with it. Now that Paco was gone, it was Maruja's task to collate the information received from furtive visitors, to add whatever she could from her own observations in San Andreas and at the Plains Bank, and pass the report on to the man who knocked at Felix Mora's door at eleven each Friday evening.

Sometimes he would be an itinerant tamale vendor and would wrap the report in a stained cornhusk, placing it among unsold tamales. Again, he might be a teamster with a span of mules, or the man who played the *guitarron* in a strolling band. It delighted her to be a part of such mysteries. It never occurred to her that she might herself be in danger because of these fascinating activities.

"There!" she said one night, closing the door and turning with sparkling eyes to old Felix. "There, Papa, goes another report to our Invincible General! This one had a lot of good information in it, too. There was a long list of guns shipped from the Agua Fria Depot and where they were going. Someone—I suppose a man who works at Agua Fria—kept a record for us."

"For General Villa," Felix corrected gently.

"*Si. Para el General, el General Invincible.*"

After Felix went to bed, she sat for a long time at the kitchen table, looking at the flame of the coal-oil lamp. In the smoky chimney she could always see images, pictures, things that had been, perhaps things that were coming to pass. Sipping her coffee, she watched the passing show. Tonight it was Paco, Paco Mora.

Paco, she murmured to herself. Ah, Paco!

In the rounded globe of the chimney she saw him, sombrero tipped rakishly over his black curls, eyes flecked with fun, a smile on the wide-lipped, generous mouth.

Ah, Paco, she thought, where are you tonight?

Since the Plains Bank robbery she had not heard from him, nor did she expect to until he had delivered the money to the general. Even then, it would probably be dangerous for him to cross the border; he might have to stay in Chihuahua until the Invincible General defeated Pineda and his *colorados*. But Maruja Cruz was a good *soldadera*. In Chihuahua were thousands of *soldaderas*—women soldiers—who followed and supported their men, even carrying guns and fighting alongside them in General Villa's army. It was the least Maruja could do here in Roosevelt.

Near midnight she took off her dress and stockings and lay down on the sagging davenport, blowing out the lamp. Roosevelt was noisy this Friday night. A football game had been played at the high school. During the day a livestock sale brought many buyers into town. And it had been payday at the Agua Fria Depot. A lot of the Depot workers were in Roosevelt, drinking and whoring away their salaries. Thank God, they did not often come into San Andreas itself.

It was hot, an end-of-the-summer hotness. She lay for

a time in her damp shift, seeing Paco's face in the darkness, in every corner of the stuffy airless room. It was almost as if he were there, comforting her, his arms around her, his fingers feeling gently for her breasts. She slipped slowly, imperceptibly, into sleep.

Sometime later, she awoke, startled. For a moment she lay not moving, hoping old Felix had heard the door and would answer it. But Felix slept like a log. When the knock sounded again she got quickly into her dress and went to the door with bare feet.

"*Quien es*?" she called. "Who is it?"

"Maria?" a male voice asked. "Maria Cruz?"

"Yes," she answered. "I am here. What do you want?"

There was a pause. Then the voice said, "I have information you can use. Please let me in."

No one would give her information—information for her report to the *Division del Norte*—in English. And no one called her Maria, though that was the name on the Plains Bank's employment records. Maruja was her *apodo*—her nickname.

"Who are you?" she called.

Another pause. Then, "Mason. Jerry Mason. I'm a mechanic at the Agua Fria Depot. Open up, will you? I'm not going to harm you. I just want to talk."

She knew no Jerry Mason. Quickly she ran back to the davenport and picked up a stocking. The garter was still in it, the garter holding the slim leather sheath and the knife Paco insisted she wear. It had sounded silly, and at times she feared the outline showed through her dress. Now she took the knife in one hand; holding the lamp in the other, she opened the door a crack.

"What do you want with me?"

The man was dressed in stained coveralls and a dirty baseball cap, a heavy silvery watch on a bracelet at his wrist. The rays of the lamp shone on the massive timepiece. She had never before seen a man wear a watch on his wrist.

"May I come in? I'll only be a few minutes."

He seemed polite enough. For a moment she stared around the room, wondering what to do. Then she decided.

"My—my father is asleep in the back room," she warned. Then she stepped aside, and he strode past her. "Be quiet." She closed the door and stood holding the lamp high to better see him, the knife still concealed.

"May I sit down?" he asked.

She shrugged. He sat down in Felix Mora's old seat-sprung rocker, and Maruja let her own weight down on the arm of the sofa, half sitting and half standing, dropping the knife into the space between the end cushion and the arm, where it could not be seen but was ready at hand.

"What do you want?" she asked again.

Mason fussed with the stained cap, denting the greasy crown with blunt fingers, then pulling it back out again.

"I hear you're interested in information."

"I don't know what you mean. What kind of information?"

He smiled, a creasing of angular features that did not seem genuine. "Miss, I work at the Agua Fria Depot. I know a lot about what goes on there. I see all the manifests, bills of lading, things like that—what goes where, and how much. With stuff like that, it's easy to figure out Pershing's plans; where he'll go next, where the soft spots are, where the cavalry regiments are strong and where they're under strength."

He seemed to be waiting for her to speak. After a while she set the lamp on the kitchen table and asked, "What has all this got to do with me?"

"I guess you don't understand." Conspiratorially he leaned forward. "We know—I mean I know Villa has got a lot of gold. His men aren't called the *dorados* for nothing, you know! And there's sympathy for Villa in the States. A lot of people prefer Villa to Carranza."

"So?"

"So I'm offering you information. I'm for Villa, too. He's the champion of the poor, isn't he? Isn't that what they call him? I'm poor, you're poor. So I'm selling you information, information Villa wants and needs; cash on the barrelhead, preferably in gold. What do you say?"

She could hear old Felix breathing noisily in the curtained alcove at the rear. From over in the Anglo part of town came a whoop of alcoholic glee. Someone fired a gun. She started nervously.

"What do you say?" Mason insisted.

Paco had not prepared her for anything like this. The offer could be genuine. Maruja was old enough, cynical enough, to know that men would do anything for gold. Perhaps even the gold could be arranged. Paco had told her to use her head. But at that precise moment Mason shifted his position on the sofa, crossing his legs, folding his hands over the stained cap. The big silver watch on his wrist—*caray*, what an odd place to wear a watch—caught the rays of the lamp. No man, she thought suddenly, no enlisted man has the money to buy an expensive bracelet watch like that!

"I don't know what you're talking about," she said. "I'm only a poor girl who scrubs floors at the Plains Bank. I don't know anything about the Agua Fria Depot, or Villa and the gold you say he has. Maybe there is another Maria Cruz. Maybe you have the wrong person."

He sidled close to her. "No, there is only one Maria Cruz." His hand closed around her arm, and he pulled her toward him. "Look, Maria, you don't need to be afraid of me!"

"Stop it!" Desperately she tried to pull away. She glanced toward the curtained alcove. "I told you my father is asleep in there!"

When he did not release her, she snatched up the knife and cut him quickly and deeply across the hairy forearm.

"Jesus!" He drew back, appalled. "Why in hell did you do that? I was only—"

"I told you to let me go!" she spat.

He stared at the wound. "Jesus!" he said again, and found a clean handkerchief, neatly folded, to mop at the wound. Enlisted men, she thought with some satisfaction, did not send their laundry out to be neatly folded and ironed.

"You probably cut a blood vessel or something!" Mason grumbled. He swore, horribly.

"Get out!" Maruja ordered. She opened the door and stood beside it, slim knife still in her hand.

For a time he stared at her, holding the handkerchief closely against the wound. "You greaser!" he said finally. "You damned greasers!" He went to the door and stood there mopping at the blood, the flow of which had slowed. She was grateful for that; she had not wanted to hurt anyone.

"No," Mason said. "No. There is only one Maria Cruz. Only one."

Still Felix had not waked, so she waited until the next morning to tell him of the incident. Listening to her, he ate his eggs and tortillas. Finally he said, "This game is too dangerous for you to play, child. And I am sure Paco would not want you to get into trouble."

"But who can get me into trouble? Who knows?"

He sopped a piece of tortilla in liquid egg, chewing slowly. After a while, he said, "Who knows? Perhaps many men, but even one is too many, Maruja. That man, I believe, was trying to trap you. It is plain you are suspected."

She was suddenly afraid. "What can I do?"

"Go to Paco! That is where you want to be, anyway, is it not? Do you think I am blind to the ways, the many ways, you miss my son? No, you must go to him. Only with him will you be safe."

The El Paso *Herald* had carried a dispatch with a Chihuahua dateline describing the fight at the Guzmán station on the MNR line. Maruja and Felix both believed that had been Paco Mora and the *tropa*. But where was Paco now? The *tropa* had left the railroad near Colonia Dublán after tearing up several hundred feet of track and dynamiting the engine.

"He is in the *sierra* someplace," Felix said. "We do not know exactly where, of course, but I suspect near San Miguel de Babícora. His Aunt Mercedes was born there, in San Miguel. And when you get in that country, there are always friendly people—poor people like you and me—who will know where Paco is and see that you find him."

Maruja was frightened. Born in San Andreas, she had gone to school there, lived all her young life there. Though Spanish was her native tongue, she had never been across the border, did not know the people of Chihuahua or their ways. How could she ever make her way to San Miguel and find Paco?

Papa Felix patted her on the shoulder, saying, "There, there, child, no need to worry!" He upended a vase and took out a small roll of bills. "These are my savings. But an old man like me does not need very much. I do not have a long time anyway." He scribbled an address on a piece of paper. "This is now Saturday, and you do not work, so no one will expect you at the bank. They will not know until Monday that you have gone away. Go to this address. It is one of Paco's powerful friends in El Paso. He will help you get to Cumbre Pass on the MNR railroad. From there it is not far to San Miguel de Babícora and Paco's aunt."

"But what will you do?" she asked.

Felix smiled. "I can take care of myself. Do not fear."

"But if they come to you and ask where I have gone?"

"When one grows old," Felix smiled, "his body weakens, true. But as compensation the good Lord often makes the brain more clever. Don't worry, I will handle them."

At Ciudad Juarez, across the El Paso, everything went smoothly. She suspected that General Villa had friends among the officials of the city, the bureaucrats and petty functionaries of the MNR. A mixed train of freight and passenger coaches was scheduled for Guzmán, Colonia Dublán, Casas Grandes, and Madera, leaving the following day. Maruja sat all night in the dingy station, wearing the long skirt and heavy sandals of a poor country woman. A gunnysack at her feet contained extra clothing, a kilo of tortillas, and some of the hard dense Mexican cheese. She still carried the knife in the sheath strapped to her thigh.

As seemed customary, the train pulled out several hours behind schedule. Box cars carried ammunition, crated rifles, small arms, drums of gasoline and oil. Each car was guarded by two or three swaggering *colorados* in brown uniforms and red-badged caps. The passenger coaches were few in number, crammed with humanity. All Mexico seemed to be on the move. Women carried trussed fowl, children played in the aisles, old men dozed in the scanty sunlight filtering through the cracked and broken windows. The car smelled of coal smoke, of urine and spoiled food and sweating bodies. From time to time an officious corporal bustled through the cars, checking papers, asking clumsily phrased questions in an obvious effort to trap someone. Her papers were in good order, but when the corporal came to her, the heart seemed to stop in her chest. But the friends of the Invincible General—Paco's friends, too—had done a good job. The corporal handed her papers back, pausing only to pat her cheek and let his hand fumble for a moment against her breasts.

At Guzmán station workers were rebuilding the station, heavily damaged by fire after the recent battle between Villistas and the *colorados*. Maruja pressed her cheek tightly against the window, wondering where Paco had stood, where he had fought, trying in her mind's eye to visualize the fight, the shouts, the moans of wounded men, the fingers of flame that licked at the building. Now she was here; Paco, though, was gone.

A one-legged youth, rude crutch lying on the floor beneath a single bare foot, was strumming a guitar and singing. Maruja became aware of the words of the ballad:

"He stood like the pine tree, roots deep in our soil.
Against him came the *colorados*, with their
cannon and guns.
But he killed them all; now a pine tree grows
where he stood."

Because of hotboxes, a breakdown in the locomotive valve-gear, and intermittent alarms of Villistas, it took two days to travel the two hundred and fifty miles to Cumbre Pass, high in the *sierra*. There Maruja Cruz gave ten pesos to a man hauling freight from the railroad to San Miguel de Babícora. He did not want to take her there in his wagon. "Señorita," he warned, "the *colorados* are in our little town. They hanged our *alcalde*—the mayor. When they left, there remained behind a small detachment to keep order, they said, and to prevent anyone from giving help or supplies to the Villistas. Now San Miguel lives in fear. No one knows when the *colorados* will knock on the door at night, drag someone away to be accused of treason."

She had come this far and knew no other destination. So he reluctantly took the ten pesos and let her ride the night on his cargo of pails of lard, cornmeal in sacks, drums of oil.

The sun was well up when they reached San Miguel. Pausing at the edge of town, the man pointed to a whitewashed house with a red tile roof, clinging to the side of a hill.

"There is a *Doña Mercedes* who lives there," he said. "Maybe that is the aunt you seek. But it is better to get off here and climb the path. If you are in the wagon when I unload in town, the *colorados* will be watching. Since your face is strange, they may take you away to question you. Then—" He broke off.

"*Que caray!* Who knows what those brutes might do to a pretty young girl?"

Shawl pulled over her head, she trudged up the path outlined by bits of whitewashed stone. It was cold; winter was coming early to the *sierra*. The scanty tufts of grass were white with frost. A cock crowed, a browsing goat looked at her, then went to wrenching bits of grass with its strong teeth.

She was almost at the tile-roofed house. She could smell woodsmoke and tortillas frying on a hot griddle, hear someone grinding corn, when a man in *colorado* uniform stepped from behind a twisted juniper hung with washing frozen stiff in the night.

"Where are you going, *chica*?" he asked.

She tried to twist away, but his hand had a tight grasp in the flesh of her upper arm. Dropping her sack, she screamed, and tried in vain to reach the knife in its leather sheath against her thigh. He pawed at her, pulling away the blouse from her shoulder. The revealed flesh only fired his lust.

Laughing, he dropped his rifle and threw her to the frost-hardened ground, burying her beneath his weight. The last thing she clearly remembered for a long time was the scent of cheap pomade on his bristly hair.

Chapter Six

At Rucio, only a few miles from Colonia Dublán, the *tropa* rode into the mountains, the seemingly endless chain of the Sierra Madre Occidental that ran south all the way to the Gulf. Paco Mora failed to find General Villa at Colonia Dublán; now the *tropa* retreated until their leader decided what to do next.

The mountains were covered with stands of pine, cedar, juniper, and wax-leafed black oak. Now in the early autumn they passed through occasional patches of snow. One morning it was so cold that men and animals had icicles hanging from hair and whiskers. But as they went higher and higher into the *sierra*, all felt relieved. No one could find them now, lost as they were in the folds of this tremendous country.

David Pine, hunched miserably in his saddle, rode between Café and Luisito. All that identified him as a lieutenant of the U.S. Army was the tattered identification card in his pocket. He wore borrowed *calzones*—the rough homespun pants and shirt of the peasant—along with a colorful sarape and a steeple-crowned straw hat. His beard had grown long and unaccountably curly, and he had the indignity of fleas.

As soon as they reached the basalt caves where Paco Mora intended to hole up, David decided to have it out with Paco. The situation was monstrous; having sworn allegiance to the United States, David Pine was now traveling as a member of a band of Mexican insurgents. He had broken regulations by driving recklessly into Mexico; he had fired on his own countrymen in the battle of Guzmán station; he had been responsible for the death of Sergeant Henry Acton. Never should he have accepted parole. What he should have done—what he now saw clearly he should have done—was to try escape at the first opportunity. That was the honorable thing Henry Acton had done. Perhaps the country did swarm with *colorados*. Perhaps they would shoot him on sight and ask questions later. Perhaps, if he reached Parral with his skin in one piece, he would be court-martialed and punished. But all these uncertainties were easier to live with than the present certainty, that David Pine, lieutenant, U.S.A., was riding into the *sierra* with Villa's men.

Luisito was tootling the song again on his homemade bamboo flute, the song about *El Pino*.

"Don't you know anything else?" David protested.

Luisito looked hurt, but Café only grinned and said, *El Pino* is right, *hombre*. Play us a chorus of '*La Adelita*.' "

"*La Adelita*" did not improve David's dark mood. It was a lugubrious ditty:

> "If some day I must die in battle,
> If some day on the *sierra* I must lie,
> Adelita, if God will allow it
> You'll go to the sierra and cry."

They were heading for a place called the Cerro de las Ventanas, a high ridge of basalt honeycombed with caves. "They call it the Hill of the Windows," Café explained, "because at the top of the ridge a lot of holes go all the way through. At night, when the moon is low in the west, it shines through the openings and the ridge looks like a beautiful palace with lights in the windows."

Climbing steadily upward, they at last reached the basalt ridge. What Paco called his "brush telegraph" had worked well. Several men were there, poor farmers who had lit fires and were roasting a calf. The *tropa* ate beef until their bellies could hold no more and drank goards full of *pulque*. Finally they lay down in the caves, wrapped against the cold in sarapes and ponchos.

The following morning the men lounged around the camp, taking an unaccustomed ease. They had carried away cartons of Alfonso, Belmonte, and Virginia cigarettes from the looted train, and there was plenty of liquor. David played a card game called *conquian* with Café and Luisito, while Paco Mora and Dr. Saenz held a council of war in a larger cave.

"I am glad," Café said, nodding toward the cave, "that I am not in there! It takes a lot of brains to command a *tropa*, to be responsible for people!"

"To be responsible for so much money, too," Luisito observed. "Dr. Saenz wants that money, I think. He does not trust Paco with it!"

They huddled together over a small flame, the roof of the cave a rich greasy brown from the fires of centuries. Though the sun shone brightly, there was a chill wind that kept them inside.

"I wish they would finish," David complained, playing an ace.

"Why, *hombre*? What is your hurry?"

"I've got to talk to Paco."

Café shook his head. "I do not think this is a good time to talk to the *jefe*. He and Dr. Saenz are having an argument. Listen!"

They could indeed hear the sounds of raised voices, sounds of arguments, of anger. A voice shouted insults.

"They say," Luisito offered, "that General Villa has gone to Santa Cruz de Villegas. They say he was shot in the leg at Colonia Dublán and is very sick."

"No one knows where the general is, and that is his safety," Café said. "After every battle, Villa separates his men into small factions. They go here and they go there to wait for him to call them together for another battle. So he could be here and he could be there. Our Invincible General could be at Tomóchic or Madera or anywhere. But it makes it very hard for *tropa* to join up with him."

At last the conference in the big cave broke up. Paco and Dr. Saenz emerged, blinking in the sunlight. Paco called the band together.

"We have decided," he announced, "to stay here in the caves for a few days. We will send out scouts to talk to the people, to try to find out where General Villa is."

Dr. Saenz's face was flushed from its usual gray hardness; there was an angry twitch at the corner of his mouth.

Paco had detailed assignments for each man. One was to go to the Santa Maria valley. Anoher was to visit El Valle, a third and fourth to Colonia Chuichupa and Namaquipa. Finally all were accounted for except Café.

"What about me?" he demanded. "Where do I go?"

Paco clapped him on the back.

"Someone, *amigo*, must remain here with the women until we return."

"But—"

"You have such a way with women, *compañerito*!"

"But—"

Paco was suddenly angry. The strain of command was showing.

"*Caray*! Why do you cross me so? I gave the order; now let it be obeyed!"

Café shrugged and went back to shuffling the deck of dirty cards.

David got up, dusting his hands, and walked across the clearing. Paco and Dr. Saenz were bending over a map. After a while he cleared his throat. Surprised and sullen, Paco Mora looked up.

"The business of the parole," David said. "It's finished."

Paco took a deep breath, almost a sigh. His eyes were bleary, there was a fine stubble on his chin. He sat down on a big rock, handing the rolled map to Dr. Saenz and motioning him away.

"What do you mean, *amigo*?"

"I am going to go away from here," David said. "At the first opportunity, I am going to escape. I am going back to Roosevelt and Agua Fria and El Paso where I belong."

Paco slapped the sombrero angrily against his thigh. Motes of dust rose to sparkle in the thin sunlight.

"You saved my life," David went on, "and I'm grateful. But I can't stay here any longer. Come what may of it, I've got to go back."

"It is very dangerous. You saw what happened to your Sergeant Acton."

"Yes."

"It is a long way. Over three hundred kilometers."

"I know that."

"Even if I were to let you go, we could not spare a horse. The ones we have are few and weak after long riding. Last night the saddle blanket stuck to poor Chispa when I took it off. Sweat, *hombre*, and blood from the creature's sore back!"

David only looked at him. Seeing the decision in David's eyes, Paco got stiffly up from the rock. "All right!" he said. "All right, old friend. But let us be reasonable about these things. You are a quartermaster officer?"

David nodded.

"General Villa has a lot of *gringos* working for him. Adventurers. Good men who work for anybody who pays them regularly in gold."

David frowned, wondering where this was leading.

"*Bueno*," Paco explained, "what General Villa needs now is a supply expert, someone to buy arms and military supplies, to warehouse and account for them, to see that the peoples' army is well provisioned." Paco grasped his arm. "You know, for a while the general even held Mexico City itself! Now I hear there are new plans, exciting plans. The general is going to join Zapata in the south, take Vera Cruz. Then he will require a good supply officer. *Hombre*, you can become rich on what he will pay you! What do you say?"

David started to speak, but in his enthusiasm Paco cut him off. "I know you are on our side, David! You are one of *La raza*—the people—and you have a great love for them! You saw the cruelty of the *colorados* against the poor farmers of Chihuahua. So come with us! You can be a rich man, and you will help the people!"

David took a long time answering. Finally he shook his head. "It's no use, Paco. I—I've got to go back."

Paco's smile faded. He dropped David's arm.

"Do you mean it?"

David nodded.

"*Caray*!" Paco swore. He became angry. "You insist on being stupid! Go, then! I do not want you here anyhow!"

"My parole—"

Paco broke in, face flushed and eyes hard. "You know what you can do with your parole!" He turned away, shouting over his shoulder. "I am going to Tomochic! When I return, I do not want to see your ugly face in this camp!"

Angry, Paco mounted his horse and spurred clattering down the slope.

The *tropa* followed—Saenz, Pedro, Mirón, Luisito, the rest—all of them, going to search for Villa, for word of Villa, for any clue to where the Invincible General might be.

The camp became quiet. The wind dropped; the *tropa*'s women came out of the caves. Some washed their tortillas, a few simply basked in the autumn sun, combing hair, sewing, singing in soft tones. Café sat atop a high rock, rifle cradled in his lap, smoking a cigar.

David, disturbed by Paco Mora's tongue lashing, clumbed on the rock and sat beside Café. A shy young woman brought them coffee in tin cups.

"*Gracias, chica,*" Café said. "Ah, Señor David Pine, this is the very stuff of life, this coffee! Until I have had coffee, I am only half a man. After"—he rolled his eyes over the rim of the tin cup—"I am three men! No, five! Perhaps ten."

David was silent, staring moodily into the distance, arms locked around his knees. He had been given leave to go away, but how was it to be managed? Paco was right; rescue was a long way off. He had no arms, no provisions, no horse—nothing.

"That Paco," Café said, wiping his mustaches.

David looked up.

"That Paco," Café repeated. "He is very worried. About the money, I mean. He has sworn to get it to General Villa."

"I guess so," David said.

"You must not take Paco's words too seriously," Café explained. "Paco is not himself. He is worried about the money. Then, too, it is hard on a man to be responsible for a *tropa*. When someone is hurt or killed, it is hard on Paco. It is as if one of his own children has died."

David knew what Sergeant Acton would have done. Acton could not even speak Spanish, but Acton would have tried anyway. Really, David Pine owed the sergeant this much. He slid down off the boulder.

"Wait!" Café called. "Where are you going?"

David dusted the seat of his *calzones*. "Back to Roosevelt. You heard what Paco said. He does not want to return and find me in his camp."

Café laughed. "*Hombre*, you are a brave man, but do not be a fool! You will never get there!"

"I must try."

Suddenly Café broke off the banter, staring at the screen of chaparral surrounding the camp. "One minute, Señor David!" He put out a hand, palm down, in a gesture to take cover, and whistled shrilly through his teeth. The women of the camp, the *soldaderas*, fled into the caves. All was silent except for a rustling of the dry leaves in the wind, the squawking of a jay atop a pine tree.

"What is it?" David asked.

Café crouched behind the boulder, rifle resting atop it, watching the chaparral. "Did you hear that?" he whispered.

David listened. Someone was coming through the brush.

"Hey!" Café yelled. He squeezed a shot into the air. "Come out, whoever you are! You are seen! You are surrounded!"

After the echoes of the rifle shot had died, they listened again. No rustling, no footsteps in the dried leaves. "I see you!" Café shouted. "I have a bead on your heart, *cabron*! Come out very slowly, hands above your head!"

David doubted if Café saw anything, but a small withered man, very old, crept out of the brush with his hands high.

"Don't shoot!" he begged. "Señor, spare me the few years that are left!"

"Come here!" Café ordered. He stood atop the boulder, aiming the rifle at the old man's cowering form. "David Pine, have the goodness to see if he is armed!"

David patted the visitor's shirt and pants, ran his hands inside the rough garments, around the thin trembling chest with its tangle of white hair.

"No," he reported. "He is unarmed."

Café slid off the boulder, motioning the man to come near. "What are you doing, *viejo*? What do you want in the camp of Paco Mora's glorious *tropa*?"

The ancient held his tall-crowned hat nervously, gnarled fingers working at the brim. "Senores," he said, "I come from San Miguel de Babícora. I ask for your help."

Café twirled his fierce mustaches. "Help? What help?"

"As you know," the man said, "it is the custom of the *colorados* to leave a few men in each town, to keep order, they say, to make sure no one gives help to the Villistas. But, senores, in our town they hanged the *alcalde*—the mayor—because he had a picture of General Villa under his mattress. The *colorados* terrorize the town! They lie all day in the jail, drinking *pulque*, and at night they come out drunk and abuse the womenfolk. Even now they have a young girl in the jail! We have heard her screams! Please, senores, help us! Help the town of San Miguel de Babícora! For the love of God, help my *patria chica!*"

Café did not hesitate. He went into the cave and came out with several heavy cartridge belts slung across his chest. In his belt were stuck two Colt .45 caliber automatic pistols identical to the one David Pine had carried at Fort Bliss. David wondered how modern U.S. arms had gotten so quickly to Paco Mora's *tropa*.

"How far is the village?" Café demanded.

The old man pointed. "Just below that peak, there. Ten kilometers, maybe less. Two hours walk."

"Listen," David said to Café. "There are four of them, the man says! Paco told you to guard the camp, watch out for the women!"

Café laughed. "Four *colorados*? I eat them for breakfast! Anyway, Paco would approve. And the women can take care of themselves until I return."

"You called me a fool," David objected, "for trying to get back to the border. But who is the fool now? You will walk into that town at odds of one to four, *hombre*, and the *colorados* will kill you, hang you up to dry like jerked meat!"

Café fondled his mustaches. "Ah, señor, when does a man get a chance to be a hero and not have to share the occasion with someone else? Such a happening is rare. I intend to take advantage of it!"

David felt confused, baffled. His system of values was changing, and he was not sure he liked it. Decisions in Chihuahua were difficult.

"That's very foolish," he said. "At least wait until someone comes back to help!"

Until someone comes back to help. Saying the words, he felt uncomfortable, ashamed. But Café did not appear to notice. He only went on adjusting his fighting gear, packing it on and about his barrellike frame in a workmanlike manner. Café had made his decision; David made his.

"Look!" he said. "You have been kind to me, *hombre*, and I owe you something. I remember, too, what the cursed *colorados* did to Don Jaime and Doña Ana at the rancho that time. These things are very clear to me, and I have taken them into account. But I've got to go back! This whole business is none of my affair! Do you understand?"

Café took a last sip of coffee.

"You owe me nothing. You owe this poor man nothing. You owe Mexico nothing—*la raza*, nothing. That is true. And each man does what he must. I do not judge you."

David's mouth felt dry; he licked his lips. He had never wanted any part of violence. He was only an unsuccessful accountant playing at soldier. The Quartermaster Corps was not the Army, not really. The Corps was only clerks and file cabinets and warehouses. The Army, the real Army, was with Pershing at Parral. Yet a perverse fate was playing with him, pulling strings. Somehow, each day, violence was forced more and more heavily on him.

"I judge myself," he finally said.

Café's voice was pleasant, casual, almost unconcerned.

"And, señor, you find?"

David looked at the trembling old man from San Miguel de Babícora. He took a deep breath, feeling it catch and tremble as it came out.

"I'm going back," he decided. "Back to the border. It's where I belong. *Buena suerte, hombre*, good luck. I will remember you."

Café shrugged. The old man plucked at Café's sleeve.

"Senores, can we not hurry a little? There is the girl the *colorados* have taken. I am worried about that Maruja. They abuse her, those brutes. Perhaps, when they are done, they will even kill her! I have heard her cry out—"

"Who?" David Pine grasped the old man's skinny arm. "The name, again?"

The ancient looked puzzled. "Señor?"

"The name of the girl!"

With dignity, the old man drew away his arm. "She is caled Maruja."

In Mexico there were hundreds—perhaps thousands—of girls called Maruja, or Marisa, or some variant of the common name Maria. It was certainly only a coincidence. Still . . .

"I'm going with you," he blurted.

Café looked at him curiously. "But this is not your affair, señor! If you want to help, stay here and watch the females until I return. Then you can go away and try to reach your people, up there on the border."

Doggedly, David shook his head. "You said the women could take care of themselves. Give me a gun, I'm not going to let you go alone!"

Café pursed his lips, stared at David with flat impassive eyes. "Help yourself," he said finally.

David went into the cave, a kind of armory for the

tropa, and took two bandeliers of Mauser ammunition and a rifle. He stuck a loaded revolver of ancient vintage into his belt, filling his pockets also with munitions. Maruja. Could it be?

"*Bueno*! Café applauded when he emerged. "Señor David, you look like a true revolutionary! Even Dr. Saenz would approve!"

"Hurry!" the old man beseeched them. "Senores, I beg you! Let us go quickly!"

With the ancient as a guide they took a winding sinuous path through the heavy brush. Downhill they went, ever downhill, vines and branches tearing at them, tripping, falling, scraping hands and knees in the rocks and shale. It must have been noon, the sun overhead, when they came out on a granite outcropping overlooking the town.

San Miguel de Babícora dozed in autumn sunlight. The street was a deep rich red clay. A tethered burro dozed in a patch of shade. The cornstalks were yellow. Smoke came from chimneys. Someone patted tortillas into shape; the slapping sound came faintly to their ears. All seemed peaceful, normal—except that no one was in the street. From the square building in the middle of the town came a sound of singing, drunken singing. As they watched, a man in the greenish *colorado* uniform walked swaying from the adobe building. He staggered to a watering trough, plunging his head into the water. For a while he blew and puffed, wiping hands over his wet hair.

"That is the corporal," the old man muttered. He bit his knuckle in hatred and contempt. "He is the judge in the court they hold! He is the one who sentenced the *alcalde* to hang!" Café held the man for a moment in his sights, saying, "I would like to sentence him right now!" But with a sigh he rolled over and sat like a Buddha, rifle across his lap, rubbing his chin.

"Four of them?" he asked.

The old man nodded.

"Will they all come out of the jail?"

The old man nodded. "Each afternoon they promenade around the town to see if someone has disobeyed their orders." He squinted overhead. "In perhaps an hour. After that, they sleep the siesta until it is time to bring them food."

"We wait, eh?" Café asked David. "When they come out—all four of them must come out for us to do a good job—I take two, you take two."

"I understand," David said. He shoved a clip into the magazine of the rifle and lay flat, propping the gun on a ledge of rock.

After a chilly morning, the noon-time sun was hot. They lay together on the granite outcropping, screened by bushes. San Miguel was silent, ominously silent, except for snatches of drunken song from the jail.

Sweat ran down David's forehead and stung his eyes. A small lizard ran across his hand, darting away when he jerked. "Patience," Café murmured. "They have not long to live, anyway! Let them enjoy their last hours singing and drinking!" He offered a small black cigar to David. When David declined, he took one himself and lit it, puffing carefully so as not to betray their hiding place.

At perhaps two in the afternoon their wait was rewarded. The corporal emerged, looking warily around. He barked a command and the other *colorados* emerged, hitching up pants, adjusting cartridge belts, buttoning coats.

"*Atencion!*" the corporal commanded. He formed the three men into a ragged line by pushing here, shoving there, cursing steadily.

Café nudged David Pine. "I take the corporal, eh? And the fat man."

"*Bueno,*" David said. "I take the man with the long arms—the one that looks like an ape—and the other."

"At my command," Café murmured. A moment later he barked, "Now! Fire!"

There was only one sound from the two Mauser rifles going off simultaneously. The corporal threw up his arms and fell. The lanky man with the long arms folded like an accordion and sank into the earth.

"*Carramba*!" the old man shouted. "*Ay, caray!" He* jumped to his feet, yelling in triumph.

They fired again, but were not so fortunate. Dancing a jig, the old man kicked David Pine's elbow and his shot went wild. When Café squeezed his trigger, there was only a quickly expiring hiss. The ammunition was old and had misfired, jamming the action.

"*Ay, cabron*!" Café said between set teeth. He jerked vainly at the bolt. Below, the corporal staggered to his feet, calling out for help. The remaining two had already fled into the jail. The corporal shuffled sidewise, like a wounded crab, into the adobe building behind them. As David Pine was squeezing off another shot, the heavy iron-studded door closed.

Again San Miguel was quiet, except for the distant echo of their shots, carroming fainter and fainter down the valley until lost in the wrinkled blue mountains. The fat man lay in the dust and did not move.

Café swore quietly to himself. He took out a knife and managed to dig free the defective cartridge. "We got one of them," he said. "And another is in bad health, I think."

David peered over the ledge. The old man squatted beside him, saying, "*Lo siento mucho, señor*—I am very sorry! I did not mean to disturb your aim! But when I saw those pigs fall—"

"No matter," David said. "It doesn't matter."

"But it does!" Café complained. "We can not go away and leave them holed up there! When they get out, they will hang everyone in San Miguel! On the other hand, how are we to get at them in the jail? The walls are thick, the door is heavy!"

"Give me your knife," David said.

Café looked surprised. "The knife?"

"And your cigar."

Puzzled, Café handed them over. When he saw the red sticks of dynamite David pulled from his ragged pants, he scrabbled suddenly away. The old man recognized the dynamite, too, and dodged into the bushes.

"Put that stuff away!" Café urged, his voice trembling. "Do not come near me with dynamite! It is very dangerous!"

David cut a short length of primacord with Café's knife and crimped a cap onto it with his teeth.

"Don't worry," he said. "My stepfather taught me all about dynamite." With the point of the knife he scraped a small hole in the red papers of the bundled sticks and stuffed cap and primacord into it, leaving a trailing length of fuse.

"Now," he said. He borrowed Café's smoldering black cigar and place it between his own lips. "I am going down there and blow a hole in the wall of that place." He handed his rifle to the old man. "Do you know how to use this?"

The man patted the worn stock. "I have never had such a good gun," he said, "but I know what to do with it. Kill *colorados*!"

Strangely, David was not afraid. His voice remained steady, surprising even himself.

"Café, when I give the word, you and our friend cover me with heavy fire. If I can reach the wall, I will be safe. With this knife I dig a hole in the adobe and light the charge. When you hear me yell—"

Very practically, Café asked, "Yell what, *hombre*? We do not want any mistakes here."

It seemed melodramatic, but David said, "*Arriba los pobres*! Up with the poor people!"

"That is a very good sentiment," the old man said approvingly.

"When I yell, I run into the brush to get away from the explosion. After the charge goes off, come down and help me with those *cabrones* in jail. See, I have a pistol, the three of us can certainly finish them off."

Café grinned. "Back there"—he nodded toward the camp of the *tropa*—"I said it would be dangerous for you to try to run away, to try to reach the border. But I think this thing of the dynamite is more dangerous!"

"I am going now," David said. "When you see me come out of the brush near the jail, start shooting!"

Cigar between his lips, one hand holding the dynamite and the other the old pistol, he made his way through the tangled brush. He could hear excited chattering inside the jail. Someone moaned in pain, probably the wounded corporal. The muzzle of a rifle poked through the iron bars of a window and David shrank back into the brush. His heart was pounding, sweat beaded his forehead. A hero, he thought, remembering Café's words. A chance to be a hero. David Pine made a poor hero.

Suddenly making up his mind, he ran out of the brush. The rifle poked again from between the iron bars, but David was already crouched against the wall; the man inside could not bring his weapon to bear. Digging furiously with the knife, David excavated a tunnellike hole in the crumbling adobe bricks. Then he stuffed the bundled dynamite deep.

Spitting on the loose dust to make a crumbly mud, he packed it carefully around the dynamite, finishing off the tamping with a fist-sized rock so that only the fuse cord showed. From where he crouched against the wall he could not see the rocky ledge where Café and the old man waited, but from time to time they fired to keep the *colorados* penned in the *cuartel*.

Sucking deep on the cigar, he watched the coal glow into flame. Shielding it with cupped hands he lit the fuse. It sputtered into life and he scrambled away, yelling as loud as he could.

"*Arriba los pobres*! *Arriba los pobres*!"

He had almost reached the cover of the bushes when

the bundled sticks of dynamite went off. The concussion drove a blast of hot dusty air at him; the ground seemed to shake. Stunned, he lay under a bush, wondering if he had been killed. From a distance he could hear shrill yells. Shakily he got to his feet, revolver in his hand, and ran toward the gaping hole. Café and the old man were there before him, firing into the cloud of dust that boiled from the shattered wall. One man ran out, screaming in terror, and Café dropped him with a bullet precisely through the head. The other stumbled dazedly through the wreckage, and the old man killed him. The corporal was dead, lying like a bundle of old clothes draped over a section of the broken wall.

"*Bueno*!" Café called. "That is all of them!"

Together David and Café plunged into the wreckage, searching. The shattered interior was filled with dust, the acrid smell of explosives, a rich rusty odor that was blood, human blood. In the rear of the wrecked building cowered a girl. Her face was smudged and dirty, her clothes torn, but she was apparently unharmed.

"Maruja!" he called, unbelieving.

The girl was indeed Maruja Cruz. With a little cry of mingled terror and relief she ran to him, huddled in his arms, weeping. "David! David Pine! It is you!"

After the heavy boom of the explosion, after the fusillade of rifle shots, the afternoon was quiet again. People crept silently from wattled-rush huts, shady *ramadas*, to ring their rescuers. Café searched the remains of the building and came out carrying rifles and small arms and belts of cartridges.

"Here," he said, "and here." He handed guns and cartridge belts to the astonished villagers. "If they come again, use these against them. Have confidence. The people in their wrath are strong!"

His arm about Maruja Cruz, David Pine sat down on a huge block of adobe blown out of the wall. She still wept and clung to him. "I was searching for Paco," she said. "That was all I was doing. But what they did to me—those brutes!"

Awkwardly he patted her shoulder.

"There," he said. "There! Everything's going to be all right now."

He felt very tired; after the tension, the explosion, the killing, he was almost nerveless, paralyzed. The villagers surrounded them, holding hats against chests in respect. One old lady shuffled up to Café and kissed his hand. A lame man leaning on a staff looked at David Pine and his lips worked soundlessly.

"Well," Café said, "I guess we have done it, eh? That was a good fight. *Cristo*, what a noise that dynamite made! Dynamite makes me very nervous. But you, *hombre*, it was like you were sitting in church, lighting only a candle!"

The old man's lips still worked. David suddenly realized what the wrinkled lips were saying, the words they were framing. That song Luisito was always singing! *El Pino. El Pino.* He grimaced.

"Yes," he said to Café. "We have done it, *hombre*. But if one more *colorado* were to come out of that building, I think I do not now have the strength to defend myself." To Maruja Cruz he said, "Let us go home, Maruja."

Chapter Seven

The small rawhide box containing the money from the Plains Bank robbery was a problem. Paco kept a watchful eye on it—ten thousand dollars or more was a lot of money—and the box was never far from his side. Now, traveling to Tomóchic for news of the Invincible General, Paco decided he would certainly take the box with him. The *tropa* were all honest men. Dr. Saenz was a representative of General Villa himself, and David Pine in this hostile country was virtually a prisoner anyway, parole or no parole. But men would do anything for enough gold, and ten thousand dollars was enough. Paco did not want to put temptation in anyone's way, so he strapped the awkward parcel to his horse's rump, covering it with a blanket and a sack of *pinole*, along with a canteen of water.

He abandoned the sombrero, the tight pants and fringed jacket, wearing instead a straw hat, rough *calzones*—the homespun cotton everyday wear of the peasant—and the leather leg protectors used for chasing cattle through cats claw and scrub juniper. Exchanging his black gelding for one of the land-hard, half-savage ponies of the *sierra*, he looked like a poor cattle herder.

Late in an autumn afternoon he reached Tomóchic. Watching below, he sat the horse on a brushy ridge; the *colorados* were surely in Tomóchic, as they were everywhere in Chihuahua, and he would have to be careful. The sun slid behind the mountains and he shivered in the breath of cold air that instantly rolled off the peaks. In the half-light his breath showed in vaporous puffs.

A tracery of oil lamps began to illuminate the main street of the town. In dwellings, the embrasured windows became rectangles of mellow light. A few electric bulbs winked on, and Paco heard the muffled sound of an electrical generator. He heard also the squeaking of *carreta* wheels behind him, coming down the trail. A moment later an old man, driving a load of firewood, appeared.

"*Buenas tardes*," Paco said politely.

The old man halted his burro. Perhaps he saw something in Paco's bearing in spite of the rough clothes. He took off his hat, saying, "The same to you, señor."

There was a Villista formula current in the *sierra*, a shibboleth to distinguish friend from foe.

"I hear," Paco said, "that our President Carranza now has a beard."

The ancient looked at him thoughtfully. "Yes," he agreed. Seeming occupied with scratching the burro's ears with a stick, he began to whistle tunelessly. But there was enough tune for Paco to recognize. It was a bit of doggerel that said:

"With Carranza's beard
I am going to make a little cockade
To adorn that hat
Of his master Pancho Villa."

When the old man finished, Paco cleared his throat and sang in a husky tenor the rest of the rhyme.

"*Bueno*!" the old man cried. "How may I serve you, son?"

Paco gestured toward the town. "Do you know the lawyer Mondragon there? Roberto Mondragon?"

"*Ah, si, señor!* A great and good man!" The woodcutter dropped his stick and came quickly to Paco's stirrup. "Tell me, *hijo*, are you—are you—*El Pino*?"

Paco was annoyed. "No, I am not *El Pino*, though I know him well! In fact, he is under my command. Tell me, uncle, can you take me to lawyer Mondragon?"

"Of course!"

"But are there soldiers in the town? *Colorados*?"

"And brutes they are!" the old man said. "They hang everyone they suspect of being a revolutionary! Why, in our own plaza they hanged two good citizens from a laurel tree! The *colorados* call it 'General Pineda's fruit tree' and laugh!" He bit his thumb in anger.

"Nevertheless," Paco said, "I must go down there and talk with Mondragon and others whom he will call together."

"That can be done, señor," the old man said. Quickly he pulled branches from the wagon. "Tie your horse here, to that oak. No one will bother him for the night. Then get into my wagon. I will pile wood on top of you to hide you."

Paco took the rawhide box with him and curled himself up in the wagon while the old man piled brush and fagots on top.

"Ready?"

"Ready," Paco responded.

It seemed an eternity before the squeaking wagon reached the outskirts of Tomóchic. Paco was thrown this way and that, jolted, poked by the branches that covered him. Through the maze he had limited vision. He saw oil lamps lighting the street, an occasional dim and flickering electric bulb, heard the cries of venders hawking fried chicken and enchiladas, smelled the rankness of *sotol*—the cheap liquor made from the roots of a weedlike plant. A moment later the wagon stopped.

The old man came to help him emerge from the load of wood.

"I live down there," he said, pointing to a small dwelling with a brush-thatched *ramada* for cooking and eating. They had turned into a dusty side lane. "My name is Villareal. They call me Chucho. Everyone knows Chucho the woodcutter." He indicated a heavy door, barred with iron, set deep in an adobe wall. "This is the house of the lawyer Mondragon. When you have finished, señor, have the goodness to send for me, and I will take you back to the ridge where your horse is tied."

The lawyer Mondragon came to the door holding an oil lamp high, peering through his spectacles. He was a small intense man with a fierce brushy mustache and sad gentle eyes.

"Who is there?" he demanded.

"Roberto!" Paco said. "It is Paco, Paco Mora." Slipping inside, he closed the door and dropped the heavy bolt into place.

The lawyer stared at him, then embraced him. "Paco, it is really you! In those rough clothes I did not know you!" He drew back smiling. "In these days when the revolution seems to have died, it is good to see a man who is still fighting." He adjusted the spectacles and peered. "What have you brought in that box, eh?"

Paco grinned. "It is a gift to the cause, Roberto. Something of value which I must deliver quickly to General Villa." He set the box carefully on the rough table. "*Amigo*, could I have a little something to eat? I have ridden all day with nothing but a mouthful of *pinole*."

While Paco wolfed beans wrapped in a tortilla, Roberto Mondragon sent a son to call together the little cell of Villistas in Tomóchic. They came furtively, one after the other, scratching at the door, until there were almost a dozen.

"This," the lawyer told them, "is my good friend Paco Mora. It was Paco's brave *tropa* that captured the MNR train at Guzmán station, dynamited the locomotive, and blocked the tracks."

Impressed, they gathered around Paco to congratulate him. But then a kind of dispirit descended. The men sat silently, some smoking, others only watching. Roberto Mondragon sighed.

"As you see, Paco," he said, "the revolutionary spirit is flagging in Tomóchic. The *colorados* have us under their heel; they watch us day and night. If they even suspect a man of a little night work, that man is hanged the next morning without a trial."

There was a chorus of assent.

"What can we do?" a farmer asked.

The pharmacist spoke up. "How is it possible even to strike a small blow for liberty when we are at such a disadvantage?"

Paco finished his tortilla.

"First things first." He licked his fingers and pointed to the rawhide box. "I have here a little present for General Villa. But first I must find him. My *tropa* went to Colonia Dublán. That was where the Invincible General was last reported, collecting taxes from the Mormons there."

In spite of their gloom, they laughed. The nature of Pancho Villa's "taxes" was well known.

"But our general was not at Colonia Dublán. And now no one seems to know where he is. Since my *tropa* is under orders to join him at the first opportunity, can anyone tell me where he can be found?"

There was an instant babble.

"Madera! Parral! Casas Grandes! Galeana!"

It was obvious no one really knew. One man insisted General Villa had been killed at San Francisco del Oro. The pharmacist had it on good authority that the general had received a bad leg wound and was being cared for in La Junta.

Roberto Mondragon shrugged. "You see how it is, Paquito. It is no wonder that people are discouraged. We do not even know where our general is, whether in fact he really lives! How can we fight a revolution when for all we know our cause is dead, our leader has died, or perhaps fled the country?"

Paco was himself disappointed. Roberto Mondragon had good connections all over Chihuahua. If the lawyer could not give him information on General Villa's whereabouts, no one could. But for the sake of the others, he tried hard not to let his face show disappointment.

"Listen!" he said. "Listen to me! This is nothing unusual! We all know the general's custom of dispersing his men and disappearing like a puff of smoke after a battle! That is simply to make easier the supply problems, and no one should worry about it! Why, at Madera only last month he defeated the Seventh Regiment of Pineda's forces, did he not? And the poor *pelados* Pineda forces into his army as recruits desert at the jingle of Pancho's spurs! No, believe me, our Invincible General will soon be on the march again!"

Warming to his task, he walked among them, clapping one on the back, shaking hands with another. "Listen!" he said. "Listen! The *gringos* know they will soon have to fight the Germans in Europe, so they are bound to go home in a few months, leaving Pineda and Carranza to us! If we can hold out only a little longer, General Villa will whip Pineda like a cur dog!" He snatched up the rawhide box and held it high. "Take courage from this!"

"What is it?" someone asked.

"Last month my *tropa* robbed the Plains Bank in Roosevelt, across the border. With Pineda's *colorados* swarming through Chihuahua, we rode right through them and struck!" He unstrapped the box and lifted the lid. "Ah, if I were to tell you how many rifles, how much ammunition, this little leather box can buy!"

With a triumphant gesture he upended the box. But instead of the shower of gold coins and lush green bills, there was only a drifting down of papers, leaves, dirt, a handful of rocks.

The lawyer was the first to speak.

"What is this, Paco? A trick of some kind? A joke?"

Paco stared at the box, ran his hand through the debris. What had happened?

Another man spoke. "Are you poking fun at us, Señor Paco? *Caray*! I do not think it is funny!"

He had been so careful to guard the box and its treasure. Face pale, hands trembling so he had to grip them together to still them, he sat down. The room was silent, expectant. In the stillness he wondered if they could hear the panicky throbbing of his pulse.

"I have been robbed," he said finally. "That is to say, we, the Villistas, have been robbed." He got to his feet, looking again inside the box as if by some miracle the money would still be there. "There was," he said, "in this little box ten thousand dollars or more, dollars we took from the Plains Bank in Roosevelt, dollars for General Villa to buy rifles, pistols, ammunition, supplies, medical goods. But someone, a traitor, robbed us!"

At the mention of so much money they sucked in their breath. Ten thousand dollars—unnumbered thousands of pesos!

"Who could have done such a thing?" the lawyer demanded.

"Are there traitors in your band, señor?" the pharmacist asked. "*Caray*, can we depend on no one any more?"

Miserable, Paco shook his head. "I do not know."

They had hoped for encouragement from him, something to lift their flagging spirits, but the loss of so much money again pressed down their hopes. Someone sighed, a long deep quavering sound. A man got up and went to the door, taking down the bar and standing it in the corner with a kind of finality. Others only stood awkwardly, looking toward Don Roberto for a sign of dismissal.

"Well," the lawyer said.

Rapidly Paco's mind scanned his *tropa*. Café? Luisito? Pedro Miñon? Perhaps—even Dr. Rafael Saenz? His mind was in a whirl. "Someone," he muttered, "someone in my own band is a traitor!" He turned toward the little company, pleading. "Do not be discouraged! Such things happen! I swear I will get the money back, that I will deliver it in person to the general, that everything will be all right!"

He broke off, seeing them bid farewell to Don Roberto, open the door, creep into the dark chill night.

Roberto Mondragon sighed. "I am always glad to see you, Paco Mora—you know that. We have been friends for a long time and are bound together by the revolution. But is it not reasonable to say, Better this time you had not come? *Caray*!" He gestured toward the door. "They—we—are now more discouraged than ever!"

Angrily Paco kicked the empty box. "Roberto, I am sorry you and your people are so easily discouraged! But to be discouraged is only to know we must fight harder, risk more!" He clenched his fist, shook it angrily. "That money meant more to me than a gift to the revolution! That money meant I would be a captain on General Villa's staff, maybe even a major or a colonel! I could be somebody! So *I* do not become discouraged so easily as you and your people! I will sift the dust of Chihuahua for the rascal who stole my money!" He flung open the door, not caring who heard his shout. "I will find that man and the money, too—or die!"

Roberto Mondragon ran after him.

"Stop shouting, Paco! You will raise the dead!" He caught Paco's arm. "Wait a minute! Old Chucho brought you, did he not? Wait a minute, *hombre*! I will ask him to come with his wagon!"

Paco shook off the lawyer's arm. "There is no time to skulk about or hide! I know the place where my horse is tied. *Adiós*, Roberto! I am in a hurry!"

Walking through the narrow streets, wiping the sweat from his brow, he suddenly realized how his haste, his anger, might betray him. At any moment a soldier might step out of the shadows and want to know his business, see his papers. But that night he had the luck that protects children, drunken men, and fools. From the plaza he could hear loud voices singing a chorus of drunken oaths. Quickly he walked away from the singing, taking advantage of the patches of blackness where the overhanging roofs blocked the moon's rays.

Tomóchic was a ghost town. Whitewashed houses shone palely in the moonlight, deep embrasured windows were like sockets in a bleached skull. A dog started to bark and was quickly choked off, as if someone had restrained the animal.

After blundering through a thicket of cats claw and barking his shins painfully on a fallen log, Paco's passion slowly cooled. He was foolish, back there in Tomóchic, to rush angry and distracted from the lawyer's house. All was not yet lost. Saenz? Surely not Saenz. David Pine? He made an effort to think calmly, logically, to plan how he would confront the thief.

Halfway up the ridge he heard an inquiring nicker. It was the mountain pony. He clucked to the animal, reassuring it, and mounted. Together they moved into the blackness of the trail.

David squatted beside Maruja Cruz in the cave. It was a cold day, a hint of snow in the leaden clouds. A small fire of twigs burned at the entrance. Pedro Mirón had gone to a nearby *rancho* and brought back across his horse's withers a rude bed made of barrel staves interlaced with rawhide thongs. Now Maruja lay on the bed, covered by a red Villista blanket, her hand in David Pine's hand.

"They caught me," she wept. "The brutes caught me. They took me and abused me. But I am all right now, David. If I will see Paco soon, that is enough medicine for me! Please, I want to get up."

Gently he pushed her back. "You've had a bad time. You must rest." Old Elena was tending the fire, and she brought Maruja a cup of broth. Maruja was hungry, seizing the cup with both hands and draining it.

"Thank you, Elena," she said to the old woman. As David tucked the blanket again around her, she added, "Elena is a *bruja*—a witch. Did you know that?"

Elena nodded proudly and poked the fire.

He shook his head. "I didn't know."

"She makes good soup. Also, Elena makes magic tea, tea from wild herbs and grasses and cactus. She is going to make for me a special tea, a drink to stop a child from growing inside of me." Her smile faded, and she turned her face to the rocky wall. "Ah, those brutes! David, I can not tell you the awful things they did to me! I am ashamed."

"They have paid for it," he said. "They are all in hell, roasting over the everlasting fires."

After a while, her breath catching like that of a small child after much weeping, she slept, still holding his hand. Squatting beside her, his legs cramped, he did not move for fear of waking her. Around him were the familiar sounds of the *sierra* camp—joking, laughing, a woman grinding corn, someone singing to a guitar, Café instructing a youth in the proper guerrilla use of the pistol.

"I have watched you, *hermanito*," Café said magisterially, "and you have trouble with that wall-eyed horse of yours."

The young man swore. "No, except that he is a devil, that wall-eyed animal!"

"It is not that at all. When you shoot your

pistol . . ." Café paused, and David could imagine him cocking a stubby forefinger. "When you shoot your pistol, shoot always to the side if you can. When you shoot forward, over the horse's neck, splinters of lead are shaved from the bullet where it enters the barrel. These splinters strike your horse in the neck. They sting him and frighten him. Do you understand me, *hombre*?"

The fine points of guerrilla warfare! In the last few weeks, David Pine had learned a great deal. An undistinguished QMC officer, he might now be capable of teaching a course in "Tactics of Irregular Cavalry" at the Staff School. It was all very strange and unsettling.

He shifted his weight uncomfortably on cramped legs. That once-familiar world of the QMC, that place and time of manifests, warehouse receipts, neatly-sharpened pencils, ledgers—it had become shapeless and indistinct in his mind. The now and here of life was this guerrilla band; he wondered at the ease with which he had slipped into their ways, their customs, perhaps, frighteningly, even their way of thinking. Yet Paco had always been the warrior. He smiled ruefully at the irony of it.

Maruja stirred, opened her eyes. He lit a cigarette for her.

"What were you smiling about?" she asked.

"Was I? Oh, thinking. Just thinking."

Elena went out for firewood, and she held his hand to her cheek, burrowing deeper and deeper into the comfort of the blankets. "Do you know something, David?"

"What?"

"Elena can see far into the future. Into the past, also. My past, your past, Paco's past. She says that when you first came to the *tropa*, she knew."

"Knew what?"

"That you and Paco were brothers. Oh, not in blood. No. No, something stronger than blood. And when you came back to the *tropa* from San Miguel de Babícora, bringing me and my shame, Elena says she saw a bright light around my head, just as she sees on you and Paco. It means, Elena says, that our fates are intertwined. She says whatever happens to one of us happens to all. We are linked together by fate, she says, and have always been so, even when we were children playing under the chinaberry tree."

He was uncomfortable. "I don't believe in that *bruja* stuff!"

"Nevertheless!" Maruja insisted. "Strange things have happened. For example, you are *El Pino*, are you not?"

He shrugged. "I guess so."

"What do you mean, you guess so?"

"Accidents!" he cried angrily. "A lot of cockeyed accidents. Things that would never happen again in a million years!"

"But these accidents did not happen to just anyone, David Pine! They happened to you—and to Paco, and to me! What better proof that our fates—the fates of the three of us—are twined together? Elena knows. She is very wise, I tell you."

Exasperated, he poured himself a cup of coffee. Luisito was sitting on a rock outside, blanket wrapped about him, playing a new verse of *El Pino* on his flute.

"I have been wanting to tell you, David," Maruja said. "Before I ran away from Roosevelt there was a long piece in the El Paso *Herald* about *El Pino*, how the people of Chihuahua are making up songs, how *El Pino* will come and save them from the *colorados*. The reporter, a man in Mexico City named Worsham, said that everything that happens to the *colorados*, every ambush, every defeat, the people believe that it is *El Pino* again. Now that our Invincible General seems to be in hiding, the people must believe in *El Pino*. It is no longer Villa's war, it is the war of *El Pino*, the Pine Tree War."

"That's ridiculous!" Angrily David threw out the dregs of coffee. He suspected she was making fun of him. "Look here now, Maruja—"

A shot sounded. Drawing his revolver, David rushed to the cave entrance. But a moment later Pedro Mirón walked from the brush with Paco Mora behind him, riding a weary pony and looking tired and angry.

"I almost shot you, *jefe*!" Pedro protested. "That is very dangerous, to ride up on a sentry and not give the password!"

"To hell with the password!" Paco swung down from the pony and dropped the reins over its head.

"But, *jefe*, you yourself—"

"Café!" Paco barked. "*Bueno*! Luisito! *Bueno*. Where is Eufemio? Ah, there you are, *hombre*!" He prowled about the clearing, seeming to be counting, ticking off names on his fingers. "Guillermo?" He saw David Pine standing at the cave entrance, pistol still in hand. "Ah, David! So it was not you. *Bueno*!" He went on down the line, calling the role, while the *tropa* stared at him, puzzled by the strange conduct. "Sanez. Saenz?" Paco's eyes narrowed. "Where is Dr. Saenz?"

Pedro Mirón shrugged. "*Jefe*, I don't know. He has not yet returned from the journey you set for him."

Paco sat down on a rock, pushing the straw hat back on his forehead. His black curls were damp with sweat, his face pale. "Yet all the others have come back?" he asked.

"Yes, *jefe*."

"And Dr. Saenz has not?"

"No, *jefe*."

"Then I suppose I must give him a little more time."

No one knew what Paco was talking about. They looked at each other in astonishment. But there was a wild look in his eye; no one wanted to cross him, even to ask what it was all about. Finally Pedro Mirón ventured, "I went to El Valle, as you ordered, Paco. No one there knew where our general was."

"In Namaquipa there was a lot of wild talk," Luisito reported, "but no one knew, actually, where General Villa was."

The rest reported failure also. Paco listened to them quietly, only chewing at a corner of his mustachios. At last David Pine came to him, saying, "Paco, Maruja is here."

"What? Maruja?"

"Maruja. Here." David nodded. "In the cave. But she is not very well. When she—"

Paco started to run toward the cave. David caught his arm and said, "*Calma, amigo*! *Con calma*!"

"Not well? Has she been harmed somehow? What has happened?"

"They suspected her of spying for Villa. She ran away from Roosevelt to find you. But the *colorados* at San Miguel de Babicóra caught her and abused her. Café and I went there and took her away from them. That is how it happened."

Paco rushed to the cave. David left then alone together.

Later that day the *tropa* dined on roast pig—a *javelina*, the wild pig of the *sierra*—that Eufemio shot and roasted over a fire. David was tearing stringy meat from a foreleg with his teeth when Paco joined them, still looking preoccupied.

"How does it go with you, *jefe*?" Pedro Mirón asked.

Paco shrugged and took a bit of pork on the point of his knife. He looked thin and haggard, but did not seem very hungry. "Well," he said. "It goes well." To David Pine and Café he said, "Thank you for what you did for Maruja Cruz. You were worthy of the reputation of this *tropa*, to go to San Miguel, into the very teeth of the soldiers, and take Maruja from those filthy rascals. I commend you both."

While the rest watched, Paco stared at the fire, chewing on the pork. They all knew something was troubling him. Still they wanted to talk to him, to receive instructions, to establish again their role as loyal men under his wise command. But Paco did not speak, only staring into the fire and chewing, the veins on his temple standing out in the firelight.

Later, Pedro Mirón came to David, uneasy. He nodded toward where Paco sat in the firelight, a lonely and brooding figure.

"What do you think, señor?"

"Think? About what?"

"Him." Pedro nodded again. "I came to him to ask a question about the rotation of guards for the night, a necessary and proper question, and he cursed me under his breath, told me to go away!"

David shrugged. "I do not know. Perhaps it is concern about Maruja Cruz. They are very fond of each other. It must trouble Paco greatly, the experience Maruja has gone through."

"I do not think it is that. If it were so, would he not be with her, comforting her?"

"Then perhaps he is worried about Dr. Saenz. The rest have returned, but Dr. Saenz has not. Saenz has been gone a long time."

Pedro spat into the night. "He would not worry about that one! No, Paco would be happy if Saenz disappeared and never came back. At first it looked like a good arrangement, to have the personal representative of the Invincible General traveling with our *tropa*. But two in command is a bad idea, in a household as well as in a *tropa*. No, they have always been like two cats stalking the same rabbit!"

"Then I don't know," David said. "But I will speak with him, Pedro. I will try to find out. It is not good for the *tropa* to be without a leader."

"*Bueno*!" Pedro said. "You and Paco are old friends, señor. He needs an old friend now, to talk to him."

When David approached, Paco did not look up. He

continued to scratch the ground with a stick, intent on the design he was making.

"*Amigo*," David said, "something is troubling you. The men notice it too. What is wrong?"

Angrily Paco broke the stick and threw it away.

"Ah, David, it has turned out to be a very hard life, that of a revolutionary, the leader of a *tropa*! There are many things that trouble such a man."

"What do you mean?"

Paco lit a cigarette; his fingers trembled as he held the wax match. "I did not want to tell anyone about it, but it seems as if I must explain my conduct. Well, the money, then—the ten thousand dollars in my rawhide box. *Caray*, I was so careful with it! I never left it out of my sight, or so I thought. But, David, the money is gone—stolen! When I went to Tomóchic I opened the box to show the Villistas there, to show them the revolution had plenty of money, maybe even—the Virgin forgive me—to brag a little about my fine *tropa* and the raid on Roosevelt, the Plains Bank! But when I opened the box, there was nothing in it but dirt, leaves, a few stones to make it weigh right!"

David was astonished. "But you kept it with you all the time!"

"I was not careful enough, it appears."

"You suspect someone?"

"At first I suspected everyone, even you, *hombre*! That is how confused and foolish my poor brain was! But when a man steals ten thousand dollars, he does not hang around the scene of the crime, does he? So who is not here? You can count them, and see. You are here. Pedro, Eufemio, Café—all the rest. The only man not here is Saenz."

"But you can hardly suspect him!"

"Everyone else has come back from the journeys I set for them—everyone but Saenz!"

"But he was your liaison, I understood, your liaison with Villa, a man sent to work with you and to report your revolutionary value to General Villa! He was a very important man!"

Paco snorted. "Saenz would not be the first Judas to betray a man for gold! So where is he? He should have returned long ago. *Bueno*, I give him one more day. If he is not here by then . . ." The tip of Paco's cigarette glowed hot and fierce in the darkness.

"So if he is not here? If he does not come back?"

The glowing coal described a red arc as Paco flipped the butt into the air. "Then I intend to go after him! Life has no meaning for me unless I recover the money, bring it to General Villa, as I swore to do!"

Dr. Saenz did not return. The next morning Paco Mora, face tight with purpose, saddled a fresh horse, filled a sack with food, strapping it carefully in place.

The rest of the *tropa* were too afraid of Paco's mood to question him, but David Pine asked, "Where are you going?"

"To Chihuahua City," Paco said between tight lips. "Saenz lived for a long time in that city, has friends there, a mistress too, I think. That is probably where the bastard is, spending my money!"

Pedro Mirón cleared his throat. "*Jefe*, that place is full with *colorados*. General Pineda has his headquarters there, you know that!"

Paco gathered the reins in his hand. "What better place for a traitor, then? Probably the rascal thinks I am afraid to come there, under Pineda's very nose, to find him."

David shook his head. "I doubt if Saenz is in Chihuahua City, *amigo*. It would be dangerous for him too. Pineda's *colorados* would hang him at once."

"Not," Paco said, "not if he gave himself up to the soldiers, to Pineda. Not if Saenz abandoned the revolution, say, and told Pineda all about Paco Mora and his band—where they are hiding, what they are planning, where they are going next!"

Pedro Mirón's mouth dropped open. "*Jefe*, do you think he would do that?"

Luisito was incredulous. "*Jefe*, the doctor was always talking about being a true revolutionary, how we simple men must do things in a certain way to be true Villistas. Can it be possible he was a traitor?"

Paco tightened his grip on the reins. The horse danced skittishly and pawed the ground.

"I never trusted Saenz," he said. "When a man is always spouting slogans, talking big and important—" Impatiently he wheeled the pony around. "It is time for me to go!"

"But what about the *tropa*?" Pedro Mirón demanded. "*Jefe*, you can not just go away like this and leave us without a leader!"

Nacho agreed. Scratching his head, he said, "I never know what to do until the *jefe* tells me!"

"It is like that with all of us!" Luisito chimed in. "*Jefe*, what are we to do while you are gone?"

Paco's eyes narrowed. There was almost a malicious glint in them.

"Listen!" he said. "Listen to me, all of you! According to all reports, even according to a popular *corrido* which has much currency in Chihuahua nowadays, there is only one man, only one man with the brains, the valor, the skills a revolutionary leader must have!"

Pedro Mirón looked puzzled. "*Jefe*, who is that?"

"The famous *El Pino* is to command you while I am gone!"

David was so startled he could not speak.

"And remember, *hombre*," Paco said to David, "it is your first duty to get the *tropa* out of here, out of this hiding place, before Saenz's trickery brings the *colorados* on you!"

David could only stare and stammer.

"What—what are you talking about?" he demanded.

"Me? Paco, are you making jokes?"

But Paco only turned and spurred his mount down the rocky slope, the pony almost losing its footing in the shale. Incredulous, David ran after Paco, shouting.

"Paco! Wait! Stop!"

But Paco Mora was gone. The only sign of his passing was a veil of dust, rapidly dissipating in the mountain wind, the chill wind of autumn in the *sierra.*

Chapter Eight

In Chihuahua, capital of the Mexican state of Chihuahua, there was a brothel across the street from the old Jesuit college. Silver from the mines of Chihuahua had enriched many men; it was only fitting there be a bordello to cater to expensive tastes.

La Pajarita—the Little Bird—was run by a Frenchwoman who looked like a society dowager. The Pajarita was paneled in rare woods, potted palms stood about the reception hall, and each of the girls' rooms was mirrored from wall to wall. A string trio played Bach and Tschaikovsky, and a liveried attendant met guests at the door. The Pajarita was an expensive house, patronized by the colonels and majors of General Pineda's staff. Captains and lieutenants could hardly afford to go there.

For a poor provincial doctor, the Pajarita would also have been too expensive, but Rafael Saenz was no longer poor. The loot from the Plains Bank robbery, except for a small amount withdrawn by him for current expenses, was safely in a canvas sack under a loose board in his lodgings at the Hotel Excelsior, where he had rented a suite. Now he lay pleasurably in a huge bed with silk sheets, fondling the girl named Clara. Or was it Cora? No, Cora had been the first one, an English girl with golden curls and baby eyes.

"Again?" Clara giggled. "*Carramba, señor*, you are inexhaustible!"

Dr. Saenz fondled his mustachios. "The result, my dear, of long deprivation. You have no idea how boring is the continual company of men."

"You have been away, then?"

"Yes," Saenz said. "I have been . . . traveling."

Of course, the *colorados* would soon come to take him away to the Government Palace for questioning; he had anticipated that. A stranger in town with expensive tastes and money to indulge them would come under quick scrutiny by General Pineda's lynx-eyed provost marshal, Calderon. Until then, until the bargain Saenz intended to strike with the *colorados*, he refused to be concerned.

Once, of course, he had been an eager Villista. But with the Invincible General soundly beaten, not even to be found in the state of Chihuahua, doubts had crept into Saenz's mind. It was not hypocrisy. No. At one time he actually believed in the revolution. But with amateurs like Paco Mora to contend with, fools like David Pine, ignorant farmers like Pedro Mirón and Eufemio and Luisito and the rest, Saenz had begun to see things in a different light. Such men could never win a revolution against hopeless odds.

To leave Villa's cause and join the *colorados* was unthinkable; after all, Rafael Saenz was a man of some principle. But to leave Villa with ten thousand dollars in a sack and *then* join the *colorados*, that was another thing entirely, something one owed one's self-respect. Why follow a leader one could not even locate? Better recant, frankly and honestly, perhaps come by a few additional thousand for revealing the whereabouts of Paco Mora and his *tropa*, along with the foolish *gringo* David Pine, whom the stupid farmers were now calling *El Pino*. Pineda would be happy to get his hands on those two.

"Señor," Clara sighed, "I am very tired. I would like to sleep a little now."

Feeling pleased and relaxed, he tweaked her nipple. "*Bueno, mi vida*. Here, come a little closer, rest in my arms."

Saenz was not mistaken about General Pineda's provost. When he finally came down the grand staircase of the Pajarita, two uniformed soldiers awaited him in the lobby.

"Señor Saenz?" one asked.

Saenz smiled a greeting at Mme. Coudray, the proprietress, and spoke gently to the soldier.

"I am a doctor, a licensed physician in good standing. I would prefer you address me by my professional title."

The corporal, a simple man, looked perplexed.

"This is Dr. Saenz," Mme. Coudray explained. "You must call him doctor."

"*Bueno*," the corporal said. "Well, in any case Major Calderon would like to see him."

Dr. Saenz inclined his head graciously.

"I am pleased," he said, "to visit the provost marshal."

Major Calderon was a big man in a rumpled uniform, smoking a pipe filled with imported English tobacco. He looked at Rafael Saenz with eyes that were heavy-lidded, almost sleepy. But Saenz had heard of Calderon. He was careful with his words.

"I am at your service, sir. What is it you wish to know?"

Calderon puffed on his pipe. "You are a doctor, eh?"

"That is true."

"From where?"

"As a young man I lived here, in Chihuahua. But I have practiced in many places, including El Paso."

"We have information you are a Villista."

Dr. Saenz lit a cigarette. It was good to get back to a real city where he could buy Egyptian cigarettes.

"I am not a Villista."

"But you were, then?"

Saenz blew out the match and laid it delicately in the ashtray on the major's desk.

"I was," he conceded. "At least, until I saw my error. Now I am a strong supporter of President Carranza and the federal cause."

"So, what changed your mind?"

"Money," Saenz said promptly. "Is that not what usually changes a man's mind?"

Major Calderon blew a reflective smoke ring toward the ceiling. "Money is a powerful influence," he admitted. "But I do not quite follow you, Doctor. What money are you talking about?"

Dr. Saenz struck quick and hard. "The money you will give me for information I bring to General Pineda."

Calderon scratched his nose with the stem of the pipe. "You will have to be more specific. Everyone in the state of Chihuahua comes to me with information. Most of it is not worth anything."

"*Bueno*. My information is this. I know where General Pineda can find Paco Mora and his troublesome *tropa*. I know where General Pineda can find the blond man they call *El Pino*, the man who captured the Lewis gun at the Guzmán station, the man the farmers sing silly songs about, the man reported in the newspaper this afternoon as having killed four of your best *colorados* at San Miguel de Babícora, the man who—"

"That is enough," Major Calderon said. He busied himself knocking the dottle from his pipe, scraping the bowl clean with a penknife, loading the pipe again from a red tin on his desk. Finally he looked up from the desk.

"How do I know you are telling the truth?"

Dr. Saenz, feeling very calm, shrugged. "Actually, you do not know! But I think you will take the risk to get a chance at Paco Mora and *El Pino*. Anyway, if I can not lead you to them, I expect no payment. So really, you take no risk."

Major Calderon went to the window and stared out at the parish church of San Francisco.

"How much do you expect for your information, assuming, of course, that it is correct?"

"It seems to me that ten thousand pesos is an equitable sum."

Major Calderon was incredulous. "Ten thousand pesos?"

"I would ask for more," Dr. Saenz repeated, "but to a poor provincial doctor ten thousand pesos is an enormous sum."

"Do not make jokes with me, Doctor!" Major Calderon warned. "I have no sense of humor." He ambled ponderously back to the desk, puffing the pipe. Dr. Saenz was reminded of a circus bear doing a trick. But bears had teeth, vicious teeth. He was beginning to lose some of his calm. Calderon had a reputation as a cruel and inhumane man.

"I could get the information from you in other ways," the provost suggested. "In the cellars of the Government Palace we have people who can get at the truth, and interesting machines to help them."

Perhaps Dr. Saenz turned pale—he did not know how successfully he concealed his fright—but his voice was steady. After all, the stakes were high.

"Major, we are both grown men. You do not frighten me with talk of torture. There is the fact, you see, that Paco Mora is hiding in a very secure place in the *sierra*. You could perhaps wring from me under torture some information, but it would still take a very good guide, such as myself, to lead a force there before Paco and his *tropa* go elsewhere."

Major Calderon flushed. He was not used to being

talked to in such a manner.

"Besides," Dr. Saenz said, playing his trump card, "my wants are very simple. Five thousand pesos would satisfy me, Major. Five thousand for you, and five thousand for me. It could be arranged. I would be agreeable to such an arrangement."

Calderon's teeth relaxed their bite on the stem of the pipe; he almost smiled.

"Are you suggesting bribery to me, Doctor? To General Pineda's provost marshal?"

Saenz knew his man.

"I am," he said. "For your good and prompt report of this matter to General Pineda."

"Well," Calderon said, "I will see the general this evening and perhaps have an answer for you soon. You are at the Excelsior Hotel?"

"You know I am," Dr. Saenz said politely.

Arising, he added, "You understand speed is of the essence! I can not guarantee that Paco Mora and his *tropa* will remain long at that place in the *sierra* known to me."

The provost marshal had certainly known that Rafael Saenz was stopping at the Excelsior. Saenz's closet had been ransacked, the drawer of the writing desk pulled out and contents jammed back in disorder, the bed obviously torn apart and inexpertly remade. He checked the loose board in the corner, under the flap of Turkish carpet, and was relieved to find the sack with the money intact.

For a time he sat comfortably in a rocking chair on the balcony of his suite, watching evening steal over the city. Fancifully he toyed with the idea of himself as a favorite of General Pineda, rewarded with rich honors for his service to the state. Perhaps he would be appointed Pineda's chief medical officer.

It was a cold evening, gray and drear, a veil of wood-smoke in the air. Saenz shivered, went inside, closed the French doors to the balcony. Settling down to read a recent issue of the El Paso *Herald*, his eye chanced to fall on a wire service dispatch datelined Mexico City by one Harry Worsham. In romantic terms the piece discussed the mysterious *El Pino*, the *guerrilero*. People claimed to have seen and talked with *El Pino* in Colonia Dublán, El Valle, Tomóchic, Madera, even Parral itself, where Pershing was. Every raid in Chihuahua was laid at the door of the dashing Englishman, or Dane, or Swiss—whatever nationality the latest account granted him. He was tall and blond, with blue eyes, and performed incredible feats. Bullets did not harm him. There was even a song, Worsham reported. He quoted several stanzas, all badly framed. Saenz grinned. He hoped Major Calderon would read the story.

At nine in the evening he ordered a light supper and a bottle of wine brought up on a tray. When he heard the knock at the door he opened it, thinking it to be the *mozo* with the tray.

The knock was not that of the *mozo*. Standing in the dimly lit hall was Paco Mora. The oil lamp in the hall glinted dully on the barrel of the pistol centered on Saenz's chest.

"*Bueno*!" Paco said. "We are together again, eh, Saenz?"

The doctor blanched. He stumbled, half fell, backward into the room. Paco laughed, softly closed the door behind him, and bolted it.

"A very nice place," he said. "A suite, eh?" He walked about, eyeing the expensive furniture, feeling appreciatively with his toe the heavy pile of the carpet. "But then, with all my money, I suppose you are able to afford the best, eh?" Suddenly he whirled, jabbed the muzzle of the pistol hard against Saenz's ribs. "And where is my money, *cabron*?"

Saenz tried to speak. No words came. He swallowed hard and wet his lips.

"Where is it?" Paco insisted.

Saenz cried out in pain as Paco slapped the barrel of

the pistol across his head. The front sight raked his temple. He put a shaky hand to his brow, staring in horror at the smear of blood—*his* blood.

"It—it is not here!" he stammered. "It is—I put it into the Banco Nacional de Chihuahua. Do you think I would keep that much money here—in this room?"

Paco smiled, but there was no mirth in the grimace.

"Saenz, do not trifle with me! Whether I get my money back or not, I am going to kill you, that is certain! But will you die quickly, with a shot through your skull? Or very slowly, taking two or three days in the hospital, shot through the stomach?"

Dr. Saenz turned more gray than ever. He made a small croaking noise and spread his hands wide in supplication. But Paco Mora, snarling like a dog, drew a knife and sliced angrily at him.

"You had better produce the money quickly!" he said. "If you put me to any more trouble," he said striding to the French doors, pulling them open, "I will cut off your *cojones* and fling them into the street, as a start!"

Dazed, blood running into his eyes and mouth, Saenz collapsed on the bed, weeping, one hand shielding his face from the terrible raking of the pistol barrel, the other protectively over his crotch. Through the open French doors someone might hear him and call the police, the soldiers. But he was too weak to call out.

"Over . . . over . . ." He started to speak, but blood filled his mouth. He seemed to have lost some teeth. Coughing, spitting, he managed to prop himself on an elbow. "Over there. In the corner. Under the carpet, under the loose board."

Paco knelt and turned back the carpet.

"Aha!" He pried up the board. The money was in a canvas sack. Quickly he replaced the board and emptied the sack on the table. Swiftly his fingers riffled through it, fanned bills, clinked coins, sorted them into yellow stacks. "I do not have time to count it accurately, but nearly all of the ten thousand appears to be here."

When a knock sounded on the door, Paco started. Quickly he scraped the money—bills, coins, all—into the bag and knotted it.

"Who is that?" he asked.

Saenz shook his head mutely, unable to speak.

"Señor Doctor!" a voice called. "It is Alberto, sir, with the tray you ordered. There is a lovely salad here, a little cheese, a cold bottle."

Annoyed, Paco looked about. His eye fell on the open French doors. "Tell him to go away!" he hissed at Saenz. When the doctor did not speak, he gestured again with the terrible knife. "Tell the damned *mozo* to go away, that you have suddenly been taken ill!"

Saenz tried, tried desperately, but blood and mucus filled his throat so he could only gurgle. Rolling piteously about the bed, weeping with mingled fear and anger, he gagged, vomited. Paco shook his head in disgust.

"Señor Doctor!" The knock sounded again, sharper and more insistent this time. "What is the matter? Are you ill, sir?"

"I should kill you now," Paco muttered. "Oh, I should kill you at this instant, Saenz, as you lie there in your own filth! I should kill you quickly, without emotion, as one steps on a beetle, for all the harm you have done to me, to the revolution. But I can not. I can not bring myself to waste a bullet on such carrion!" Slinging the bag over his shoulder, he went to the French doors and threw a booted leg over the balcony. Then he was gone, disappearing into the screen of trees.

Saenz finally managed to get to his feet. Disregarding the knocking on the door, now frantic and insistent, he went out onto the balcony. It was dark; he could see nothing. From the distance he heard a challenge, "*Alto*!" and a single shot. Really, he hoped Paco Mora had gotten away. He wanted to deal with Paco Mora himself, on a day that would surely come, though he might have to search the whole of Mexico for him. Helplessly he wept, eyes filled with tears of rage and humiliation.

Pale and wan, but nearly recovered from her capture by the *colorados* at San Miguel de Babícora, Maruja Cruz sat at the entrance of the basalt cave they shared, looking at the white flakes falling in the *sierra*.

"It's an early snow," David remarked. He wrapped leans arms around himself, flailing his body for warmth. Still angry and upset at Paco Mora for abandoning him and the *tropa*, he nevertheless said, "I hope Paco got down the mountain before it started."

Maruja was smoking a cigarette. Wrapped in a blanket, she stared somberly at the falling snow, eyes flat and unseeing. Under the tattered bodice her breast rose and fell slowly, deliberately.

"A penny for your thoughts!" David joked.

When she still did not answer, he questioned her, concerned. "Maruja, are you all right?"

She stubbed out the cigarette. He wished she would not smoke so much. It was the last of the Belmontes they had captured on the MNR train at Guzmán station.

"My thoughts? A penny? What does that mean?"

"It's only an Anglo expression. What were you thinking about?"

She looked at him a long time. Many things seemed to waver, take form, then disappear in her dark eyes. Finally she shrugged and said, "It's Paco, of course."

He squatted beside her, sipping at a cup of thin coffee brewed from rapidly dwindling stores. "What about Paco?"

She bit her lip, shook her head.

"Come on now! We are all friends, are we not?"

She turned anguished eyes on him. "David, Paco is not the same! He has not been the same for a long time, ever since he got mixed up in the revolution. Now he has left me! I came all this way, and he has left me already, to go to Chihuahua City. He hardly took the time to hold me in his arms, to tell me he loved me!"

"He had to go away," David explained. "He had to go to Chihuahua City in search of Dr. Saenz, to recover the money."

She did not appear to hear him.

"I was a virgin," she went on in a low voice. "I had not been had by any man, and I was proud of that. It was Paco, Paco Mora, I was saving myself for. I wanted to come to him new and clean and untouched, David. That is what I thought about my Paco, what I intended to do for him! But now I am soiled, dirty!" Fiercely she grasped his arm. "Is that why he left me so quickly, to go away? Is that it?"

Gently he pulled her hand away, taking it in his own.

"You know that's not true. The thing that happened to you, Maruja, the thing you bore so bravely and honorably, that was for the revolution. Paco would honor you for that."

"He would honor me as a patriot, but not as a woman." The old quick anger welled up in her. "No, David, he does not love me any more! I think he does not love any woman! He loves only the revolution, loves only that damned money he has sworn to bring to General Villa! I tell you, David, Paco has changed, has changed greatly. He is not the good fine Paco any more; he is a Paco who wants only power, recognition! He wants only to be a big man!"

She flung herself weeping into his arms. He sat for a long time, cradling the fine slender body in his arms, feeling guilty and uncomfortable. What Maruja Cruz said was indeed true; Paco had changed greatly. But David Pine had also changed. Life was a badly-written comedy that mocked them all with its twists and turns.

"Maruja," he whispered into her hair. "*Ay*, Maruja, don't cry!" He stared at the entrance to the cave, where snow was falling, heavier now. "*Bueno*, it seems to me we have all changed, and I not the least. I've changed in a way that's not to my liking, really. I guess that's part of being an Anglo, with the cast-iron conscience Pop and Mom Cooper left me. So I've made up my mind. I'm going back to the border somehow and face the music. It's time for this insanity to stop."

A sob caught in Maruja's breast once or twice, like a child after a bad dream. She sat up. Throwing away the empty Belmonte packet, she found a crumpled and bent brown paper *Ala*. There were not many of them left, either.

"You can't go away now, David," she said in practical tones. "Too many people depend on you. Not only Pedro Mirón and Nacho and Luisito and the rest, but I also, Maruja Cruz. I do not know what I would do without you. Do you intend to abandon me also?" She bent forward to accept the light he offered. He saw the clean white line where her dark tresses were parted, and almost bent his head to touch it with his lips.

"I must," he said doggedly. "I've certainly had plenty of opportunities before this. But it was a long way, a dangerous way, back to the border, and at the time I suppose I didn't have the guts, really. And, in a curious way, I think maybe I was enjoying the experience. After all, the life of a supply officer is pretty dull."

She drew deep on the cigarette.

"*Claro*, the border was indeed a long way. But it is even farther now, and the *colorados* are all around us, thicker than flies about a milk pail."

He shrugged. "That's true. My chances aren't really worth a lot on either side of the border. I'll certainly be court-martialed; if I ever get back to Fort Bliss, that is. But I'm not a Mexican, Maruja! No matter how well I speak the language, no matter how much I sympathize with the revolution, with *la raza*, with good people like you and Paco and old Felix and Café and Pedro Mirón and the rest, I'm still an Anglo, with roots, deep roots, on the other side of the border. I belong back there, and that's where, ultimately, I've got to go!"

Maruja inhaled deeply, said nothing.

"You don't really understand!" he said desperately. "Look. Maybe you can understand it this way! I'm a coward! At first I figured it was safer to stay with Paco and the *tropa* than try to escape. And maybe, for a while, it seemed like a romantic adventure, something picked up and carried on from the days when you and I and Paco played uner the chinaberry tree. But it's not! It's all a dream, a bloody dream. It's death and anguish. And people—good people—like Don Jaime and Pop Cooper and Doña Ana murdered. I myself was responsible for three U.S. kids being shot to death at the Guzmán station, in that battle there. That weighs on my conscience, Maruja. I need to go back, to be punished for letting my emotions carry me away. I need to be with my own people again, to let them pronounce sentence on me for my sins! Do you understand?"

She took a deep breath. "Of course I understand, David. Maybe I am part Anglo, too. I lived across the border, in Roosevelt, for a long time, went to school with the Anglo kids. You are all alike, I guess. So I suppose it could not be any other way. The children under the chinaberry tree died long ago. But for a little while, I hoped."

She went to the doorway and beckoned him.

"But before you make any decision, David, look!"

Even in the mouth of the cave, away from the smoldering fire, it was cold. But outside, in the falling snow, it was colder. Pedro Mirón stood there, waiting, blanket heavy with snow, rifle slung over his back. Luisito the *telegrafista* was there too, without a hat, black curls heavy with flakes. Café cupped his hands around a tin cup of coffee to keep them warm, and Nacho, the Yaqui, sat on a rock, rifle across his knees, motionless, like an ancient idol drifted with snow.

Others of the *tropa* walked slowly back and forth. When they saw David Pine they stopped their pacing and looked up.

"You see?" Maruja murmured.

He saw and was moved.

"They are waiting for you," she explained. "Without a leader, they do not know what to do. They are farmers, most of them; a blacksmith, too—a potter and some herdsmen and shepherds—people who gave up their tasks to fight for something better, something not for them but for their children. Paco was a hope. Now Paco is gone, and they think he will not come back. So they depend on you. And without you, without a leader, these poor men will sooner or later hang on one of General Pineda's fruit trees." She clutched his arm. "David Pine, does not all this move you, sway you, make you want to cry out for justice, fight for justice, die for justice?"

He almost wept with the unfairness of it.

"I didn't ask for this!" he shouted. "How does it concern me? There's injustice everywhere—in the States, too! But it's not my job to play God, to right wrongs!" Angry, he stalked back to the small warmth of the fire and lay down on the blanket. He did not want to meet her eyes.

"David, ah, David!" She came to kneel beside him, soft dark hair falling about her face. A hand stroked his cheek with tender fingers. "I am cruel to talk so! I know that!"

"No, you're not!" he said roughly. "It's just that—that—"

"You belong back there, in your Anglo world. I will help you. Café and Luisito and Nacho and the rest will help you. Our fight is not your fight, that is so. The *tropa* will be glad you were once with us. They will say, *'Gracias, señor Pino,'* and that will be the end of it. It is a good ending for a legend, I suppose."

She was crying again; the muffled weeping tore at his

heart. He pulled her to him, kissing the tear-stained eyes, the smooth cheeks, the lips red and full without cosmetics.

"Maruja," he said softly. "Maruja! Can I bear to leave you?"

Their bodies flowed together, curve for curve. He felt a warm tingling in his loins, a flush throughout his body.

"David," Maruja protested, "we should not be here, like this!" She tried to pull away from him; hungry, he only pressed her tighter.

"Listen!" Maruja said suddenly. "Do you hear that?" She held up a warning finger.

Cheated, he relaxed his embrace of her, propping himself on an elbow. "Hear what?"

"That! That noise!"

The fire made small hissing, crackling sounds. He closed his eyes, concentrating. Then he heard the needlelike drone.

"I hear it," he said. "It's an airplane!"

The sound grew louder. Wrapping the blanket around him, he ran from the cave. Through the trees and brush he could see only small patches of gray sky dimmed by the falling snow. But the needlelike droning grew, increased in volume. It was indeed an airplane. The *colorados* had no airplanes. It must be one of Pershing's R-2 Curtisses, called for by General Pineda to scout the *sierra.* But in this weather—snow falling—at over two thousand meters high? The pilot must be a brave man—or a fool.

"Jefe," Luisito said, "it is one of those airplane things again. Is it looking for us?"

"Should we hide in the caves until it goes away?" Pedro Mirón asked.

"Can it hurt us?" Nacho shook snow from his shoulders and came to stand beside David Pine. "Jefe, what should we do?"

In the heavy growth of trees, the only clear spots

studded with boulders the size of houses, and with the snow falling, it was unlikely the airplane could spot them. But possibly the smoke from their fires . . .

"If it comes near," Nacho threatened, raising his rifle, "I will shoot it!"

If they were reconnoitering the mountain, the *colorados* might soon advance toward them. David Pine had no illusions about what would happen then. Burdened as they were with women and children, low on food and ammunition, there could only be one outcome. But how much time did they have?

He snapped orders. "Nacho, take three men and go down to the south lookout where Eufemio is! That is the only way the *colorados* can get in here. Send a man back to inform us if you see any soldiers. The rest stay there and watch until relieved. Do not fire at them. That will give away our position. But if they come too close before you are sent for, shoot as many as you can and return quickly to the camp. All the rest of you—women and children and all—pack things on the horses and get ready to move."

"But where are we going, *jefe*?" Enrique demanded. "And what about Paco?"

"We can't wait for Paco. We have got to get out of here quickly, before we are trapped and die."

There was a chorus of dissent.

"We should not abandon our Paco!" Pedro Mirón protested. "What if Paco comes back here and we are gone?"

"Maybe we should stay here and let them come against us," Luisito said. "One revolutionary is worth a dozen of those *pelados*! We will give them a hot time!"

"Listen!" David said. "Listen to me!"

They kept chattering, slapping each other on the back, making contemptuous gestures in the direction the federal soldiers would come.

Angry, David shouted, "*Por Diós*, listen to me!"

There was a new note in his voice, a sharpness, an

authority, they had never heard before. Suddenly silent, they listened, eyes wide and mouths hanging open. This was not David Pine, this was not even the blond *El Pino*. This was someone else.

"You are all talking foolishness," David said. "You are like little boys boasting and bragging. Listen to me! You are caught, here on this mountain! *Colorados* will probably advance up this mountain soon. And there are not many of us to fight such a superior force. Our women, too, are here, and the children. What about them?"

There was a babble of voices, a waving of hands, and insistence on being heard as one man shoved another, trying to speak. Everyone had a plan. But David Pine shouted them all down.

"I am leading this *tropa* now!" he told them. "You all heard Paco! Well, he gave over command to me, did he not? And I will make the decisions!" He put a hand on the pistol in his belt. "Does any man here challenge my authority?"

No one spoke. They looked uncertainly at each other. Nacho dropped the muzzle of his rifle. Pedro Mirón looked astonished, then pleased.

"No, *jefe*," Café grinned finally. "We do not challenge you. No one challenges you. You are the leader. That is what Paco said."

It had been their way of testing him. He grinned back at Café and said, "*Bueno, hombres*! Let us now have a council of war to decide what to do."

In the cave David rolled flat a tattered map. "Here we are," he said, pointing. "And the *colorados* will probably be advancing from the railroad at Madera—here. The airplane may have spotted us, and maybe it has not. It probably has a wireless set—"

Pedro Mirón frowned. "*Jefe*, a what?"

David could as well have been talking to a Stone Age man about a Victor talking machine. What was it Paco Mora said that time? "Commanding a *tropa* is a hard task.'' *Caray*, it was indeed.

''*Hombre*,'' he said to Café, ''you know the *sierra* well. Is there a way out for us to the west, over the mountain to Sonora?''

Café, squatting on his heels, sucked in his breath.

''*Ay, carramba*! There is a back trail yet, but only for sheep and goats! Even then, only in the summer! With this snow . . .''

''No other way?''

Café shook his head.

''Then we go over the mountain,'' David said. ''There is no other way.''

''Wherever you tell us, *jefe*,'' they agreed.

''And after that,'' David took a long breath, ''well, there is something I am going to tell you. After that, after we arrive in Sonora, and that is not yet certain, I am going to go away. I am going back to my own country. Do you understand?''

Luisito looked puzzled.

''*Jefe*, how can you go back to the *gringos*? They will not like it very well that you fought side by side with us in the *tropa*, will they? Does that not make you a—a—'' Luisito paused, delicately.

''A traitor? Yes, I suppose it does.''

''Will they not shoot you then, the way the *colorados* shot your Sergeant Acton?''

Café made a snorting sound. ''The *colorados* did not shoot Acton!''

''But that was what was given out!'' Luisito protested.

''True,'' Café said, ''but the *colorados* still did not shoot Acton. Dr. Saenz himself shot Acton, when the sergeant tried to run away to be saved.''

David grabbed Café by the arm. ''Is this true?''

Café looked hurt. ''*Jefe*, I do not tell lies! I was there, beside Señor Acton when he started to run. Dr. Saenz took aim, so—'' Café cocked his thumb, and pointed with his forefinger. "Bang! Dr. Saenz said he was trying to escape, so he killed him!"

It had been long weeks since Henry Acton's death, but David Pine felt a fresh upwelling of grief. Saenz had killed poor Acton! In an involuntary gesture he made the sign of the cross on his chest, the simple and common gesture of the *tropa* in the presence of death. Then he was annoyed at himself. In Roosevelt he had gone to the Baptist Sunday School. *Que caray!* Had he already become some sort of cross-breed?

But he could not now encumber his brain with thoughts of revenge. There was a more pressing matter, the matter of the *tropa*'s escape from the Cerro de las Ventanas, the Hill of the Windows.

"So we go over the mountain to Sonora," Pedro Mirón said with an air of finality.

"I have told you what I will do then," David said. "But what are you all to do, then? I do not want to leave you, but I must, as I have told you."

They looked at each other. There was a shuffling of feet, a clearing of throats. Luisito's brown toe described a pattern in the dust. Nacho rubbed the barrel of his rifle with a gnarled thumb. Finally Pedro spoke.

"*Jefe*," he said, "do not worry about this. Sonora is a place where we all have friends." He swept his arm around. "All here. We have roots, too, *jefe*, as you do. We have friends, relatives—in Bavispe, in Nacozari—all the way to Hermosillo where Luisito and I have cousins. Although I do not like to think so, perhaps the revolution is over. Perhaps we have lost, *la raza* has lost. But there will be another time. If a man waits, there is always another time."

Café gruffly cleared his throat. "As for you, *jefe*, you will go with God to whatever waits for you across the border. But we will remember you. We do not forget easily." He grinned. "*Caray*, what you did with that cursed dynamite at San Miguel de Babícora!"

They called in the guards at the lookout, who had thus far seen no *colorados*. Perhaps the weather was too bad for federal troops to move up the mountain. The *tropa*, a long file of riders and pack horses, started up the rocky trail. From David Pine's rough estimate, the summit was at least a thousand meters above them still. As they rode, snow fell more thickly. The wind rose. It was hard for one rider to see the next in line. Animals, men, women, children—all lost their outlines in the mantle of snow.

Maruja rode beside David Pine, head bent and shawled against the wind. Reaching up with a numbed hand, he felt a thin crunch of ice around his mouth where the breath had already frozen.

"Are you all right?" he asked Maruja, shouting against the noise of the wind.

She looked at him and nodded, smiling.

From somewhere in the file behind came an eerie tootling, the music of a flute. Luisito had added another verse to the song of *El Pino*. David wanted to be angry, but he could not. It was a measure of his change that he felt a perverse pleasure.

Paco Mora had changed, changed from the boy under the chinaberry tree, so long ago. Maruja Cruz had changed also. But perhaps the greatest change, David Pine realized, had been in himself. It was well that he was going home before he became unrecognizable, even to himself.

Chapter Nine

General Pineda y Flores dined late at the Government Palace. While his staff officers stood, hats in hand, he carved a slice of breast from a roast fowl. He chewed slowly, sensuously, savoring the flavor of the meat as he savored the success of his campaign against Doroteo Arango, the upstart whom the people called Pancho Villa.

"I have driven the rebels from the field," he announced, severing a wing. "My campaign in Chihuahua has been successful. Our President Carranza is pleased. But we still have unfinished business in Chihuahua."

The harsh eyes stared for a precise interval at each officer, sparing none.

"Although Villa and his so-called *Division del Norte* have been beaten and dispersed, there remain pockets of resistance. These small pockets can be likened to tiny centers of infection in the body of the state. Without removing them, as a surgeon lances a boil, there is the possibility of reinfection that again will sicken the whole of Chihuahua."

Pineda y Flores had an affection for words. At times he thought himself a poet.

"There is the matter of the *guerrillero.* Paco Mora,

and others of his type, like the troublemaker they call *El Pino*. Mora, you recall, robbed the *gringo* bank at Roosevelt, captured an MNR train and tore up the tracks. Only recently he, or others like him, attacked our outpost at San Miguel de Babicora and armed the farmers there against us."

Mora had made Pineda look foolish not once but several times; the newspaper *Excelsior* in Mexico City ran a cartoon showing a worried man who looked like Pineda y Flores slapping ineffectually at a gnat labeled Paquito.

"There are," the general said, pouring himself a goblet of Monopole champagne, "other such bands, also. But if we can make an example of Mora and his followers—hang them, for example, in the plaza of the city of Chihuahua—that will do much to discourage the others, especially now that Villa is driven from the field."

Most of the officers were old hands, knowing enough to limit their reaction to wise and knowing nods. But a lieutenant in the artillery, young and inexperienced, spoke up.

"Sir, where is the *guerrillero* Mora?"

It was not an unreasonable question; an artillery officer does not want to set up his piece without knowing the location of the target. But the rest of the officers blanched, drawing apart from the artillerist as if from a leper. Intelligence had been searching for Paco Mora and his *tropa* for months. Their lack of success had drawn down on them the frequent wrath of General Pineda.

"That is a good question, *hijo*," the general murmured.

There were baited breaths as the others waited for the lightning to strike.

"A very good question," the general repeated, dabbing at his lips with a napkin. The small eyes swept the company. "You, Major Gomez, do you know where Paco Mora is?"

"No, Excellency."

"You, Aguilar? Colonel Meraz? How about you, Major Sifuentes?"

Sorrowfully they shook their heads.

"*Cristo*!" The general beat his fist on the table. The bottle of scarce Monopole overturned, the carcass of the fowl rolled off the platter. "Is there a real soldier in this room? Does anybody here understand the art of war? Must I do all the thinking and the planning here, wipe your noses and change your diapers and tuck you into bed at night?" He blotted ineffectually with his napkin at the puddle of champagne. "May the Holy Virgin deliver me from such dolts and simpletons!"

In the silence that followed there was a small clamor at the door of the general's suite.

"In my time," Pineda y Flores continued, "when I was a young officer on the staff of the general—that is to say, Porfirio Diaz himself—such inefficiency would not have been tolerated! The old general would have seen you all immediately reduced to private soldier set to cleaning latrines!"

The clamor at the door grew. Loud voices were heard.

"Nowadays," General Pineda mourned, recovering a turkey wing from the carpet, "our soldiers are frightened *pelados*, our officers, toy soldiers merely stuffed with sawdust!"

In the hall outside the suite someone shouted, the door rattled.

"Aguilar!" the general commanded. "See what the devil is going on out there! A man can hardly hear himself think with that commotion!"

Major Aguilar went to investigate. A moment later he returned, saying, "Sir, there is a man out there, a wild man, it seems, who demands to speak with you!"

"About what?"

"He says—" Aguilar broke off as Rafael Saenz escaped the grasp of a guard and burst into the room.

"I will tell you what he says!" Dr. Saenz shouted. Wild-eyed, a bloody handkerchief wrapped about his head, he stood spraddle-legged before Pineda y Flores, a hand clutching his throat as if to subdue himself to a calmer state. "Sir, I have come to tell you how to catch the rascal Paco Mora and his *tropa*!"

Major Aguilar drew his pistol to threaten the intruder, but the general raised his hand. "Paco Mora, you say?"

"Yes, your Excellency."

"And what do you know of Paco Mora? Who are you?"

Dr. Saenz licked gray lips, face drained of blood by his passion. "Sir, I am only a poor country doctor. I—ah—perhaps I had better explain."

"You had better," the general warned. "I do not take kindly to poor country doctors interrupting my staff meetings!"

Saenz was thinking rapidly. His emotion had suddenly brought him on to dangerous ground. It would not do to have told Major Caleron one story and General Pineda another. On the other hand, circumstances were now different. When he had discussed the matter with Calderon, Saenz had had ten thousand dollars in a sack under a loose floorboard in the Hotel Excelsior. Now he had nothing but a badly bruised head.

"I was at one time a Villista, that is true," he admitted. "I was even on General Villa's staff for a short time, before being detailed as liaison to the *guerrilero* band of young Paco Mora. I traveled for a while with Mora's band, but soon I came to see the revolutionary cause was in error. Then I ran away, you see, and came to this city to set up a medical practice. I wanted to forget my brief deviation."

"Yes, yes!" General Pineda urged. "Go on! What is all this about Mora?"

"I am now a good social defender!" Dr. Saenz's eyes shone with the fervor of repentance. "I believe now in President Carranza and the well-being of the state. Long live the state! *Viva Carranza*!"

General Pineda's eyes narrowed.

"If you knew the whereabouts of Mora and his gang, why did you not immediately inform my provost marshal when you reached this city?"

"I did so!" Dr. Saenz protested. "Indeed, I offered at once to lead your federal soldiers immediately to Mora's hiding place in the *sierra*." He looked indignant. "But Major Calderon demanded money from me first, money in exchange for bringing this information to your Excellency's ears!"

The general pursed his lips. He spoke briefly to a staff officer; the officer made notes in a leather-bound book.

"We will see about that," the general said. He picked up a drumstick and pointed at Saenz's head. "Your skull," he said, "seems to have suffered some maltreatment. What is the story behind that, eh?"

Dr. Saenz chose his words carefully.

"Mora's ruffians followed me to this city. When they found I had even spoken to the provost marshal, they beat me unmercifully to show what would happen if I gave them away."

"Listen to me!" the general said. "If Paco Mora had found you here, talking with my provost marshal, he would have cut your throat and not let you off with a beating. Is that not true?"

There was silence. Dr. Saenz stood his ground. He had given the general the best story he could think of at the moment. Pineda y Flores stared somberly at him, holding the drumstick like a baton. Finally he spoke.

"Doctor, I was not born yesterday! What do you expect to get out of this cock-and-bull story?"

Dr. Saenz swallowed. This was getting near the core of the matter.

"Sir," he said, "I am thinking only of my country. All I ask is the pleasure of assisting the state, putting an end to the depredations of the bandit Mora." He shrugged. "After that, if the state should see fit to reward me in some small way . . ."

Pineda found some champagne in a nearly empty bottle and poured it into a glass. Good champagne was very scarce, what with bandits looting trains.

"So that is the way the wind blows, eh?" He sipped at the champagne. "I doubt you are telling the truth, you rascal. There is more here, much more then meets the eye. But I have no choice. I find myself forced more and more to investigate every lead to Paco Mora, no matter how gamy it smells." He leaned forward. "And where is this place, where you say Mora and his men are hiding?"

Saenz breathed a small sigh of relief, hidden by a spell of coughing behind a handkerchief.

"Sir, near Cumbre Pass, in the *sierra*. It is a place known only to me, and very difficult to find."

General Pineda glowered. "Do you know what will happen, señor country doctor, if you are pulling my leg?"

Dr. Saenz drew himself up with dignity. "Sir, every word I have spoken is the truth! I swear it on the grave of my mother!"

The general took another sip of champagne, stared hard at the contours of the goblet. Finally he said, "Major Aguilar! Turn out a company of the Seventh Regiment and go to Cumbre Pass with this rascal! If Paco Mora is indeed found, capture the bastard and bring him here to me."

Major Aguilar saluted. "Yes, sir. And if Mora is not found?"

General Pineda drained the goblet to the dregs and rose, wiping his mouth with a napkin.

"If Mora is not found, hang this so-called doctor to the highest tree you can find in the whole cursed *sierra*!"

Major Victor Aguilar was a great trial to Rafael Saenz. Aguilar did not believe in moving against the enemy until he outnumbered, outgunned, and outsupplied him. Consequently, Aguilar took with him a great store of Mauser ammunition, enough rations for six months, and many other items of supply which might be needed. All these were loaded on flatcars of the MNR for transport to Cumbre Pass. The leisurely procedure made Rafael Saenz dance with impatience.

"We are wasting time, valuable time!" he protested. "Mora has no more than two dozen men with him and is running short of ammunition. Let us get rid of all this cumbersome baggage and ride quickly to Cumbre Pass on horses! *Caray*! By the time we reach the rebel camp they will have disappeared again!"

Aguilar was a small, sad-eyed man, accustomed to having everything in proper order. He had once been a government clerk.

"Patience!" he urged. "My good Doctor, patience! Half the battle is won by a well-prepared campaign. This is a military matter you do not understand."

Dr. Saenz cursed well-prepared campaigns.

"It is my neck that is at risk!" he shouted. "If we do not hurry, I can not promise anything!"

Major Aguilar shrugged. "We are prepared for everything, you see." He held up a coil of rope, raw yellow in color and smelling of newness. "Absolutely everything, Saenz."

Dr. Saenz mopped his forehead. "*Cristo*, this is not fair to me, you know, delaying thus!"

At Madera there was more delay while Aguilar prepared papers in countless copies for a Vickers-Maxim mountain gun requisitioned from the commandment there.

"Preposterous!" Saenz spluttered. "Why do we need a blunderbuss like that?We can never get it through the narrow passes in the mountains!"

Major Aguilar's logic was unassailable.

"Are we not going into the mountains to seek Mora? Well, then, this is a mountain gun, suited for operations in the mountains. Therefore—"

"Therefore," Saenz interrupted, "you are a fool, Aguilar!" In his panic he began to be abusive. "I beg you, forget mountain guns and let us get on with this business of trapping the bandit in his lair, before he goes to some other place!"

Aguilar only went placidly on superintending the loading of the mountain gun and a great deal of ammunition on a flatcar. Cursing, Dr. Saenz sat on an ammunition locker and wept. His head hurt, and he was almost out of his favorite cigarettes. Aguilar was a fool, but he—Rafael Saenz—was a bigger one. The money was stolen from him, vanished, and Paco Mora gone back to his *tropa*. Perhaps the doctor should have let well enough alone—at least, his neck had been safe. Now, with his foolish appeal to General Pineda, he had gotten that same neck into a noose.

Before the MNR train reached Cumbre Pass, a dozen or more of the soldiers deserted. Many came from that country, and when the chuffing train slowed on mountain grades, when they saw familiar country, they swung off and disappeared in the brush. They were indeed *pelados*; once free of Chihuahua City and Pineda's military police, they decamped, taking their rifles with them. Major Aguilar, however, was not concerned.

"By the time we reach Cumbre Pass," Dr. Saenz protested, "there will be only you and me, Aguilar, to face Paco Mora and his desperadoes!"

The major rolled sad eyes. "A certain attrition is normal," he assured Saenz. "You are not a military man, remember. You do not understand these things."

While they were unloading at Cumbre Pass, Major Aguilar telegraphed northward in an effort to persuade the Americans to send out an airplane to confirm whether Paco Mora and his *tropa* were still in the *sierra* above them.

"But this is insanity!" Dr. Saenz exploded. He shook an angry finger under Aguilar's nose. "They will hear that airplane and flee immediately, if they have already not done so! They are not simpletons, Aguilar! They have seen airplanes before, and they know that airplanes have wireless sets, too!"

Aguilar shook his head pityingly.

"My dear Saenz, you had best leave these matters to a soldier. There are, I beg you to believe, ninety-four thousand square miles in Chihuahua. To go up that mountain uninformed, except," he smiled, "except for your somewhat tardy information—well, that would be to search a haystack for a needle."

Saenz clenched his fists in anger.

"Tardy? Whose fault is that, I ask? We have wasted valuable time while you equipped yourself with a Roman army to capture some ragged rebels! I myself could have taken a few good men and finished the job by now!"

The airplane finally came. It dipped its wings as it flew overhead and departed. No further information, however, came from the Americans. Eventually the expedition of Major Aguilar inched its way into the *sierra*. Horses and riders fell into chasms and were lost, the cumbersome "mountain gun" had difficulty traversing the narrow passes, a whole chest of 2.95 inch ammunition for the gun fell into a gully and could be retrieved only by men carrying up individual shells and stowing them again in packhorses. Dr. Saenz himself clambered down the cliff to help with the process in spite of a headache. It was the least he could do, he felt.

The weather turned bitter; finally it began to snow.

The column passed through isolated mountain villages which were starving, the *colorados* having requisitioned the village stores of grain. Old men and children followed their horses, picking from the dung undigested grains of corn. Sad-eyed mothers lined the square, cautioning their broods to silence as the soldiers passed. One woman was smoking a tattered corn-husk cigarette and handed the butt to a child as they passed. It reminded Saenz he was down to his last pack of Egyptian cigarettes. His hands trembled. Hurry, that was what they must do! Ignoring Major Aguilar, who rode at the head of the column in a bulky greatcoat, the doctor spurred his own mount along the length of the file, urging the men to greater speed.

"Hurry!" he shouted. "Come along, boys! The sooner we get this job over with, the sooner you will all be back in Chihuahua with your sweethearts again!"

More of the *pelados* decamped. Remaining was a hard core of more or less professional soldiers. Most of them were noncommissioned officers of one rank or another. Pineda paid them well, for soldiers. For the time being their allegiance was to the federal cause. Saenz had a feeling, however, their allegiance was a shaky one.

At another mountain village, a sprawl of huts high in the *sierra*, the mayor himself came to greet them, hoping the federal government was bringing them much-needed food. The old man was disappointed, but retained his courtesy.

"At least," he said, "perhaps, señores, you can tell us what the date is?"

Major Aguilar put his head out of the thick collar of his coat and stared with wind-reddened eyes.

"The date? *Caray*, it is the last day of November! You do not mean to tell me your village is so backward as not to know the day of the month!"

In ragged dignity the mayor drew himself up.

"Sir, until recently there was a telegraph wire from

here to Cumbre Pass. That was the way the news, the government's decrees, all these things were passed to us. But the rebels cut the line and took away the copper wires. Since then we have lost our way of reckoning the date. Some people said it was one thing, others thought it was another." He spoke to a young boy beside him, shivering in a thin blanket. "Geraldo, write it down. This gentleman says today is the last day of November."

They rode away, Major Aguilar shaking his head. "Ignorant people!" he complained. "How can a country tolerate such imbeciles? They are completely untrustworthy, too. The minute our backs are turned, they give aid and assistance to the same rebels who deprived them even of the day of the month!"

As the force approached the Cerro de las Ventanas, as Rafael Saenz saw again the familiar landmarks, his spirits began to rise. With the unseasonable heavy snow, it was probable the *tropa* had decided to stay in the basalt caves, believing it unlikely that soldiers would ascend the mountain in such weather. He rubbed his hands briskly together and spoke to Major Aguilar.

"There—do you see that huge boulder, the one that looks like a giant crouching animal? We are not three miles from the hiding place of the rebels. I suggest, Major, you detach scouts to reconnoiter forward. The main body, with the mountain gun, makes so much noise it will frighten them away."

Major Aguilar smiled a confident smile. "In the face of the enemy, Saenz," he explained, "one does not divide his forces. That is exactly what happened to the *gringos*' General Custer. At the crucial moment he divided his forces. I am not about to fall into that trap."

The doctor argued in vain; Major Aguilar would not be moved.

"*Bueno*!" Saenz shouted. "If you persist in being a fool, then, we will probably find the camp deserted. Then what will General Pineda say, eh?"

Aguilar shrugged. "It is not my concern to predict what the general will say. It is only up to me, then, to find a suitable tree and hang you, as I was instructed."

Saenz shivered, not completely from the cold.

"It is unfair!" he muttered. "*Carramba*, it is completely unfair!"

"After all," Aguilar said, "most wars are unfair. The innocent suffer with the guilty. And it is not up to me to separate guilt from innocence, Doctor. It is my sole duty to carry out the orders of General Pineda."

Saenz finally guided them near the basalt caves. Snow fell heavily, masking the sound of their approach. Major Aguilar was at last moved to action. He ordered the soldiers to dismount; he motioned Saenz to accompany him to a wind-scoured ledge where they could see the clearing below.

"Where are they, Mora's people?" Augilar demanded, poking through a screen of snow-laden bushes and staring below them. His face was pinched from the cold, drooping mustaches frosted. The wind howled about the basalt crags and made it seem even colder.

Rafael Saenz, pistol drawn, stared also at the clearing. There was no sign of human habitation. The openings to the caves yawned like sightless eyes. The worst had come to pass. Paco and his *tropa* had gone.

"There is no one here," Major Aguilar complained.

In the dusting of snow there were, however, windblown tracks, human and animal. In the only trail leading up the mountain the *colorados* had not encountered Paco and his people. Where were they?

"Saenz," Major Aguilar said, "it seems to me we have come finally to the end of a fruitless search." The mournful eyes took on a sudden hard glitter. "Are you ready, then, to be hanged, which was part of the bargain?"

"Wait!" Dr. Saenz pleaded. "Wait! Let us not be hasty! There is still a chance!"

"Where are you going?" Aguilar demanded.

Saenz started to clamber down the rocks toward the clearing. "Down there." He gestured with his Luger.

"For what reason?"

Saenz was impatient. "Why, to see what has happened, where they have gone!"

Aguilar shook his head. "That is immaterial. You promised to lead me to Paco Mora's *tropa*. You have not done so." Seeing Saenz continue to scramble down the slope, he became alarmed. "Stop! In the name of the federal government I forbid you to go farther!"

Still picking his way carefully through the icy rocks, Saenz called back, "Are you afraid?"

Aguilar was stung. "I am afraid of nothing! I have three medals for bravery!"

"Then come on!" Saenz invited.

Unwillingly, Major Aguilar clambered down after him. Puffing, he at last reached Saenz's side on the level ground before the caves. He looked cautiously at the yawning black opening of a cave.

"I think," he said, "it is better to have some of my men with us at this point." He drew a brass whistle from his pocket and placed it between his lips. Saenz laughed.

"What are you laughing at?" Aguilar demanded.

"Are you afraid?" Saenz jeered. "You said yourself, Major, there was no one here. Do we need a detachment of soldiers to look at an empty cave?"

Squatting, Saenz poked a finger into the ashes of a fire. "Cold," he said, half to himself. "How long can they have been gone?" An idea suddenly occurred to him. He scratched his chin, eyes scanning the abandoned camp. Though fresh snow had fallen, it was possible to see a scattering of prints concentrated to the far side of the camp, the uphill side, where there was a saddle in the encircling crags. Up there? Had they gone that way? But it was impossible.

"Where are you going now?" Aguilar demanded impatiently.

Saenz walked slowly up the rise in the direction of the saddle, the new idea forming slowly in his mind. The tracks, though indistinct, grew more numerous. There were horse droppings, an abandoned stone grinding trough, a child's corn-husk doll, half covered in snow. Of course, they could have been gone for days, a week or more, perhaps.

Gazing upward, he estimated the saddle at almost a thousand meters above them. Any pass through there would by now be deep in drifts. Once Paco and his people reached the top of the mountain, there was still a long and difficult passage through the very peaks of the *sierra* until they reached the Sonora side and the long and meandering descent.

"Well?" Major Aguilar, slapping his arms against his greatcoat to keep warm, stumbled up.

Saenz nodded toward the high saddle. "They went that way, into the *sierra*."

"But that is impossible!"

Saenz shrugged.

"Then," Aguilar said, "they are all frozen to death and no further concern of mine."

Saenz pulled his hat down tighter on his bandaged head.

"But we must follow them."

Aguilar looked incredulous. "Follow them? Are you mad, Doctor?" He shook his head. "I was against this foolish expedition from the first! Now there is nothing left to do but struggle back down this damnable mountain. That, and—" Again he raised the brass whistle to his lips. "That, and the matter of disposing of the liar and traitor who so wasted the resources of the federal government!"

Aguilar was about to blow a blast on the whistle to summon his man when Saenz, the idea completed, shot him through the heart. With the moaning of the wind, and the fact that Saenz had pressed the muzzle tightly against the major's breast before pulling the trigger, the sound was almost inaudible. Major Aguilar stared in surprise, the sad eyes were puzzled. Then he toppled slowly, falling backward in the snow, arms and legs outspread.

Saenz lingered for a moment above the body, peering back toward the heights where they had left the soldiers of Aguilar's command. When nothing happened, he retrieved the major's whistle, still unaccountably in the major's mouth. Grinning, he pointed his Luger skyward and fired the rest of the clip into the air, at the same time shrilling blast after blast on the whistle. He started to run, awkwardly, in the snow and rubble. He was halfway up the slope, panting for breath, when Aguilar's sergeant stepped from behind a boulder. Behind him were the rest of the soldiers, rifles at the ready.

"They have gone!" Dr. Saenz wheezed, clutching his throat. "Mora and his people have gone! But they left behind snipers! *Que caray*! I was speaking to Major Aguilar, and suddenly a bullet took him through the heart!" He wheezed again, for good measure. "Poor fellow, he never knew what struck him!"

Covertly he watched their reaction and was pleased to see he had judged them correctly. Most of the *pelados* had deserted. The handful left were hard-bitten professional soldiers, men who had probably fought on both sides of an issue at one time or another, going wherever the pay and chances for booty were highest.

The sergeant scratched a stubbled chin. "That is too bad," he said. "Major Aguilar, I mean." Ordering the men to fan out behind him and search the boulders that ringed the abandoned camp, he drew his pistol and prowled down the slope, looking about with battlewise eyes. Dr. Saenz followed.

"There he is," Saenz said, pointing.

Together they stood over the late Major Victor Aguilar. The sergeant nudged the body with his toe.

"Dead," he agreed. "Yes, he is certainly dead." He

looked at the soldiers, scattered wide, now descending the slope. "Where did the shot come from?"

Saenz shook his head. "I don't know." Quickly he squatted over the body and unbuttoned Aguilar's coat, carefully folding back the lapels to cover the scorched hole. *Caray*, he had been careless! Perhaps the sergeant had seen the powder burns in the cloth, but Saenz did not think so. To cover his discomfiture, he made a great pretense of medical examination. "Directly through the upper chambers of the heart," he said professionally. "Yes, death was instantaneous."

The sergeant sighed and fingered his mustachios.

"*Bueno*," he said finally. "Well, we must somehow bury him, that is clear." He told off a detail of diggers, then turned to Rafael Saenz. "As to what action to take now, I am not too clear. Doctor, have you any suggestions?"

The rest of the soldiers crowded round, listening. They paused in their tasks.

"Well," Dr. Saenz said, "I suppose I must now reveal to you a certain secret I was previously sworn to keep. But your commander is dead, and circumstances have changed."

The sergeant, whose name was Montes, lifted an eyebrow.

"General Pineda," Saenz said, "was of course very put out at the depredations of Paco Mora and his *tropa*. But more to the point is the fact that a great deal of gold was concerned."

He had their attention. At the mention of gold, they listened raptly. Saenz felt encouraged. These were the kind of men he understood.

"You must know," he went on, "that Paco Mora and his ruffians robbed the Plains Bank in Roosevelt, New Mexico, across the border, last September. Since then he has been carrying about Chihuahua an enormous amount of stolen money, intending to give it to Pancho Villa. But the so-called Invincible General was nowhere to be found, after his many defeats. Even Paco Mora could not find him. So, my friends, the money is still with Mora."

He gestured toward the snow-choked mountain passes.

"The *tropa* left here—how recently I do not yet know—to flee over the mountain. They have women and children with them, a lot of animals, household effects, things like that. They will be traveling slowly and are greatly encumbered."

He paused, letting the implication sink in. One man wiped a running nose with a sleeve. Another spat into the snow. Sergeant Montes lit a cigarette with chapped hands cupped carefully about the match.

"I am not exactly a military man," Dr. Saenz said modestly. "Oh, at one time I was an officer on Villa's staff, that is true, but I am primarily a doctor, a simple country doctor. But I know enough of this military life to know that the lot of the common soldier, such as yourselves, is a hard one. A man risks his life, perhaps he is spared only to grow old and unwanted in the service of the state, starve after a devoted career. Who needs a soldier, eh, after he has done his duty and the enemy is dispersed? Now I want to say to you good men that with Paco Mora is enough gold so we can share in it ourselves, become men of property. What do you say, eh?"

Sergeant Montes, cigarette dangling from his lips, looked at his fingernails. "I say some would call it mutiny, señor."

Saenz felt a chill. Had he miscalculated?

Suddenly one of them, a *mestizo* with a cast in one eye, started to laugh. One of the grave diggers, grinning, took the late Major Victor Aguilar by one booted foot and dragged him unceremoniously into the hacked-out hole. The rest looked at each other, started to guffaw. Sergeant Montes laughed, too.

"What are we waiting for?" he asked. "After all

these years, here is a campaign with something in it for the common soldier."

Dr. Saenz clapped him on the back.

"You are a good man, Montes!" he said. "Now let us go!"

He had, of course, no intention of ever sharing the treasure with the brutish *colorados*.

Chapter Ten

Perhaps there was a trail—David Pine was never sure—but Café always figured out a way to get through. They picked their way through boulder-littered canyons, deep with snow, only to find themselves blocked, the canyon narrowing until it appeared they were in a fatal dead end; fatal, because with the snow and the wind and the freezing temperature, they did not have enough strength to turn and retrace their steps. Café, sided by the keen-eyed Nacho, took them into narrow defiles where it appeared impossible for a horse and rider to pass. Just as their spirits sagged the lowest, just as it appeared they were irrevocably trapped, the two would discover a narrow outlet, sometimes with rocky ledges towering above to form a kind of roof. At times the whole party was forced to dismount, leading the horses. They way became at times so constricted it was necessary to unload pack animals and drag sacks and bales and bundles by hand through a rocky corridor. Continually the snow fell; not a heavy snow now, but a wet and clinging downfall that dampened their clothing as well as their spirits. And always the way was upward, ever upward.

At night they crouched in whatever shelter they could find, huddled for warmth over a small blaze of juniper twigs. Many of the *tropa*, especially the women and the few small children they brought with them, developed colds. Some had chests that rattled when they coughed, and a baby was having trouble breathing. Old Elena coated the baby's chest with a poultice of mountain herbs, ground into a powder between two flat rocks and stirred to a paste with a little *sotol,* but the child did not improve. Maruja beside him, David sat on a rocky ledge, wrapped in a threadbare blanket, and considered their chances.

"How much farther?" he muttered, half to himself.

Maruja turned a pale face to him. "Café says it is not far. Soon we will be over the highest ridge. From there he says it is all downhill to the river, to Bavispe and Colónia Morelos and Bacerac."

He shook his head, discouraged. "Some will die before then."

She pulled the blanket tighter about her. "A revolution is bought by deaths. All of us understand that."

He looked at the camp, the few tiny fires winking in the twilight under the rocky ledge where they had stopped for the night. In the mountain hideaway there had been laughing and joking, tricks played, plenty to eat, huge warm fires in the basalt caves. The women sewed, chatted, combed their hair; men lay at their ease, smoking and drinking; children played, or slumbered in nests of warm robes and blankets. Now the snowy camp was silent, except for the small whimpering of a child. No one spoke. A few clustered silently around a cooking pot, waiting for a scanty meal of beans and tortillas. Others tried to sleep, men, women, and children all pressed together for warmth. But there was little sleep. They were too fatigued with the constant struggle against snow, altitude, and the rocky way.

Café plowed through the drifts to them, beating his arms against his sides for warmth. "Ah, what I would give for a cup of hot coffee, *jefe*! Just one cup!" He shook his head; wet snow fell from the brim of his tall-crowned hat.

"How are the animals?" David asked.

Café shrugged. "They are very tough, these animals of the mountains. Look!" He pointed to where a wiry, spring-legged mare wrenched with her teeth at a snow-laden bush. "They will eat anything if they have to." He sighed; taking off the hat, he beat it against his thigh to dislodge the clinging snow.

"*Que pasa, hombre*?" David asked. "What is troubling you?"

Café shrugged, "Ah, it is nothing! A foolish thought."

David put a hand on his burly shoulder. "Tell me."

Café took a deep breath. "*Jefe*, for days we have struggled through rough country, some very rough country. All in all, we have done well, considering. Some would have thought it impossible, what we have done, with women and children, too."

"It is due to you," David said. "To you and to Nacho. You found the way."

"True," Café admitted. "We found the path. But it is you, *jefe*, who ride back and forth, encouraging the people, lightening their loads by taking more on yourself. It is you who joke with them, sing songs with Luisito, keep up our spirits. And it is you whom they know will take them to safety, trail or no trail. Somehow they know you will do it. *El Pino* will do it. That is the truth, their truth. So they keep on." He put on the steeple-crowned hat again, carefully tucking his long black hair up into it. "But those soldiers, *jefe*, the ones who were coming up the mountain. Whenever we come to a high place, I find myself looking back into the *sierra*. I do not want to think so, but I have thoughts of seeing soldiers, back there, coming after us. If we have advanced this far, through this bad country, is it not possible the *colorados* can do the same?"

Maruja shook her head.

"That is foolish, *hombre*, to think so! Those soldiers are *pelados*, the poor exploited ones. They have no spirit, no valor. Their officers would have to drive them with whips into the *sierra* in weather like this! Most of them would desert."

Café turned to David Pine.

"What do you think, *jefe*?"

David got up and teetered for a moment on legs cramped and wooden from the cold and his rocky perch.

"I think," he said, "that we have enough worries without creating new ones. And I think that it is time I made the rounds of the camp to see that everything is all right."

The next day the sick baby died. The snow had stopped falling, they were all grateful for that, and stood bare-headed in the thin sunlight while David Pine put into Spanish what he remembered of the 23rd Psalm from his Baptist days in Roosevelt. They put the tiny shawl-wrapped form into a shallow crevice and piled stones on top to protect it from animals. The mother did not cry, only staring with stone-dead eyes at the barren landscape.

"*Lo siento mucho, senora,*" David said, pressing her hand. "I am very sorry."

"The child, too," Pedro Mirón said, hat in hand, "was a soldier of the revolution."

The trail steepened, as if in a last desperate effort to bar their way. One of the coughing women died and was buried. A horse and rider, along with three pack animals, fell from a rocky ledge and were lost in a canyon that yawned far below them. Much of their precious food was on the lost pack animals. They were reduced to a handful of *pinole* each day, dried and ground corn sweetened with a little mesquite-bean flour, which David Pine carefully measured out. But still the *tropa* stumbled on, pitting the residue of their strength against the mountain.

David rode continually along the column, trying to cheer them. Some of the mountain ponies gave up the struggle and lay down in the snow to die. Finally David, with many others, was reduced to walking, leading his own mount with a burden of an older man who had what David thought was pneumonia, a dying man out of reach of Elena's most powerful potions. The old woman herself was afoot too, but striding through the snow with a powerful gait, supporting herself with a staff.

"I am too old to die!" Elena said. "The devil does not want me!"

It had been over a week since they left the security of the *sierra* camp. Slowly and more slowly the column climbed, fighting for each inch as they approached the summit. David could see the life, the spirit, of the *tropa* leaking away, like grain spilling slowly from a rent sack. People no longer talked to each other; they saved their meager breath. Frostbite was everywhere, and a more serious freezing of extremities. There were few good horses now, and most of the *tropa* walked, stumbling, falling, picking themselves up one more time, and then again one time.

"*Adelante*!" David cried. "Forward! Look there—do you see? We are almost at the top!" He grabbed Luisito's arm and shook it. "*Hombre*, sing! Sing a song for us!" When a man stumbled and fell in the wet snow, without strength to rise again, David rushed forward, a lanky rag-wrapped figure, and hauled him to his feet again. "Only a little while longer!" His voice sounded thin and unreal in his own ears. "There! Up there!" He pointed at the watery sun. "On the other side of the ridge, we go down. Down! I swear it to you!"

The man only stared at him with dazed, lackluster

eyes.

"Come!" David pleaded. He got one arm under the man's shoulder and staggered forward, almost dragging him. "Up! *Adelante*! Forward!"

Atop the snow-choked saddle finally, the *tropa* stopped, winded, exhausted. Café stumbled and clawed his way up a jumbled pile of boulders and scanned the horizon.

"What do you see?" David called.

Café whooped. He pointed.

"What is it?" David called.

Café was too overcome to speak. He only jabbered, stabbing his finger toward the west and making incoherent sounds.

With what he was sure was the last of his own strength, David clambered up the rocky incline and stood on a flat ledge beside Café. A cold wind whipped the blanket about his legs, and wind-driven particles of dry snow flailed his cheeks.

"There!" Café finally said, his voice choked with emotion. "*Jefe*, look!"

David looked. "What is it? I don't see anything."

Café grabbed him, turned his head, forced him to stare along the lean arm, the pointing finger. "Down there! Do you see it? That little patch of green far below? *Jefe*, that is the Rio Bavispe!"

David stared, squinting his eyes into the chill wind. Was there—was there—green?

"It is warm down there!" Café babbled. He seized David's hand and danced a wild jig. "It is green and warm. There are houses and food!

"*Jefe*, there will be coffee! Hot black rich coffee! Think of it!"

David shook off Café's arm, shading wind-reddened eyes with his hand. Yes, surely there was green. A faint whisper of color, a thread of emerald seen through a rocky slit. Green! What a beautiful color, after this eternity of gray rock, white snow, black despair!

"Come up!" he howled. Looking below, he beckoned the remnant of the *tropa*. "Come up! There is a beautiful sight here! *Amigos*, we are over the top! The Rio Bavispe is below. Plowed fields, houses, food! Come up!" He grabbed Café's arm and they danced together, howling with laughter.

The rest of the *tropa* struggled up the hill, strong helping the weak, well helping the sick, young helping the old. Maruja, wrapped in a ragged poncho and with the soles of her boots flapping, came to stand beside David Pine. Her eyes filled with tears.

"Ah!" she murmured. "Ah, it is indeed beautiful, that green!"

He thought she was weeping with relief, but she went on to say, "If Paco were only with us now! If Paco were only here to see that green valley, the valley of the Rio Bavispe!"

He gave her a quick comforting hug. "Do not worry about Paco, *hermana*. He may join us soon!"

She turned away, shaking her head. "Paco is dead," she said in a low voice. "I had a dream. *Verdad*, the soldiers killed him. It is true. Never will I see him again." And in spite of his protests, she would not have it any other way.

After the struggle to the summit, the rocky trail that stitched down to the Rio Bavispe seemed almost a lark. Men, women, children, animals clattered cheerfully lower, and David had to slow the breakneck pace.

"*Mas despacio*!" he called. "Slowly, my friends! Do not hurry so! We do not want any broken legs!"

Though the Rio Bavispe seemed near from the lofty perspective of the summit, it soon became apparent there was yet a long way to go, obstacles to be surmounted. The joyful pace slowed, humans and animals were forced once again to pick their way through boulder-littered canyons and across treacherous patches of rotten snow where there was constant danger of breaking through. Muscles ached from the new downhill altitude. The sun breaking through leaden clouds brought a swarm of small stinging gnats. Another child died from congestion of the lungs. An old man complained briefly of chest pain and died only a few minutes later. Still, ragged and footsore, the *tropa* inched down from the *sierra*, breathing gratefully the air now substantial and reassuring in the chest, observing thankfully the junipers and an occasional hardy oak that clothed the previously bare and stony flanks of the mountain. After what they had been through, this was now a good time, a time to laugh, to tell jokes, to speculate on the taste of fresh-cooked tortillas, beans in a thick sauce of their own marrow, maybe even a little goat meat—*cabrito*—roasted over coals.

"And coffee!" Café insisted. "Hot and black and meaty enough for the spoon to stand upright!"

Many little towns were scattered along the gorge of the Rio Bavispe. Riding down the rocky trail, the *tropa* first reached Santa Teresa de las Cuevas, a tiny settlement on the banks of the river. Fields of green and hardy crops grew in the winter sunlight, the air was warm and sweet, fat cattle grazed. It was nearing dusk, the sun a red ball sinking into the cleft of the canyon, when the ragged band rode into Santa Teresa.

Their coming had been noticed. No one was in the streets, not even children, nor dogs. As they rode into the plaza, a shot rang out, ricocheting off the cobblestones before them. As if by magic, armed men rose from behind walls, behind doors and shutters, on the tiled roof of the town hall itself.

"*Alto*!" someone called. "Stop where you are! We have you surrounded!" The voice was that of a small fat man in a green sash, a fierce-looking man with tremendous mustaches and an ancient fowling piece. From the doorway of the building he aimed the gun unwaveringly at David Pine's chest, demanding, "Who are you? What do you want here?"

David raised empty hands. "We are only poor

travelers, señor, who have had great misfortunes."

The little man walked carefully from the doorway, holding his aim. "Are you bandits?"

"No, señor. We take nothing from the people."

"I am the mayor here," the little man said. "We must be very careful, you understand." In the dusky golden light he squinted his eyes, staring hard at David Pine, at the band of shabby men, tired women, children fallen to sleep in older arms. "Are you—are you—"

He stepped back and spoke under his breath to one of the men who stood behind him, guns at the ready. They conferred, speaking behind cupped hands while the sun slid lower and lower. Finally the mayor cleared his throat and took off his hat.

"Señor—are you—perhaps you are—*El Pino*?"

David nodded. "I am."

The mayor's breath whistled sharply between his teeth.

"And this is your *tropa*?"

"It was the *tropa* of Paco Mora. Now Paco is dead, we think, and I command."

The villagers emerged from shelter and stared up at the rocky heights the *tropa* had lately descended. In the failing light, the *sierra* was grim and forbidding, capped with snow.

"And you came over there, over the mountains, with your people?"

"The *colorados* were after us, and there was no other way out. Yes, that is the way we came."

Suddenly the people were all about David and the *tropa*, babbling with excitement, trying to shake his hand. The villagers helped women down from spent mounts, brought fresh tortillas, pots of richly-spiced beans, meat that had been roasting on a grill.

"Señor," the mayor cried, "we are honored! Santa Teresa de las Cuevas is honored! Eat, drink, rest in our homes, sleep! Everything is for you, for the great *El Pino* and his famous *tropa*!"

David was still wary, keeping one hand on the stock of his Mauser rifle in the saddle scabbard.

"Are there *colorados* here, in this valley?"

The mayor shook his had. "Señor, they are all in Chihuahua, searching for Pancho Villa! Here we are in Sonora. The soldiers do not come here, along the Rio Bavispe. Even the tax collectors—" He grinned, patting the stock of the ancient gun. "Even the government tax collectors do not bother us here, in this great fold in the mountains!"

Suddenly David Pine's legs were weak, his knees like hollow vessels filled with warm and enervating fluid. He had been leaning against the bony mountain pony, and when he tried to stand erect he almost fell. All those days in the *sierra* something had kept him upright and functioning, but now he was near collapse.

"*Con permiso, señor*?" the mayor said, offering his arm for support.

But David waved him away, thanking him. First he must look to the *tropa*, see that they were all well, were all fed, were made comfortable. And when he finally decided everything was all right, saw even Café was sitting in a cane-bottomed chair on the veranda of the mayor's house, sipping a cup of his beloved coffee, he collapsed on a cornhusk mattress. He slept that night through, and a great part of the next morning.

It was December, but the weather was mild when they left Santa Teresa, riding down the precipitous canyon toward Bacerac, toward Colónia Morelos and El Pozo. At the end of the canyon, spreading out into a broad valley, was Agua Prieta. Directly across the border was the city of Douglas, in Arizona. David tried not to think of it, not at the moment, because that was where, soon, he would turn himself in to the Military Police. And that would be the end of it. That would be the end of *El Pino*, the beginning again of Lieutenant David Pine, a prisoner in the dock, a prisoner of his own conscience, charged with enough crimes to hang a dozen men.

So he rode with the *tropa* in these last days and sang and joked. Together they enjoyed the winter sunshine, the tent of blue that spread over them, the rich grass for their mounts, the food and drink, the beans and beef and *pulque* the people of the canyon pressed on them. Luisito sang a new stanza every day. The farmers listened with awe and respect and pressed to touch the hand of *El Pino,* the remaining symbol of the revolution. After all, no one had seen or heard from General Villa for a long time. The Invincible General, the Centaur of the North, had disappeared.

One by one, two by two, the members of the *tropa* asked permission to leave, and David granted their requests. Many of them knew this country, had relatives in Huasabas or Cumpas or Arizpe. David knew how they felt. At one time some had talked of preserving the *tropa*, of fighting on in Sonora. But few hearts were really in the proposal. The revolution had not succeeded, and now the call of the land was too strong for them. Spring would come soon. Spring was a time of preparing the earth, a time for planting and sowing, a time for growth and renewal. Fighting was for another season. Too, there were other reasons for dispersal. As the mountains gradually broadened into the plain of the Bavispe, the *tropa* became more conspicuous, more vulnerable, exposed to federal troops that might be deployed along the border.

"*Adios*," David said finally to Pedro Mirón. "You are *puro corazon, amigo*—a great heart." "*Hasta luego*," he told Luisito. "You have much music in you, *hombre*. Some day people will pay money to come and see you on the stage." He only wrung Eufemio's hand, and Eufemio his, but they understood each other. Enrique and his wife left, first asking his blessing. Old Elena insisted on leaving her silver ring on David's finger, and Quillermo bid him a gruff farewell and went quickly away so *El Pino* should not see tears in his eyes.

They came at last to El Rusbayo, only a few miles

from the border. There were left by now only Café, Nacho, David, and Maruja Cruz. Café had an uncle beyond El Rusbayo whom he wanted to visit. Nacho was reticent about his plans, seeming only to want to be near to David Pine, like a silent dog watching over his master. "There is time to decide," the Yaqui muttered. "There is no hurry! I will go away soon, but there is no need to hurry." Maruja was only silent and uncommunicative; David did not press her, feeling she was deep in some personal problem. All of them had had to make hard decisions. He had made his, the *tropa* had made their's, now Maruja was making her own.

In El Rusbayo they stopped at a small hotel run by a Swiss. David Pine took from his wallet the tattered remains of a few U.S. dollars to pay for rooms for himself and for Maruja. Nacho insisted on sleeping in a chair in the hallway, and Café spent the night drinking coffee and chatting with M. Renaud, the proprietor. In the morning Café would go on with them to the house of his uncle, a few miles north of the village.

Putting back his wallet, David paused for a moment to look at the worn and creased identification card: Lieutenant David Pine, QMC, U.S.A. In a way, it was his only link with the past, back there across the border. He had a sudden impulse to tear it up, to destroy it. He was in Mexico, he was practically a Mexican anyway in speech and dress, there might even be a good job here for an accountant, a man familiar with payrolls and gross sales and inventories. But he folded the card, tucked it back into the wallet.

That night, sitting in a rocker in his room, he picked up a dog-eared copy of the El Paso *Times*, several weeks old. There was obviously some kind of celebration going on El Rusbayo; when they rode in, it had been decorated in greenery and colored lights, and even now he heard a choir of childish voices singing in the plaza. Leafing through the paper, ringed with coffee stains, he sat suddenly erect. No, it could not be! He leaned closer to the kerosene lamp, peering at the smudged newsprint. The Americans were withdrawing from Chihuahua! Already Pershing was gone from Parral, and the bulk of U.S. forces in the state were withdrawing across the border!

He shook his head in disbelief. Reading further, he began to understand that a precarious accommodation had been established between the U.S. and the Carranza government. Pancho Villa had apparently been beaten, and the U.S. was becoming too concerned about an approaching European war to be diverted any longer by Chihuahua bandits. The border, for better or worse, was now felt to be secure; Carranza could mop up any remaining pockets of revolution.

Poor Paco! Paco had died in vain; his sack of gold would never be delivered to the Invincible General. Poor Maruja; the cause for which she gave so much was lost! And Pedro Mirón and Eufemio and Enrique and Luisito and the rest—what good had it done, their bravery and sacrifice?

Gloomy, he folded the paper under his arm and walked down the hall to Maruja's room. He did not want to tell her the sad news. The singing in the plaza below was louder now, and the melody tugged faintly at his memory. What was that song?

At her door he knocked softly. They were near the border; he did not want to compromise her, a man entering her room at night.

"Maruja?"

She did not answer. He thought he heard muffled weeping.

"Maruja! Are you there? It's me, David. May I come in?"

She unbolted the door, holding a candle. She was dressed only in her shift, and her eyes were indeed red.

Awkwardly he stood near, holding out the *Times*. "There's a story, a long story, in here, all about Chihuahua and Pershing and General Villa. The

Americans have given up. They're withdrawing across the border. The article says General Villa has been defeated for good, and now Carranza can pacify Chihuahua."

She shook her head at the offer of the newspaper and went to sit on the bed, legs folded under her on the ragged coverlet, her head bowed.

"I suppose it had to end that way. Somehow, I knew it. Really, there was no chance for Paco and me, for Luisito and Pedro and Elena and all the rest. Well, perhaps that is all there is now. Some will go on fighting, I know, but there is not much hope." She sighed and turned soft eyes on him. "David, do you know what night this is?"

He shook his head. "What night? What do you mean?"

She managed a small smile.

"It is *la Noche Buena*—Christmas Eve—in this year of 1916."

Now he understood the greenery, the songs, the air of anticipation in El Rusbayo.

"Christmas," he marveled. "Christmas!" He had almost forgotten there were things like Christmas.

In the flicker of candlelight her eyes were moist and luminous. "Merry Christmas, David Pine! *Feliz Navidad*!" In sudden lithe movement she rose from the bed. In the candle shine her eyes shone moistly. She stood for a long moment, one arm upraised toward him, in a gesture that made him think of some classical naiad in a long-forgotten book.

His mind a welter of confusion, he fumbled with the newspaper, not daring to look at her, but unwilling to turn his eyes away.

"Maruja—" His voice was thick and strained. He dropped the *Times*, or perhaps threw it away; he did not know which. His body tingled, his reaching hands trembled. "Ah, Maruja!"

She came close, still looking at him with that strange

look as she swayed gracefully near. Her long fingers brushed at his cheek; he flinched as if from an electrical shock.

"I have no money," she murmured in his ear, breath soft and clear as a baby's. "I can not buy you a gift, David, for all you have done for us. All I have is my love."

He took a trembling breath and folded his long arms around her. "Maruja," he whispered. "*Ay*, Maruja!"

Locked together, they knelt on the creaking bed.

"But it is not all for the revolution," she whispered. "I am grateful, we are all grateful, David. But I would have given myself to you anyway. Always I loved you, I think, but did not know it. Even back under the chinaberry tree, so far away and long ago."

The singing was louder now, seeming almost under their window. He pulled her warm body down beside him. "And I you," he said. "And I you, Maruja. I knew it then, and I know it now. I have always known it."

They lay for a long time in the sagging bed, bodies close, hands linked. The village bells tolled midnight; the singing in the plaza softened, whispered out, departed. El Rusbayo was silent in the moonlight. The winter night was cold, the window was open, but they were warm in their passion.

"What will you do now?" David finally asked. "Where will you go?"

For a long time she was silent. Then she said drowsily, "I do not want to think about it now. Let us not think about anything. Let us just lie here, close to each other. That is enough for now. Tomorrow . . ." She fell silent.

For a while he slept, or thought he slept. Maruja lay contentedly next to him, a rounded arm thrown over his chest. Shafts of moonlight lay on her dark hair, and her breathing was deep and easy. How fate had played tricks on them all! He wanted desperately to take her with him, back across the border. But it was not fair to drag her into the consequences that lay ahead of him. He would have to face them alone.

Suddenly he stiffened, hearing muffled footsteps in the hall. He sat up, and Maruja asked, "David, what is it? *Que pasa*?"

The steps paused; there was a faint scratching. Not at Maruja's door; it seemed to come from farther down the hall, perhaps at his own. Quickly he sprang from the bed, reaching for his revolver. *Colorados*? Police?

With careful fingers he slid back the bolt and opened the door. The hallway was dark and silent, only moonlight filtering through the barred windows. He called softly. "*Quien es*? Who's there?"

In the shadows someone moved. "We are here," Café said. "Nacho and I!"

David drew a breath of relief. "But there is someone with you!"

They came toward him, shuffling slowly and carefully, supporting a man between them.

"Señor," Café said. "Here is Paco Mora."

Chapter Eleven

Quickly and carefully they laid Paco Mora on the bed in David Pine's room, crowding around him in the dim yellow light of the kerosene lamp. It was after midnight. The town was quiet, seemed to be listening. They spoke in whispers.

"*Jefe*," Café muttered, "this is a miracle! We had given you up for dead! Where did you come from?"

Rifle cradled in his arm, Nacho stood respectfully at the foot of the bed. Even his stolid Yaqui face showed emotion. Maruja knelt beside Paco to touch his stubbled cheek with her fingers.

"*Ay, Paco, querido*. You are hurt!"

David tried to open Paco's blood-soaked shirt, but it was difficult, with Paco clutching so tightly the stained canvas moneybag.

"So you got the money back," David said. Carefully he peeled blood-stiffened cloth away from the wound. When he saw it he swallowed hard. A small black hole just below the ribs oozed blood, thick dark blood with an unpleasant smell.

"It is a bad wound," Café said. "I have seen bad wounds before. This one needs attention right away."

Paco's forehead was beaded with sweat. He winced as David's fingers touched the inflamed flesh around the wound. "Not so bad!" he protested. "Those federal soldiers are poor shots! It was only an accident that I was hit as I ran from Saenz's room!"

"But *jefe*," Nacho asked, "how did you get here, all this way from Chihuahua City?"

Paco smiled, almost gaily.

"You know that the revolution has friends everywhere! I managed to get as far as Tomóchic, where Roberto Mondragon hid me and got a surgeon to treat my wound. There it was heard that Saenz and a force of federal soldiers had been sent to the *sierra* after you, and heard also from farmers at San Miguel de Babícora that the *tropa* had escaped over the mountain. So the lawyer Mondragon put me in a wagon with trusted friends. They brought me along the river, around the mountains, all the way to El Rusbayo. Ah, we had some close calls, I can tell you that!"

"Where are they now, these friends?" David asked.

Paco waved his hand. "Once I was sure you were here, David, I dismissed them, ordered them to return under cover of darkness. They had taken enough risks for me, and, besides, El Rusbayo is very close to the border." Suddenly frowning, he looked round. "Where is my *tropa*, eh? Eufemio, Luisito, Enrique, the rest?"

David spoke gently.

"Paco, they have gone. The revolution is over. No one can even find General Villa; the *colorados* have won. The men said it would soon be time to prepare their fields, to plant crops. When they asked, I said it would be all right for them to leave. So they went away." He gestured to Café, Nacho, Maruja. "We are all that is left. And I myself am going soon across the border where I will turn myself over to the authorities. It is all finished."

Paco stared at him. In spite of Maruja's restraining arm he raised himself on an elbow. "But the revolution is not over! The truth is that the Invincible General is even now planning an attack on the Hacienda Palomas! He has fully recovered from his leg wound and is once more gathering his men!"

They all knew that place. It was a great land and cattle company, owned by the Americans, not far south of El Paso.

"He has changed his strategy!" Paco protested. "I learned all this in Tomóchic! The Americans are leaving, you see. But if we are left then to Carranza and Pineda and the *colorados*, that is indeed the end of the revolution. Our only hope is to keep Pershing and his *gringos* engaged. There is then a chance they will finally become disgusted with Carranza and force him to leave the presidency. Then someone more sympathetic to the revolution may succeed. That is our only chance! And that is why General Villa is planning an attack on this American-owned company at Palomas!"

David shook his head. "We have heard so many tales."

"But this is true! Believe me, I know!" Exhausted by the effort, Paco fell back on the bed, face chalk-pale in the rays of the guttering lamp. Café brought him a cup of water, and Paco swallowed a few drops.

"You see," he said, "all that is necessary now is for me to reach Palomas with the money. And that will be the end of it." He closed his eyes and swallowed. "This wound," he said, "this wound is really nothing. It was all right until that rough ride in the wagon. Shortly after we approached El Rusbayo, it broke open again and started to bleed. If it had not been for that—" He patted the soiled canvas bag. "But this is the real concern, is it not? Here we have the money at last, the money to deliver to General Villa, who needs it badly for bullets, bullets for the new campaign that will start in the spring."

David shook his head. "That wound is very serious. You couldn't stand another mile of travel."

Paco snorted; there was almost a mischievous amusement in his eyes. "Of course, *hombre*! Bullets do not come out unless someone takes them out! But many men walk about with a little lead in them. Café here still has a government bullet in his shoulder. It pains him only when the weather is damp. Is that not so, *amigo*?" He did not wait for an answer. "In any case, that is immaterial. We go at once to Hacienda Palomas and meet General Villa there."

In spite of restraining hands, he swung his legs over the edge of the bed and sat up. "I have returned," he said. "And though it appears there is little left of Paco Mora's famous *tropa*, Mora still commands."

His own weakness accomplished what their entreaties could not. He swayed for a moment; the blood left his face. Passing a shaky hand over his brow, he fell back on the bed. "I am weak," he admitted. "Let me rest a moment. It will pass. Then I will be ready."

David Pine spoke quietly to Café. "*Amigo*, find a doctor if you can and bring him here at once. Be very quiet. Do not disturb the town. That bullet must be gotten out, and quickly."

Café scratched his head. "*Si, señor*. But what do we do about this business of the Hacienda Palomas?"

David shrugged. "I do not know. That is to be decided later. Now go!"

The doctor was a small waspish man with an overcoat hastily thrown over a nightshirt. Turning up the lamp, he lifted Paco's shirt and made a clucking sound.

"This is very bad," he said. "A gunshot wound, eh?"

Paco, eyes closed, moved his lips. "An accident," he said. "A lucky accident."

"Not for you, *hijo*," the doctor said. "Not lucky for you." He turned to David Pine. "I can do nothing here. This is a serious wound. He must be taken to the government hospital in Agua Prieta, where they have facilities for handling such cases."

Agua Prieta was directly across the border from Douglas, in Arizona. The town was probably swarming with federal soldiers.

"We can not go there," David said. He pointed to the doctor's scuffed leather bag. "Do you not have surgical instruments with you?"

"Of course! In this violent country one must go prepared. But he should have a sterile operating theater, nurses—" The doctor picked up his bag. "*Bueno*, in any case, whether you move him to Agua Prieta or not, I must report the incident to the government authorities."

"No," David said.

Adjusting his spectacles, the doctor peered at him. "*Como*? What is that?"

"You will report this case to no one," David said. He took out his pistol. "Doctor, this man is a revolutionary. You must have suspected that. And we are his friends. Get out your instruments. The bullet must be extracted from the wound, or our friend will surely die."

"I protest!" The doctor scowled. "I am a licensed physician. I have given my best medical opinion. You should not force me to operate!"

David cocked his pistol. "We are wasting time," he said.

Paco opened his eyes and looked at David Pine. "You know," he said, "the doctor is right. I object also." There was a hint of fun in his drawn face, but something very serious also. "I object, unless, that is, you—David Pine—promise me something."

"Promise what, *hombre*?"

"Promise that when this good doctor has cut me open and taken out the damned bullet—that damned lucky bullet—that you will then take me without further argument to Hacienda Palomas." He swallowed hard and winced in pain. "I know I can not get there by myself any more, so I depend on you, David Pine, my old childhood friend, to help me in this matter. It—it is all I will ever ask of you again, believe me!"

"We will see," David said. "After—after the

operation, we will see."

Paco shook his head and tried to arise. Maruja put her arms around him and gently persuaded him to lie back again.

"No!" he insisted. "No! That is not good enough, David. Promise! Promise me!"

"But—"

"Promise!"

David went away to stand at the window. He took a deep breath, smelled from somewhere a fragrant, night-blooming vine. He was trembling; for a moment he put his face in his hands. The irony of the situation simply overwhelmed him.

"Well?" Paco insisted.

He turned back from the window and put a gentle hand on Paco's shoulder.

"I will promise," he said. "And I will do all I can do." He looked toward the doctor, who was reluctantly preparing a cloth cone for the anesthetic, dribbling ether on it from a can.

"Now lie quietly," he said. "Everything is going to be all right, Paquito."

At dawn, twenty miles east of El Rusbayo, they came from the hills into the broad flat plain of the Casas Grandes river. They untied the indignant doctor and set him on a mule, one of several Café had quietly bought at El Rusbayo during the night, along with a two-wheeled *carreta* to carry the bandaged and groggy Paco Mora. Some gold from the canvas bag had done wonders.

"There is a village to the north," Café said, pointing to a far off greenish smudge in the dun desert. "Señor Doctor, you can get food and water there. It is a long ride back to El Rusbayo. When you return, you may then speak about us and our wounded friend to anyone you please. By that time, it will be unimportant to us."

The doctor's mustachios quivered in indignation. Even the hundred dollars in gold David had given him did not mollify him.

"You are bandits, all of you!" he cried. "Dangerous and violent men! The country would be better off without you! Soon I hope to see you all hanging from a gallows!"

"*Adiós,*" David said, "*y muchas gracias.*"

From El Rusbayo to Hacienda Palomas it was almost going back into Chihuahua again, with consequent increased danger of being discovered by Pineda's soldiers, especially in the broad plains, studded only with *saguaro, pitahaya*, and the flat, plate-leafed *cardon*. In the distance a wavering green line marked the course of the Rio Casas Grandes itself. But in the parched plain where they now traveled there was little water. The tributaries of the river disappeared in crackling white rims of alkali. Vulnerable and unprotected on the featureless plain, they were forced to travel by night.

Paco did not do well. His face took on a waxy pallor, his lips a bluish tinge, and fresh blood soaked the dressings the doctor had applied after the midnight surgery. But he called out to them frequently, apparently alert, wanting to know how far it was yet to Hacienda Palomas, urging them to greater speed.

"For," he said to David Pine, "there may not be much more time for me, *amigo*." He clenched his teeth in pain, small sparkles of perspiration dotting his forehead. "*Carramba*, that butcher of a doctor! David, why did you let him cut me so?"

"The bullet was very deep," David said. He poured Paco a little water and held the cup while he drank. "Now sleep, *hombre*. Try to get some sleep. You are very weak."

Paco nodded. He lay back, holding the canvas moneybag on his chest. He refused to let anyone take it from him. "You are right," he said. "David Pine, you are always right." The ghost of a smile lingered on his lips. "I owe you very much, *amigo*. It is a shame I can never repay you."

"Never mind that," David said. "Just close your eyes and try to sleep."

They passed the day in a shallow canyon, slaking their thirst with alkali-tasting water from a brackish pool in the rocks. Finally the sun slid down the wrinkled mountains to the west. Squatting over a fire of mesquite twigs, David spread out the tattered map that had guided them in their flight over the *sierra*. Maruja Cruz knelt beside him, waiting for the coffee to boil. Café slept. Nacho, never seeming to need sleep, sat on a little rise, rifle cradled in his lap, scanning the darkness that lay around them like a thick and impenetrable blanket.

"Three days more to Hacienda Palomas, I make it," David said folding up the map again.

Maruja was silent, watching the flames. Then she pulled the shawl more tightly about her and asked, "Will—will he live, David? To Palomas, I mean?"

He shrugged. "God knows! But the desire is very strong in him. And that means much."

He saw a dark shadow of compassion in her eyes.

"It is hard for me," she murmured. "It is hard for Paco. But for all of us, I believe it is hardest for you, David Pine." She put a hand on his sleeve. "I know how it is with you. You do not need to explain to me. I know."

She knew indeed. They all knew; it was the final irony. Paco Mora had robbed the Plains Bank, and in the process Pop Cooper had been killed. Now David Pine was taking both robber and booty to Hacienda Palomas to complete the business that had begun that September night so long ago, that hot violent night in the streets of Roosevelt, New Mexico.

"Café!" he called.

"Señor?" Café sat up, stretching his arms and scratching. "Is it time?"

"It is time."

"Ah. Is there coffee?"

"Fresh coffee," Maruja said, pouring him a cup. "Hot and black, the way you like it."

Nacho brought in the grazing mules and harnessed them to the *carreta*. They rode silently, their only light the faint starshine, the only sound the creaking of saddle-leather and the grinding of the *carreta* wheels. From time to time David Pine, always watchful, halted the caravan, twisting in his saddle to look, and listen, behind them.

"Did you hear anything?" he asked Nacho.

"No, señor. Only a small bird and the yucca leaves scraping together in the small wind that blows."

They did not call him *jefe* anymore. Paco Mora, though grievously wounded, was with them again.

"*Bueno*." David clucked to his mare. "Let's go."

Riding toward the faint glimmer of Orion's belt, low on the horizon, he was still uneasy. With every plodding hoofbeat, every grinding revolution of the wheels, they were nearing the border. The long journey from the *sierra* to El Rusbayo, and now from there to Hacienda Palomas, had been difficult; still, in a way, it had been too easy. They had outwitted any pursuers, apparently. Yet . . . He shook his head, trying to free it of the clinging, uneasy feeling. Was there something he had neglected, some precaution he should have taken but failed to do?

Near dawn they approached the line of trees marking the course of the Casas Grandes. Willows were green along the edge, and there were patches of rich grass where cattle grazed. Somewhere in the glow of the false dawn, a calf bawled piteously. Café, riding forward, found a white-faced heifer spraddled in quicksand at the river's edge. Getting his rope around it, he backed his horse and managed to pull it free. Wet and trembling it ran to its mother, still bawling.

"There was not much light," Café told David Pine,

"but the brand on the big cow looked like a *P*, a *P* in a circle."

Everyone in Chihuahua knew that brand. The cattle belonged to the Palomas Land and Cattle Company. They were finally nearing their rendezvous with the Invincible General.

They followed the course of the river northward now, grateful for an end to the dry and arid country they had passed through. Though he had never been here before, the character of the land was familiar to David Pine. The Casas Grandes eventually flowed into Lago Guzmán, the same Lago Guzmán where Don Jaime and Doña Ana had lived. In five months David had made a complete circle: from Roosevelt to Lago Guzmán, to Colonia Dublán, into the *sierra* to the rebel camp, then across the snowy summits and down to the valley of the Rio Bavispe, Santa Teresa de las Cuevas and the other villages scattered along the Bavispe. Finally, El Rusbayo, and now across the desert again to Lago Guzmán—and the border.

The morning was still only a faint glow in the east when they rode into the little town of Barra de Navidad. A sable cat, the only sign of life, sat on a red-tiled roof to watch them pass. No smoke came from the chimneys, no slapping palms making breakfast tortillas; it was too early. They turned the animals loose to drink in the reedy shallows of the Casas Grandes. While the rest waited, David knocked on the heavy wooden door of the principal building, probably the city hall, mayor's home, police station, administrative headquarters—the all-purpose adobe blockhouse they called the *cuartel*.

No one answered, though he thought he heard a muffled sound from within.

He knocked again. "*Hóla*!" he called. "Is anyone there? We are travelers and want only to eat and rest." In the silence he waited. "We have money," he added, "and we are friends."

In the east he could see a long streak of saffron, lit

pinkly from below. Day was coming; the sun would soon be up. David became impatient. He wanted to inquire about the presence of *colorados* in the vicinity, to ask also if there had been any sign of the Invincible General and his red-saddle-blanketed troops.

He clenched his fist, intending to bang hard on the door, but it opened a crack. A candle glimmered.

"Who is there?"

"Travelers," David said, relieved. He pushed the door open. A small bearded man with curly hair around a bald pate stood within, pale and frightened.

"Do not worry," David said kindly. "We mean no harm." He pointed to the *carreta*, the grazing animals. "We have a sick man there. All we want is a little rest, a bit of food, perhaps some information."

He walked into the room. It was large, bare, whitewashed, with a stairway at the rear that led up to a balcony and other rooms. A candle flickered before a statue of the Virgin, garlanded with faded flowers.

In the formal Mexican way, David asked, "Whom have I the pleasure of addressing?"

The little man seemed uneasy. He took out a soiled handkerchief and mopped his brow, though it was cold in the room and there was no fire. It was odd, moreover, that at this early hour, with no other sign of life in the village, the mayor was up and fully dressed, even to an incongruous silk cravat with a large glass stickpin.

"I am the mayor of Barra de Navidad," the little man said.

Again David felt that uneasy prickle about his scalp, the tautness between his shoulders, a vague feeling of disquiet. It was like one of those pictures in a cheap magazine, offering great rewards if a reader wrote in and cataloged the errors in the picture. In the magazine the errors would be patent: a man wearing one white shoe and one black, a cat with two tails, a portrait hanging upside-down. But where were the errors in this cold whitewashed room? What was wrong in this cold silent room, the light of coming day filtering through a high-grilled window, the mayor fully dressed, as if for a ceremony?

"We have heard," David said, "that there may be a little action in this vicinity. General Villa, the rumor goes, may be planning an attack nearby, perhaps even on the Hacienda Palomas."

At the rear of the room was a curtain hanging over a doorway. The kitchen, perhaps; David thought he saw the curtain move. The women of the house, perhaps, mixing dough for the mayor's breakfast tortillas?

"Is that so?" the mayor asked. "Is that so, indeed?" He dabbed at his forehead again, and sat down at the heavy plank table. "You will forgive me, señor," he said, "but my legs are old. Standing, sometimes, is a burden. I mean no disrepect. *Bueno*. General Villa, eh? No, señor, I have heard nothing of his presence here."

David remembered the tune, the song about President Carranza and his goatlike little beard, the one Pancho Villa was going to wear for a cockade in his hat. It was, Paco had told him, a kind of secret password among the Villistas. The mayor was understandably reluctant to tell anything he knew about Villa to this stranger. How did the melody go?

The mayor, too, glanced toward the sleezy flowered curtain. The old man swallowed hard, ancient Adam's apple sliding up and down. David's muscles tightened. A thickness gripped his throat. Suddenly he knew what was wrong about the scene. He drew his pistol.

"Do not move, señor," he said in a low voice. "One move and you are a dead man."

There was a smell in this room. There were many smells: hot candlewax from the icon, dust and ground corn, the droppings of chickens that in daylight must walk in and out of the door and across the earthen floor. But above all these, faint yet persistent, was the perfume of imported tobacco, the musky scent of an Egyptian cigarette. David Pine remembered that smell very well. It had been in Felix Mora's house that night the conspirators of the bank raid had met there. Dr. Saenz, Dr. Rafael Saenz, had smoked those fragrant cigarettes and was always fretful in the *sierra* when he could not obtain a supply.

Kicking out, David overturned the heavy table. The mayor shrieked, scrambled for cover with an agility that belied his ancient limbs. At the same time, shots rang out. Armed men dashed from the cover to the curtain, from the back room, the kitchen, where they had been hiding. An ambush! A hail of lead thudded into the heavy planks of the table, and David winced as splinters flew. The whitewashed silence suddenly shattered. Orange flame splashed the gloom, men cursed and yelled, the air thickened with the stench of burning powder.

As the brown-uniformed men poured over the table, trying to get at him, David heard someone yell, "Save him! Do not kill him! Save him for me, I tell you!" David caught a glimpse of Saenz through the clamor and smoke, waving a pistol and gesturing.

He emptied the magazine of his pistol, hurling the useless weapon in the face of a man with sergeant's stripes who clawed at him, trying to drag him from behind the table. The sergeant had probably been the first man to rush from the kitchen, for he wore ridiculously draped around him the remnants of the flowered gingham curtain, torn from its rod in his rush. But suddenly, as the man's big hand grabbed David's collar and hauled him triumphantly across the warped planks of the table, a fresh fusillade broke out. David Pine felt the grasp on his collar relax; the sergeant's look of triumph faded to a puzzled questioning look. He stood up, swaying a little, that same puzzled look on his bearded face. His puzzlement grew. Then, suddenly, he collapsed like a rag doll across the table, life draining quickly from him.

Dazed, David staggered to his feet, searching for a

weapon. On the balcony at the end of the room he saw with unbelieving eyes that Café and Nacho were standing, pouring a cool and murderous fire into the packed federal soldiers below. David did not know how many of the attackers there had been, but several bodies were sprawled on the dirt floor. A man sat in a corner, hands spread over a bloody face. Another threw down his Mauser rifle and bolted through the open door.

"*Jefe*!" Café called. "Are you all right? Wait there, we will be right down!"

Dr. Saenz was still standing under the balcony, looking frightened at the sudden turn of events. He was holding a pistol in one hand, a soiled canvas bag in the other. With a sick lurching of his stomach, David realized it was the money sack, the sack with the loot from the Plains Bank robbery. But what had happened to Paco? Where was Paco Mora?

"Don't move, Saenz!" Café called. Nacho slung his rifle quickly over his shoulder and threw a leg over the spindly rail of the balcony preparatory to leaping down. But Saenz suddenly spun and dashed for the open door also. Café's shot ripped a small fountain of earth from the floor.

David felt very tired, completely spent. His face was wet; when he touched it, his hand came away red. Legs like rubber, he staggered toward the door. "Stop him!" he screamed. "Someone stop Saenz!" His voice sounded faint and faraway in his own ears.

Even as he stumbled into the growing dawn, he heard the beat of hoofs. Rafael Saenz swept by him, riding madly, his mount's hoofs clattering, striking sparks on the cobblestones. Nacho fired. Café fired. But Saenz only bent low over the flying mane, and horse and rider dashed into the reeds along the river, spray flying high in the first rays of sunlight.

Café swore, snatched up the reins of his mount. But David pulled at his sleeve, demanding, "What about Paco? Where is Paco?"

Together they ran to the *carreta*. The canvas cover was ripped and torn. With a sinking heart David realized that bullets had done that. Café and Nacho saw the torn canvas too. They stopped stockstill. Slowly David walked up to the wagon.

Maruja Cruz was leaning against the end of the wagon, hands covering her face. He thought at first she was weeping, but there were no tears left in her. Her face, when she heard him come, was white and stonelike, and she spoke in a monotone, almost without inflection. She did not look at him.

"I was talking to Paco," she said. "Suddenly Café and Nacho heard something from the house, and he and Nacho ran toward the house. I watched them go, wondering—and suddenly—" She paused for a moment; her lip quivered. "Dr. Saenz came from nowhere. He shot Paco many times. I tried to get between him and Paco, but it was no use. When Paco still clung to the sack of money, Dr. Saenz shot him again, in the head, and took the sack. He ran away then, into the house where the fighting was going on."

In the *carreta* Paco Mora lay gracefully, one hand across the chest, the other behind his head as if in sleep. His face was whole and unbroken, but many savage shots had riddled his body; the blankets were sodden with blood. David Pine, standing near, felt a faint impingement on his boots. He looked down. Heavy red drops dripped from the bed of the *carreta* onto the toe of his boot.

He walked back to Café and Nacho.

"Yes," he said. "He is dead. Paco is dead."

Café wiped a hand across his mustachios and carefully reloaded his rifle. "We left him to go inside," he said. "That was our mistake. But we had seen men, strange men, enter the place from the back. It was still too dark to see who they were, so the Yaqui and I climbed up a tree into a bedroom. A woman was in bed, very frightened, and we told her to be quiet. Then, when we heard shots, we ran out on the balcony and saw you behind that table, with the *colorados* swarming on you like bees. *Jefe*, are you hurt?"

David brushed at his cheek, but it seemed the blood was only from the splinters of the table. For a moment he stared at the blood; then he snatched the rifle quickly from Café and vaulted into the saddle of his horse.

"Where are you going?" Café called.

"After Saenz!"

"But he is long gone," Café said, very practically. "You will never catch him now!" When he saw David dig his heels into the mare's ribs, he grabbed at the reins. "Wait a minute! We will go with you!"

But David Pine was already gone, clattering across the cobblestones and toward the river. A moment later he was in the head-high reeds, his mount's hoofs sucking and splashing in the sandy ooze.

"*Jefe*!" he heard Café call. "Wait a minute! We are coming too!"

The low grazing rays of the rising sun blinded him. The reeds caught at him, whipped him, serrated edges cut through his thin cotton pants and drew blood. The mare was frightened, too, not being able to see her footing. His head hurt abominably, and he became dizzy and nauseated. Swaying in the saddle, he wondered if he had been hit somewhere during the battle and had not realized it.

Everything wound around and around; the world reeled in a sunlit kaleidoscope. He slid from the saddle and leaned for a moment against the sweat-rank flanks of the mare, trying hard to catch his breath, blinking his eyes in an effort to defeat the cobwebs that were veiling his vision.

Somewhere, through the forest of reeds, he heard Café again, calling his name. They had probably seen the mare, but David Pine himself was out of sight in the high reeds, stumbling through the rotten-smelling muck, parting the reeds with the barrel of the rifle and peering ahead. Saenz was probably gone for good. Café had been right. But before him there still was a trail of flattened broken reeds, saucerlike hoofprints in the muck, filling already with water.

"Saenz!" He staggered ahead, splashing and falling, picking himself up again, trying desperately to keep the muzzle and action of the Mauser rifle out of the water. The mud pulled at, sucked at, his feet, and somehow he lost a boot.

"Saenz!" he sobbed. "*Cabron*! Where are you?"

If he followed the track and pulled himself out on the far bank, he might have one desperate chance for a long shot at the fleeing Saenz.

Through the reeds he saw a sudden patch of brown that was strange and foreign, did not belong there in the murky greenness. Blundering, sweating, cursing, he stumbled toward it.

"Saenz?"

A glint of sunlight filtered through the leafy screen, a sparkle of sun on brass.

"Saenz!" he called again and suddenly halted.

Horse and rider had fallen into the mud, the quicksand, whatever it was. Saenz was under the horse, the great weight pressing him down into the quaking stuff. The horse, seeing David Pine, neighed shrilly and fought to rise.

"Help me!" Saenz pleaded. "David Pine, help me! I am trapped in this damned stuff!"

The doctor was still holding the canvas money sack. David took a step forward, feeling the jellylike sand give under his feet. Quickly he drew back to firmer ground.

"*Jefe*!" Nacho bawled from someplace in the reeds. "*Jefe*! Where are you?"

"Hurry!" Saenz said. "There is not much time! Get me out of here!"

"Throw me the money," David ordered.

Saenz looked at the dirty sack. He hesitated. Then he arched his arm, flung the sack high to drop soddenly at David's feet.

"I don't want the damned money," he said. "Only hurry, will you? Can't you do something?"

Approaching the struggling horse carefully, David managed to grasp the reins. While the horse thrashed, kicking wildly, he pulled hard. Rafael Saenz gasped in sudden terror.

"I'm sinking! *Cristo*! I'm going farther down! Get some help, will you?"

David kept a steady pull on the reins. "Come on!" he urged the animal. "Keep coming, damn you!" He braced his heels and pulled hard, fearing that the sweat-rotted leather would snap. "That's it, keep kicking, old girl!"

The panting mare finally got a foreleg under its chest and threshed to a ridiculous sitting position.

"Come *on*!" David shouted. "Come out of there!"

Haunches scrabbled under the barrellike sweating body, the legs gathered, pushed, flung out like suddenly released springs. In a great splatter of mud the mare pulled free of the quicksand and stood for a moment beside the quaking pool, blowing and snuffling. Then, rolling frightened eyes, she galloped away through the reeds.

"Hurry!" Dr. Saenz begged. His face was white.

"You killed Acton, you bastard!" David said. "You killed Paco! You betrayed all of us! I ought to leave you here, let you be sucked down to Hell where you belong!"

The struggles of the mare had pushed Dr. Saenz deeper into the quicksand. He was submerged nearly to the chest. He tried to pull his arm free, but already it was sucked to the elbow in the viscous stuff.

"All right," Saenz said. "All right, David Pine. I did all those things. I admit them readily. But you are not going to leave me here to die. I know that. You have a conscience. All of you *gringos* have consciences. So hurry up and get me out of here. I am sinking deeper and deeper!"

David tried to uproot a canelike reed, hoping to use it to pull the struggling man free. But the reed was tough and wiry and slipped from his fingers.

"Hurry!" Saenz begged.

He was wrenching helplessly at the reed when Café and Nacho came splashing through the shallows, leading their horses. They looked at Saenz, at David, then at each other.

"Have you got a knife?" David asked.

Café hesitated. He rubbed his chin. Slowly, reluctantly, he drew the knife from the tasseled sheath at his belt. Quickly David slashed through the reed; stepping cautiously, he moved toward Dr. Saenz, holding out the reed. But the whiplike stalk was smooth and wet. Saenz's hand grabbed, slipped, caught, then lost its grip as David pulled.

"*Carramba*!" Saenz screamed. "It does not work! Someone hurry to the village, get help—a rope! *Valgame Diós*!"

David stared in amazement as Café and Nacho sat casually down on a hummock of earth. Café took out a penknife and started a leisurely exploration of the dirt under his nails. Nacho only squatted, rifle in his lap, staring without expression.

"Help me!" David cried. "For God's sake, help me! This man is going to die!"

Café shrugged. Nacho said nothing.

"We can't let him die like this!" David staggered through the mud and caught Café by the shoulder. "We've got to do something. Help me!"

Café pulled away from him. For a moment their eyes met. Something was in Café's that David Pine did not remember ever seeing before. There were a thousand years of Indian in that stare. There was slavery, cruelty, revolution, death—all mirrored in that flat opaque stare.

"Come!" David pleaded. "Help me!"

Café took a deep breath. "If there is a God," he said finally, "and if he is concerned with this man—which I do not believe—then God will undoubtedly pass a miracle to save him. I am only a simple farmer myself. I do not concern myself with God's business."

David turned to Nacho. He started to speak, to beg, to plead. But Nacho did not even seem to see him. He only stared at David, through David, seemingly back into time, far beyond such recent amenities as pity and mercy.

"Someone help me!" Dr. Saenz sobbed. His voice rose an octave, broke, screeched. "Help me!"

Café and Nacho continued to sit on the bank while David Pine struggled to save the dying man. Saenz sank deeper and deeper, screaming all the while. His flounderings grew weaker, his voice failed. Soon the villagers came to watch. They saw that the man in the quicksand was one of the hated *colorados*, and they too refused to help. Instead they only watched, squatting in a ring around the quicksand hole, staring with the same opaque gaze as Nacho, without emotion.

Finally the sandy muck entered Dr. Saenz's mouth. He retched, gagged, spat, but the quicksand soon covered the gaping mouth. Eyes rolling, Saenz snorted for a while through his nose. Finally that passage too was closed. Saenz died, sinking completely out of sight. All that remained were a few frothy bubbles.

Shaken, David Pine put both hands over his face, trying to blot out that final desperate image. Café crossed himself, rose, and handed David Pine the reins of his horse.

"We are finished here, eh, *jefe*?" he asked.

David was too horrified, too spent, to make any

judgments. He only nodded. Wearily he picked up the blood-splattered canvas sack.

"Yes," he said. "Now it is all over. We—we are finished here."

Chapter Twelve

The villagers of Barra de Navidad brought David and his company food and cigarettes, coffee, an earthenware jar of rank *sotol.*

"You, señor," the mayor asked politely, "you are *El Pino*, no?"

"I was," David said. "But no longer. That is all over." He watched the men digging graves for the slain *colorados*. The mayor followed his gaze.

"There were seven of them," he said. "Eight, with the one that called himself a doctor." He spat in the dust. "A fine doctor, that one! Anyway, they had, it seems, followed your trail for a long way, losing it in the mountains and elsewhere. When they came here and wanted to use my house for an ambush, I protested." The old man held up his wrists, and David saw the cruel welts of a rope. "They hung me up till I fainted." The mayor shuddered. "They were very cruel men. I asked them why they did not just fall on you outside my village, sparing us from bloodshed. But the doctor only laughed. An ambush, he said, was his preference!"

The mayor's wife came to the *carreta* with a beautiful Saltillo blanket, an artifact of white wool worked with complex designs in red and green and blue. She and the other women washed Paco, combed his ringlets, covered him with the precious blanket in the immemorial manner of women caring for the dead.

"That is a fine blanket," David said.

Squatting on his heels, the mayor sucked at a brown paper cigarette, holding it carefully between thumb and forefinger. "He was Paco Mora," he said simply. He sighed. "We, too, heard that tale about our Invincible General coming to Hacienda Palomas. We heard the tale and hoped. But there was no truth in it."

The villagers carried out the dead men, dumping them without ceremony in the shallow graves.

"Will there be any consequences?" David asked. "I mean federal soldiers being killed here, in Barra de Navidad?"

The mayor hooted. "What consequences, señor? I am the mayor of this village, and I am the only one to give explanations. The soldiers came, like a good citizen I offered the *cuartel* for an ambush of the rebels against the state. But *El Pino* and his men came." He chuckled. "Only four men, with one wounded. And a girl! *El Pino* was invincible! He and his followers killed all the *colorados*! My friend, there will soon be a new stanza to that song about *El Pino*!"

Nacho and Café lay at their ease in the shade while the women brought them beans wrapped in tortillas, some roasted goat meat, even coffee. Maruja sat in a cane-bottomed rocker. She rocked slowly and steadily, hands gripping the carved arms. When David Pine approached, she stopped rocking.

"I tried to cry," she said. "I tried to cry for Paco. But there were no tears left." She turned a numbed face toward him. "Does that make me wicked, do you suppose? Am I an evil person?"

Gently he touched the black shawl around her head. "No, of course not. I feel the same way. It is like a long sickness. When the worst is over, the body and mind start the long journey back to life again."

She felt for his hand, pressing it against her cheek. A

brightly-colored bird lit in the cottonwoods, looked at them with sharp eyes, then fluttered away, wheeling and diving after a mate. The air was soft, a promise of spring, a time of life and renewal.

"What will you do now, David?" Maruja asked.

He picked up the dirty canvas bag, staring at it as if trying to extract some meaning from the convoluted folds of canvas, the leather straps, the frayed threads where the fabric failed after long use.

"I am going home," he said. "I will take Paco with me. Paco and I are going home, to Roosevelt. But first there are decisions to be made." He beckoned to Café and Nacho. They got to their feet, Café surreptitiously pinched the behind of a fat lady, who giggled.

"*Compañeros*," David said, "this is the end of the thing." He nodded to the *carreta*, now garlanded with flowers. "I want to take Paco home. He was born in Roosevelt—in San Andreas, that is. His father is buried there, and there are uncles and aunts and cousins. I intend to bury Paco there and see that candles are lit for him each saint's day."

Maruja nodded silently. Nacho only blinked and continued to rub the action of his rifle with an oily rag. Café approved. "That is a good plan. Paco should sleep well back there, near his own folk, away from the fighting and bloodshed. *Jefe*, that is a very good idea."

"Do not call me *jefe* anymore," David said. "That is all over now." He held up the canvas bag. "Paco died trying to deliver this money to the Invincible General, our Centaur of the North. But the general was not at Hacienda Palomas. That was only a rumor. And no one knows where General Villa is. It is like searching for a ghost. Maybe the general does not even exist any more. But I want to take this money back to Roosevelt with me."

Café looked puzzled. "After we went to all the trouble to rob a bank for it?"

"The money," David said, "really belongs to a lot of

people in Roosevelt, poor people who worked hard for it. Maybe some of it even belongs to the people of San Andreas, people of *la raza*, like you."

No one spoke. David asked, "Is there any objection? If anyone has a different idea, he should speak. After all, I will know how you feel. There is a lot of money, enough to make you all rich."

Café took a deep breath.

"Señor David, take the money and do with it what you will. That money is cursed, anyway!" He made a fluttering gesture, half crossing himself and half tracing some ancient Indian charm against evil. "A lot of people—too many people—died for that money. Your papa, that night in the street before the bank in Roosevelt—many men of our *tropa*—the sergeant Acton, who is now revenged—Paco, certainly—Dr. Saenz himself. So I say take it! It is the devil's gold!"

Nacho nodded and went on with his endless polishing. Maruja nodded, too, and said, "Yes. That is what you should do with it, David. That is the right thing."

There were still unsettled questions.

"You, Café, *amigo*," David said. "You and Nacho. What will you do now?"

They looked at Maruja Cruz.

"We have talked about that," she said. "Perhaps, as you say, the revolution is lost. Perhaps our general has been defeated. But some of us choose to fight on. That is the least we can do for Paco, for ourselves, for *la raza*. We have horses, guns, bullets. We will go south, into Chihuahua, perhaps to Cumbre Pass and our old camp in the *sierra*, perhaps to Tomóchic, where Roberto Mondragon can help us." She shrugged. "*Quien sabe*? It will work itself out."

"You can't do that, Maruja," he said uncomfortably. "Café and Nacho, they are men. But you—"

There was a flash of the old quick anger in her eyes. Then she smiled.

"I am a woman, yes. But I am now as hard as any man, David Pine! I have been through the fire. I can kill *colorados*. I can do whatever is necessary."

He sighed. "*Ay*, Maruja!" He longed to gather her in his arms before all of them, to press his lips against hers, to say many things. That was what *El Pino* would have done. But he was no longer *El Pino*. He was a fugitive, a deserter, an unsuccessful accountant with no future beyond a federal prison.

"Goodbye, then," Maruja Cruz said. "*Buena suerte*, David Pine! Good luck!"

"Sometime—" he stammered. "Sometime—on a better day, perhaps, we will see each other again."

He saw the luminosity of tears in her dark eyes. She had not wept for Paco, yet she wept—for him? Then she turned quickly away, head averted.

He only shook hands with Café and Nacho. They all wanted to speak, to say noble and heroic things about their companionship, but they were as dumb and ill at ease as he was. "*Adiós*," was all they could manage. "*Buena suerte, señor* David Pine."

Riding away, the mules drawing the flower-decorated *carreta* and its burden after him, he paused at the outskirts of Barra de Navidad. The people, rough white garments glowing in the winter sun, stood motionless in the plaza, watching him go. Cottonwoods waved in the breeze, the Rio Cases Grandes slipped over moss-covered stones. Barra de Navidad looked simple and innocent, innocent of the gunfire and death of the morning. Barra de Navidad would go on, *la raza* would go on, David Pine would go on. Life would go on; that was the way it had to be. Turning his mount, he clucked to the mules.

"Get along," he said. "There is not much time. We must hurry."

At the Roosevelt border gate things looked much the same. The splintered wood of the gate had been repaired, but now there was only a bored corporal guarding the entrance. A customs clerk sat in a small shed and watched David Pine approach with indifference.

Before he reached the gate, he had removed the flowers; he had cut a load of branches and twigs and piled the *carreta* with them, concealing the body. He had taken off his revolver and cartridge belt, too, and hid them in the wagon. The corporal sauntered over, rifle in the crook of his arm.

"Where are you going?"

Burned dark and leathery from the sun and wind and rain, bleached hair carefully pushed up into the sombrero and a rag thrown over his neck for protection against the low-hanging sun, David Pine could pass for a Mexican, and did. He spoke in Spanish to the corporal, pointing toward the town.

"*Voy a San Andreas, para vender leña.*"

The corporal turned toward the clerk. "What's he say?"

"Got a load of firewood. Going to take it into Chili Town to sell."

The corporal poked tentatively with his rifle into the load of firewood. He called again to the clerk. "Wanna come and take a look?"

The clerk shook his head. "Naw. Lots of them old men gathers wood and sells it in Chili Town."

"Okay," the corporal said, jerking his thumb. "Pass on through."

Roosevelt looked the same. San Andreas looked the same. After all that had happened to him, David Pine, it seemed as the town, too, must show a dramatic change. But Doc Menick's office was still there as if nothing had happened, shingle swinging in the wind. Everything was the same—the icehouse, the Plains Bank, the Dodge motor-car agency, Druid's Hall. San Andreas, too, was the same; somnolent in the winter sun, a sprawl of unpainted shacks, tarpaper, corrugated iron.

It was noon in Roosevelt, and citizens were in the streets. Ranchers lounged before the restaurant, picking their teeth. Women hurried out of Pettit's Grocery with brown paper bags. Children hurried home from the school for a hasty dinner. They stared only briefly at the *carreta*, the mules, at the lean brown man who drove them. David Pine rode privately on, looking neither to right nor left. Once, from the corner of his eye, he thought he saw a blond girl in a flowered hat and a bright dress with a red ribbon around her waist. It might have been Louise Trilling, the girl he had met again that night at Druid's Hall, the Louise Trilling he had gone to high school with. But he was not sure.

He came finally to the Cooper house. The porch still sagged under the weight of the bougainvillaea vine, the entryway was a jungle of Mom's plants in old tomato cans, broken vases, spoutless teapots. Curtains still hung in the windows, a mop leaned against the house, dried gray and lifeless, but no one came out to meet him.

He drove the mules into the side yard and tied them to a sagging clothespole. Mom's old wash boiler still sat on the pile of blackened rocks. Below him, in the canyon, he could just see the top of the chinaberry tree, the tree under which he and Paco and Maruja used to play.

He went into the stable and took a shovel from among Pop's rusty tools. The buggy was still there, but old Atlas was missing. When he emerged there were people in the yard; curious children, a fat man in faded denim and a straw hat; two middle-aged women carrying groceries and whispering behind their hands.

"Is it?" he heard one woman say.

The other shook her bonneted head. "Why, it *can't* be!"

Pulling away the branches and twigs, he uncovered Paco Mora's body. Gently he lifted the blanket-wrapped form, hearing a buzz from the growing crowd. He passed before them, walking heavily down the path outlined in whitewashed stones. Near the chinaberry tree Pop Cooper, in spite of Mom's objections, had once started to dig a hole, the start of a mineshaft. Pop had never gotten very far and finally abandoned it.

Laying Paco under the tree, David Pine started to dig in the old hole, now almost completely covered with grass and weeds. The sun was hot, and soon he was sweating. He took off the straw sombrero, and his shirt, too.

As he dug, ramming the shovel into the hard earth with a bootheel and twisting it out, sweat beaded his brow, ran into his eyes, stitched the sparse golden hair on his chest. People came hesitantly down the path to watch him. One of the ladies called out, "Are you David Pine?"

"Yes," he said, and kept on digging.

"There, I told you!" the other lady said in satisfaction. "Though a body'd hardly know it, and that's a fact!"

The hole was deeper now, but the digging was hard. More people came down the path. They stared at the blanket-wrapped body, at David Pine.

"Your mom's staying in town," a half-grown boy called. "She's staying with Doc Menick and his wife. They got an extra room."

Finally the hole was deep enough. He sat on the pile of earth, breathing hard. The crowd had grown large. They watched silently, expectantly. A man came down the path, a big man in a black vest, a star pinned importantly to it. There was a stirring in the crowd. Heads turned.

"What's going on here?" he marshal said.

David had known old Marshal Fitzwilliam—"Fitz," everyone had called him—since he was a child. But old Fitz had probably died. He had been nearly eighty. The new marshal was a young man, bulky and confident.

"I'm burying a friend," David said. "An old friend, I'm David Pine, and this is my stepmother's property,

Mrs. Cooper."

Staggering under the weight, he bore the blanket-wrapped body to the edge of the grave. Boots slipping in the poor gravelly soil, he almost fell. Straining with the effort, he laid Paco Mora to rest and stood back, wiping hands on the seat of his cotton pants.

"You can't do that!" the marshal objected. "Mister, we got rules in this town! What you're doin' is against the law. We got a potter's field, take him there! Anyway, you got to have a permit from the town clerk to bury anybody!"

The sun was past the zenith. Light filtered through the branches of the chinaberry tree, making shifting patterns of light and dark on the Saltillo blanket. David picked up a handful of soil and threw it into the grave.

"I'm tellin' you!" the marshal protested. "No burials without a permit!"

He broke off as David Pine walked past him and fumbled in the bed of the *carreta*. He took out his cartridge belt and slung the pistol about his lean hips. Someone in the crowd whispered. It sounded like a word he had heard often. *Pino. El Pino.* Someone said in a shocked voice, "I'll bet that's him, all right. That's *El Pino*! David Pine! Mrs. Cooper's boy David!"

David walked back to the grave. Someone else said, "The Army's looking for him." The marshal heard the murmuring, and rubbed his chin, looked uncertainly about. "Well—" he said. "Well—" He put his hands in his pockets.

David muttered, "Goodbye, Paco." He started to fill in the grave. Slowly, carefully, he worked, firming the ground, patting it with the back of the old shovel. At last, when he had a smooth raised mound, he sat down, wiping sweat from his face with the back of his hand.

When he reached for the pistol at his belt, the crowd drew a sharp, collective breath and moved back. But he only drew it out and stuck it, barrel first, in the fresh earth. It was a kind of monument; to Paco Mora, certainly, who had lived and died by the gun. But it commemorated also the end of the Pine Tree War, the end of the notorious *El Pino*, perhaps the end even of David Pine.

His counsel was a fresh-faced young officer only recently out of the University of Pennsylvania law school. Lieutenant Barcom seemed awed by David Pine. Sitting in David's cell at Fort Bliss, the young man made endless entries in a small notebook, listened to David's recounting of all that had happened since that hot September night of 1916.

"My goodness!" He shook a carefully barbered head. "You certainly had a lot of adventures!" He closed the book, slid the gold pencil into a breast pocket. "Most of this war has been sitting at a desk for me! But it looks like I'll see action soon. Maybe in France or Belgium. The Huns are getting pretty cocky."

David frowned. "I'm not sure you understand, Barcom. I didn't mean, really, to do any of those things they're talking about. It was the force of circumstance, that's all. I'm not a brave man. I'm not even adventurous, by nature. I'm—well, all I ever was, I guess, was an accountant, and not a very good one at that. I failed in business, drifted into the Army—the rest just happened. I never meant harm to anybody!"

"I understand," Barcom said. But David knew he did not understand. How could he? David Pine himself hardly understood.

"Listen," he said. "Listen, Barcom. What are my chances?"

The lawyer shrugged. "Who's to say? There's a strong case against you, of course. You crossed the border without lawful authorization, you went AWOL, you did all those other things. The Mexican government wants you prosecuted, too. I understand General

Pineda's sending officers to testify that you fought with the rebels against Pineda's federal forces at the Guzmán station of the MNR."

"I told you!" David protested. "I explained! I was only acting to save my own life! Those damned *colorados* were going to shoot me with their Lewis gun!"

Barcom shrugged. "Three U.S. soldiers were killed by the rebels in that action, and you admit you were on the side of the rebels. No matter what the circumstances, you were an accessory to the fact, at the very least."

David put his head in his hands.

"At San Miguel de Babícora," Barcom went on, "Pineda claims you dynamited the *cuartel* and killed four of his soldiers!"

"But that was where they were holding Maruja Cruz! They were abusing her! They raped her! Maruja and I were children together! Could I just stand by and see that happen?"

Barcom went on, almost apologetically.

"And in that final fracas at Barra de Navidad—" He sighed. "Mason's Intelligence people haven't gotten all the facts straight yet, but it appears you and your people scragged a force of federal soldiers that were trying to capture you."

"Mason? Gerald Mason? The captain with the phony English accent, the big watch on his wrist?"

"He's a major now," Barcom said.

David took a deep breath. "So my reputation still stands. What are my chances?"

Barcom stood up. "Not very good, I'm afraid."

David touched his recently shorn locks. His head felt queer, free. The long tangled hair, the high-crowned sombrero, were gone. He felt almost lightheaded.

"When will the court-martial be convened?"

"Don't know. There will probably be a considerable delay."

"But I want to get it over with!"

Barcom was sympathetic. "I know how you feel, old man. But there are so many big things going on now, it's hard to convene enough senior officers for a dogfight. Now that Villa's been squelched, all anyone's interested in is the big war that's coming up in Europe. Why do you suppose they sent all those National Guardsmen down here last spring? Not to fight Villa, certainly; Pershing and the regulars were doing that. No, everyone knew the big war was coming, so they were just getting everyone together and giving them a little training, getting them ready. Your case is important to you—and to me, of course. But I wouldn't expect any quick decision."

A date was set for the court-martial, changed once, twice, three times—finally delayed indefinitely. David Pine languished in his cell, took exercise walks three times a day in the barbed-wire-enclosed compound, read a few old and tattered books from the stockade library. January passed, February. Colonel Hayden, his old CO—off for Paris on a liaison mission to the French—came to see him, brought him cigarettes which David didn't smoke, shook his head, muttered, "I'm damned if I know why you did all those things, David! You had a future in the Corps! Right now, you could make captain, at least, if it wasn't for—for—" He broke off, coughing apologetically.

Old Felix Mora, very ill, came on the SP to Fort Bliss, bringing David Mexican sweets in a box: *panoche*, chocolate, pumpkin candy. They talked in Spanish.

"I am grateful," Felix said, "for what you did for my Paco." But David could tell him little about Maruja Cruz, where she was now, if she would ever return.

Mom Cooper, too, rode the SP to visit him. She came near weeping but did not do so. She sat pale-faced and composed on the chair the stockade sergeant brought her, gloved fingers working in her lap.

"I wish you could have been there," she said. "Pop

had a lovely funeral. Everyone in town knew him, of course, and respected him."

"Mom," he asked, "how are you fixed for money?"

She tried to smile, to reassure him. "All right, Davy. Don't worry about that."

"After this is finished," he said, "I may have some back pay that I can—"

"Don't need it." She shook her head; the spray of artificial cherries bobbed. "Pop left me a little. His pension, too, though that's not much. I'm renting the old place, you know. Doc and Mrs. Menick let me have that back room of theirs, and I have kitchen privileges." She patted his hand. "No, it's you I'm worried about, Davy. When are they going to let you out of here?"

"I wish I knew," he said.

In March he had another visitor. It was a newspaper reporter, a man named Harry Worsham, who worked for one of the national wire services. Worsham was a quick, nervous little man in gold-rimmed eyeglasses who chain-smoked cigarettes. "Aha!" he said, grinning. He poked a stained finger at David Pine. "The famous *El Pino*! I must say you don't look like a killer to me!"

"I'm not," David said.

Worsham rubbed David Pine the wrong way at first. But it was only his way.

"Killer or not," the reporter said, "you've been a gold mine! My career was going nowhere until I started to file those stories about the glorious adventures of Robin Hood—*El Pino*, that is to say!" He coughed, sucked hard on a fresh cigarette.

"I don't want to hear any more about it," David protested.

Worsham grinned. "A lot of our readers do! You're a hero in Mexico, even if the revolution failed. You've got a readership in the States, too, believe me! People see you as a romantic figure. Machinists, grocery clerks, coal miners, shopgirls, waitresses—*El Pino* sells a lot of copies of our newspapers. And now I'm here to cover your court-martial! How's that for publicity?"

Wearily David shook his head. "I don't want any publicity. All I want is for this damned thing to be over, have them shoot me or whatever they intend to do."

Worsham crossed one skinny leg over the other, plucked at a black silk sock. "I can't blame the Army for procrastinating so. You're a problem to them."

"What do you mean?"

Worsham chuckled. "You're embarrassing to them! They'd like you to just dry up and blow away! There's another war coming on, and no one's got time for *El Pino*. You know, nothing fades so fast as the memory of a finished war, if you could call Black Jack's shenanigans in Chihuahua a war. Now the Army knows there's a lot of popular sentiment in the States in your favor. After all, you fought for the raggedy-ass peasants against Carranza, and no one likes Carranza since he's been playing cozy with the Germans. I tell you, if it wasn't for that damned Pineda pushing so hard, they'd probably open the stockade gates some dark night and tell you to get lost!"

On a windy April day the court-martial at last convened. The sky was blue, blue as the sky of Mexico. Small puffy clouds roamed the heavens like gamboling sheep. David sniffed the air appreciatively. His cell had come to smell musty and stale.

The case against him seemed overwhelming. He sat at a wooden table with his counsel, listening to a hatchet-faced Mexican major tell about the rebel capture of the MNR train at Lago Guzmán.

"Can you identify the man you call *El Pino*?" the presiding colonel asked.

Major Bustamante was positive. He pointed his finger at David Pine.

"That is the man," he said. "I was there. I saw him. I had ordered our machine gun to be set up, but just as it was ready to fire, this man attacked the crew. He killed them all. If it had not been for that, the outcome would have been very different."

There were many other damaging witnesses. Captain Mason—now Major Mason—testified he had long been suspicious of David Pine.

"He had too many friends in the Mexican population. The girl Maruja Cruz, a suspected spy, was one of his good friends. We tried to catch her, but she was apparently warned, and disappeared before we could put her under arrest."

Lieutenant Barcom whispered to David. "About the only good thing anyone seems to have to say about you is that you did bring the money back, return it to the Plains Bank."

When the court questioned David, he gave his answers in a low voice. No, he had not known Maruja Cruz was a Villa agent, though he probably had suspected. Paco Mora and he had been friends since childhood, but he had known nothing about Paco's plans for a raid on the Plains Bank. Yes, it was true that David Pine had technically fought against Pineda, General Pershing's ally in the search for Pancho Villa, at the battle of Guzmán station. But he had not meant to harm anyone; he had only been protecting himself in a murderous crossfire. Yes, he knew he had been responsible for Sergeant Acton, taking the non-commissioned officer on an illegal mission into Chihuahua. He was sorry about what had happened to Acton. He would have given his own life to prevent it, if there had been any way.

Allowed to make a final statement in his own defense, he told the court the truth, reading from a handwritten statement he and Lieutenant Barcom had labored over. It was not really exculpatory, but Barcom thought it was his best chance.

"I am not a brave man. I never was. But I ask you to believe that sometimes a man can get caught up in a thing not of his own making, be carried along by it. I ask the court to remember also that the *colorados* were known to be cruel and brutal men, feared by the poor, the humble, the oppressed people of Mexico—*la raza*. Perhaps Pancho Villa was not a proper savior for the poor farmers of Mexico, but neither were Pineda and his soldiers, or President Carranza. These people have always been ground down, exploited, persecuted. I knew them; I had grown up with them, shared their food, their happiness, their grief. When I was put in a position where I could help them, I guess I did. But I did not feel I was doing wrong."

The verdict came after only a short period of deliberation by the senior colonels: Dismissal for the good of the service, forfeiture of all pay and allowances, three months hard labor in addition to time already spent in custody. David, standing to receive the sentence of the court, swayed a little on his feet, unbelieving. They were not going to shoot him.

"Are you all right?" Barcom asked.

David nodded. "I'm all right."

Major Bustamante protested the light sentence, banging on the judges' table, very red in the face.

"It is a travesty! This man is an assassin, a criminal! I tell you, our government will take a very serious view of this miscarriage of justice! Diplomatic representations may be expected."

But the verdict had been handed down. David, leaving the room under guard, paused when someone plucked at his sleeve. It was Harry Worsham, the news-service reporter.

"Three months isn't long," Worsham said. "You can do it standing on your head, a tough guy like you." He fumbled in his pocket. "How are you fixed for money?"

When David didn't speak, Worsham took out a wad of bills and pressed them into his hand. "Take it!" he said. "You earned it. Anyway, you'll be out of the pokey soon, and you'll need cash."

David protested, tried to hand the money back, but

Worsham only grinned and walked away, waving his hand. Over his shoulder he called, "Keep it, friend! You made me a lot of money! I hear I even got a chance for Washington bureau chief now!"

On a hot June morning, almost a year to the day from the time he first returned to Roosevelt to visit Pop and Mom Cooper, and find out for Colonel Hayden what was going on in San Andreas, David Pine sat in Mom's rented room at the Menicks', a dish with a cup of coffee and an oatmeal cookie on his knee, and said goodbye to Mom.

"I just baked them, hearing you were coming," Mom said. "I have kitchen privileges, you know."

Carefully she did not mention his appearance. He had spent a little of Harry Worsham's gift on cheap clothes, and they hung loosely on his gaunt frame. Three months at hard labor had toughened him, but thinned him, too.

"What will you do now, Davy?" Mom asked.

It was amazing the way people had changed, but things remained the same. In the small back room Mom had arranged most of the furniture, at least the "good things," from the old house. Lace doilies covered the backs and arms of the chairs, the room smelled already of dust and furniture polish. On the round table with its pie-crust fluting, Mom's pride, rested the polished glass dome filled with dried flowers, colored pebbles, the stuffed woodpecker with the missing glass eye that so fascinated David Pine when he was young.

"Eh?" he asked absently. "Oh. What will I do now?"

He drank some of the coffee and ate a bite of the cookie. Even the cookie tasted the same as the old ones Mom used to make in the wood-burning range.

"I really don't know. It sounds foolish, I guess, but when I get on the platform at the SP station I'll probably flip a coin; east or west." He thought of Pop

Cooper's old expression. "It don't make me no never mind."

Mom coughed a little, the way she did when she was embarrassed.

"Now, I don't want you to take it the wrong way, Davy. You're a grown man now, and you're going to make your own way and come out fine, just fine. But right now I know you haven't got any money. I've got a little saved up, and—"

"No," he said, almost angrily. "No, mom. I'll get along."

At the door her reserve broke. She flung her arms about him, weeping.

"Oh, Davy, I love you so much! Things has been hard, but I never lost faith in you. And I never will!"

Doc Menick and his wife said goodbye, too, and Mom called out after him, "Now don't forget to write, Davy! Send me your address soon as you can!"

Carrying the sleazy borrowed suitcase, he walked the SP platform, looking at train notices, grateful for the shade of the overhanging roof. In the distance, to the south, the mountains of Mexico shimmered blue; sun-baked earth rippled in heat waves. Westbound No. 10 was due in two hours. Westbound? How about California? The talk was that California would be the coming thing, a place to make dreams come true.

On the other hand, Eastbound No. 24, freight with one passenger car, would be along an hour later, bound for El Paso. He did not want to go back to El Paso again, but that was the gateway to the East, to Chicago, to Washington and New York City.

He was sitting on the hard slatted bench, feeling every slat, when he knew someone was beside him. He did not see the figure; rather he felt it, a prescient tingle that flushed quickly through his body.

"Maruja!" he cried.

He folded her in his arms, pressing her tightly against him. "*Ay, Maruja*!" he said. "*Que milagro*! What a miracle!" Almost without knowing it he dropped into the liquid Spanish. There was no better language to talk about miracles.

"David!" Dark head against his breast, she clung to him. "Ah, David!" For a moment she wept. Then she pushed away from him, looking at him. "*Querido*, what have they done to you? You are so thin?"

In sudden embarrassment he looked around. But no one was on the platform. In his tiny cubicle the SP clerk riffled through papers, stamping each one heavily.

"Let's not talk about that," he said. "That's all over." He led her to the bench. "Why are you here, in Roosevelt?"

"The revolution is over, David. The general will probably fight a few more fights—there will be more bloodshed before it is over—but there is no use keeping on."

"What about Café and Nacho?"

She looked down at her hands, folding them in a kind of finality. "They did not want to give up. They would have been willing to stay in the *sierra*, to fight until they died. But I—I persuaded them, finally. It was no use."

"How did you find me?"

"Doctor Menick told me you were coming."

"Where are you staying?"

"With Señor Ruiz, the druggist in San Andreas. You remember Ruiz. Papa Felix finally died, you remember."

"Of course," he said.

"And where are you going?" she asked.

He shook his head, wanting time to think. An idea was occurring to him, a wonderful, mind-boggling idea.

"Don't you know?" she insisted.

He swallowed hard. "Maruja, I—I want to ask you something."

She did not speak, only looked at him with her soft liquid eyes. There was a churning in his stomach, a kind of vertigo overtook him. It had been like that a long time ago, when he had wanted to ask a pretty girl—maybe it was Louise Trilling—to go with him to the class dance.

"I—I—" He stammered, turned red, cursed himself, his awkwardness. It was almost as if he had never slept with Maruja Cruz, had never felt her body warm and soft beside him. Throwing himself recklessly on her mercy, he finally gasped, "Maruja, will you marry me?"

One hand crept to her throat. A flush spread on her cheeks, darkened into the cleft at the neck of her dress.

"Me? David, you want to marry me?"

He plunged on. "I'm going to California. Right now. I mean, very soon. They say there are great opportunities out there! They'll need accountants to add up all the money they make! We'll get a little house and be happy together! After all that's happened to us, Maruja, I think we can make it together! You and me—together!"

She didn't speak, only stared at him. She was beginning to cry. Joy—or regret? Which?

He grasped her arm. "Maruja, say yes! Please say yes! You remember what old Elena said in the *sierra*. I didn't believe in that mumbo-jumbo then, but I do now!" He did not speak of Paco. "You and I—we're bound together, somehow!"

She managed a hesitant smile. "*Ay*, we are indeed, David!"

Puzzled by her manner, he drew back.

"Café and Nacho and I gave up the fight, finally, and left the *sierra*," she said. "It was no use any longer, fighting, that was true. But there was something else." She flushed again and looked down at her lap.

He saw it then, the thickness of body, the growing burden of a child.

"It is your child, David," she said. "I came back because it was your child. I wanted you to see it, some day. I wanted it to be born here, in the United States, because I thought that was what you would want." Seeing the amazement in his eyes, she went on. "I had some powerful tea Elena had given me, some tea so that I should not conceive. You remember, that time in the *sierra*. But this time I did not take the tea. I let the baby come, and grow, and get big in me. Was that—was that all right?"

He sprang to his feet and whooped. The SP clerk looked curiously at him. A small boy teetering barefoot on a rail grinned and almost lost his balance. But David Pine did not care.

"Mine?" he demanded. "Mine? I mean ours? Do you mean it?"

She nodded. "Ours. David, I have a little money, but are you sure you want to take a—a pregnant woman to California?"

Carefully he got an arm under her elbow and lifted.

"You don't have to be so careful," she said. "I'm not going to break!"

They went back to Señor Ruiz's rooms over the pharmacy and packed Maruja Cruz's few possessions in a suitcase the druggist loaned her. While she packed, David Pine sat on a window ledge and watched her, proud and happy.

"She is beautiful, is she not?" he asked Ruiz.

The druggist wiped his eyes, hooked the gold-rimmed spectacles over his ears again. "All women are beautiful," he said. "But when they are going to have a baby, some special beauty comes."

Busy at the packing, she asked over her shoulder, "David, do we know anyone in California?"

He thought he heard the distant whistle of the SP. No. 10 would not pause long in Roosevelt.

"No," he said, "but we'll make friends."

There would be difficult times, he knew that. But with Maruja, he could accomplish anything. When bookkeeping palled, when eyes grew weary and dim, when numbers swam spiderlike in the lamplight, he could always close his eyes and think of those times in the *sierra*. He could remember Paco Mora, a brisk coffee-drinking rooster named Café, a Yaqui idol named Nacho. He could think of starlit nights in the mountains, the smell of roasting meat and tortillas and cigarettes, sentinel pines towering into the dark vault of sky. He could remember all those things. Who could want more? Some day, even, he might tell the child about *El Pino* and the Pine Tree War.